Deceitful Blood

Deceitful Blood

Fionn Murphy

&

Simon Bramhall

Scalpel Stories

Dedication

Jack, Jenna and Jude;

George and Maeve;

Pippa, James and Alexis;

James and Cristina

ISBN 978-1-9161915-4-9

Cover design by Fionn Murphy and Simon Bramhall

Other books from Simon and Fionn

Trick or Treat?

Charity

Just Another Saturday Night

Dilemma

Available on kindle and in paperback from Amazon

Find out more at www.scalpelstories.com

Acknowledgement

We owe so much to so many, but mostly, as always,

to our wonderful families for their love and support.

Thank you, everyone.

Your support, patience, ideas, comments and time are hugely appreciated.

Very special thanks to Ian Forster, Alipops, Tara, Estelle Spring, Lynne Ackland, Jennie Corrie, Mike Cosgrove, Lizzy Watson, Jim Burkinshaw, Lily, Jessica, Chloe, Verity, Lucy, Grace and Lewis.

Table of contents

Epilogue

Journal

Prologue

His feet had died and the cold was scaling his thighs. The floor was tiled, black and white. He had been there once, before, and recognised the sound of the heavy door that opened which did not immediately shut behind him. Heavy footsteps followed him from the outside world, where it was winter. And here, too. He heard his own bare feet slapping against the tiles as he was pushed. The blindfold had been on a long time. Strands of hair had got caught up in the knot at the back like needles and would have hurt if it had not been for the weariness of his arms. He would be dragging the weight at the end of this rope until death came to save his life.

No one spoke. Except him.

"Why? Why?"

There was no real pain, just the fear.

It was the expectation.

Suddenly they stopped.

No more pushing.

Silence, so dark it hurt.

A heavy rap on the door with something hard then ... nothing happened.

Another rap, just the same and again, nothing.

The third rap was harder. More angry. "Let me in!"

A door opened ahead of him. The same sound as the first one, just as heavy, perhaps made of the same type of wood. Maybe even the same tree he thought, before the weight at end of the rope reminded him to die.

It was warmer now. He sensed the presence of others – a crowd? No, not so many, but enough to surround him. He could feel it. He was caught.

Then he smelled the fire.

Was this why he was bare-footed and bare legged? Dressed only in a loose, white shrift like an old-fashioned night shirt with baggy sleeves that reached almost to his knees. He felt watched. Exposed. They could see through the thin cotton; were scrutinising his pale body. Imagining how it would look afterwards.

He wished he could see. Was this how it would end? In darkness? Would he ever know?

The fire was getting nearer. He felt himself being guided – not unkindly – towards it and its increasing heat. He wished he could warm his feet.

Now he was very close. He could hear the flames talking to each other in low voices. Not blazing. Not angry. Just burning, gently. Building. Someone was turning him around, and around, many times, until he had no idea where he was or what was happening and the fire seemed to be everywhere. And then it stopped. He stopped. Something was burning.

His hands were free. The rope had gone and with it, the terrible weight in his arms. He wanted to lift them up and rejoice, to reach out towards the fire and roast his palms as at a fireplace. An acrid smell of burned sisal from the severed rope drifted from behind his body and assaulted his nostrils. He wanted to sneeze.

"Sinner. Repent."

A male voice. In front of him; quite close. Deep and sonorous, the words were said slowly and without warmth. The blindfolded man bowed his head, deep, right down onto his chest. Should he fall to his knees? Yes. Damn the tiled floor. He dropped to the ground, cushioning his fall with his hands and prostrated himself, low, serpent-like, in the direction of the voice. The floor was freezing but he tried not to shiver; he did not want them to know he was afraid.

Then he felt strange hands at the back of his head, tugging at the cloth tied around his eyes and suddenly, amazingly, dazzlingly, the darkness disappeared and he could see again. Raising his head slightly he perceived that he was surrounded by reflections. The room was dim; the fire danced; its colours bounced off the shiny polished black shoes of the feet around him and splintered across the floor.

"Kneel."

A silver goblet, held in white-gloved hands, appeared before his face. Firelight fractured and danced on its surface and he smelled the liquid within. It was dark red and thick. Bitter old and rusty.

"This is the blood of our covenant. Whoever drinks of this blood becomes one of us. A brother in a bond that never can be broken.

Are you prepared to give yourself to the brotherhood?"

He nodded.

"Drink."

The goblet was thrust against his face so he drank from it. The liquid burned as it reached the back of his throat.

"Welcome, brother."

Soft, pure, white-gloved hands reached down into his and guided him upright. He realised that he was still looking at the floor; his feet were in the centre of a huge Masonic square and compass, marked out in gold on the tiles.

Chapter One

January 1977

Detective Sergeant Catherine Scott found herself staring at the bathroom mirror, as she did every morning. You would have thought she was used to it by now.

It was the only mirror in the house but it was her mirror, and it was her house, small as it was. No more being interrupted by flatmates desperate to use the toilet or using her shampoo/toothpaste/soap. At least they had never touched her make-up. And at least, now, she could put it on in private.

She had already done her legs. Not as carefully as her face, obviously, but then she was wearing tights which helped. Dark tan was the best: too dark and the white patches glared, too light and they seemed to glow. She would have loved to wear trousers for the rest of her life but as a newly appointed Detective Sergeant in a Yorkshire serious incident squad she was required, by all that was unsaid, to wear skirts. Sensible, on the knee, demure, but always a skirt. Speculation was rife and very vocal as to whether she wore tights or stockings with, oh joy, suspenders. But that was only for her to know and the rest could go to hell. Thankfully, her hands were more or less one colour.

She stared at the patchy face frowning back at her. It was winter and the vitiligo was not so bad. Always there, of course, but when there was no sun to darken the normal skin and throw the renegades into sharp relief, it was easier to conceal with make-up and present an even face to the world. No one knew about it here. Well, wasn't that why she had left London? For a new, even-coloured start.

Sighing, she reached for the palette of pan stick and began to apply it. The mirror smiled sympathetically and tried to clear the bath water steam clogging up its pores. She tried not to think about what she would do if there was a big case, or the Leeds killer ventured onto their patch and she was away from her bathroom for days on end, or woken up in the middle of night to be immediately somewhere else. Perhaps she would have to go to bed fully painted? Ironically, as a woman, she had the advantage that she could always carry supplies in a handbag, which swung from a long strap over her shoulder wherever she went. Her male colleagues would have regarded her as semi-dressed without it. No matter that she had an OU degree, a proven career record, was qualified to drive a police vehicle in high pursuit chases, (even though women, obviously, could not drive), and had earned her promotion out of uniform in a very dodgy area of south London. No – she grimaced at herself – all that men saw was that she had tits (too small), an arse (too tight), wore make-up (too much), carried a bag and made decent tea and coffee. Oh, and she could type. All the better to help the lads with their reports eh, Cath? Or was she a Kate? No. She was Catherine, but any diminutive was better than Bird, Chick, Bunny, Baby, Stella, or Shagadelic, not that she was often called that. Not to her face, anyway.

There. Face done. A finger slick of blue eyeshadow, some mascara and she was, "Bitch'n", as her colleagues would say. Could be worse.

She wished she had a dog to talk to but her garden was too small and her hours were too long.

At much the same time on an RAF station in the Midlands, Scampton, the black Labrador sat, then lay, his head on front legs stretched just as far as the boundary of the dining room of the Officer's Mess. He was happy to wait. That's what he did.

"Here Scamp," said the steward, slipping him a bit of bacon fat off a plate he was clearing from a table. "Just toast for the boss this morning. Must be a clinic day."

"It is. Then we're away until Monday. Don't feed him scraps. He'll get fat." The boss, Group Captain Leonard Potts, had materialised in the doorway.

"Yes sir. Sorry, sir." The steward spoke to the carpet and winked at the dog who pretended not to see.

"Heel."

An instruction for the dog apparently, although the steward was not entirely sure.

The green Volvo 240 estate was immaculate, inside and out. Even Scampton, sitting on the front passenger seat, knew better than to shed hairs or to leave mud within its hallowed halls. He always sat in the front, sometimes upright to keep an eye on proceedings, sometimes curled on the tan upholstery atop his own neatly folded tartan rug. The back seat was permanently folded down and the rear load cover fastened securely over the chasm. No one but man and dog had ever been known to travel in the vehicle, and no one cared even to wonder what lay beneath the weekly-vacuumed and wiped-clean cover. Something boring probably, like the Group Captain himself, who did not even play golf. Airfix model kits? An ironing board? Whatever it was, it would not be untidy. Occasionally, the mildly curious speculated about his private life, (he must have one?) and all came to the same conclusion. It was an empty room; functional; overhead lighting; bare walls; austere and cold. Buttoned up to the neck, just like its owner, with nothing to find inside or out. But that he was an excellent doctor was undeniable and surely his mania for order and hygiene couldn't be that bad if he had a dog? Scampton was a poppet. Clearly, he could not possibly be vacuumed, shampooed and laundered every week like the car.

Potts approved of the car park layout. His allotted place was close to the main entrance, as befitted his position, and he was pleased to see that maintenance had finally got around to installing a sign with his name and rank there. About time too. That was the trouble with civilian institutions; they were sloppy and slow; inefficiently run. It was not like that in the Services where orders were given and acted upon, immediately, or there were consequences. Rank, file and uniform equalled order and strength. Rank also clarified the order of things and everyone followed the rules. That was something understood by the Masons – comradeship, loyalty, solidarity. There was structure in the medical hierarchy, of course, but not enough enforcement, especially from the middle ranks. That was why he approved of Jenny Cullum. He did not like her much - no one did - but she was not there to be liked. What mattered was that she was a formidable medical Sister; would have made an exemplary NCO. Ah well, the RAF's loss was the NHS's gain and God knows, they needed it.

Scampton recognised the routine of the slowing speed and gear change, the well-controlled gradual coming to a stop exactly in the centre of the parking space, and the death of the engine. He was already sitting to attention, gazing ahead. Another busy day in the office.

Catherine always arrived at Police HQ early. Not conspicuously, but a tactful fifteen to twenty minutes ahead of time, mostly to avoid having to walk into a maelstrom of testosterone and male egos, but also so that no one would ever be able to accuse her of being typical. Women – always late, nudge, nudge, wink, wink. Oh, if only they were joking. But she would smile, say nothing and let the innuendo bounce off her masked face. Being ahead of the rush also meant that she could find somewhere to park her Morris Marina 1.3, bog standard beige, but not too badly scratched. Theirs was an unromantic relationship, based on economy and the necessity to get from A to B without drama, which suited them both. She tucked it discreetly away at the far side of the car park and enjoyed the brief walk through the cold, dark morning to the main entrance.

The first time she had arrived it had been necessary to explain to the desk sergeant that she was not, in fact, a member of the general public. Nor was she the temp sent by the agency to cover for an absent admin assistant: touch typist, 60 wpm, shorthand preferred, with special responsibility for filing. She was, however, reliable, punctual, recognisably female and knew all about confidentiality. The reason that she was not in uniform was that she was a detective and that the 'C' in her name stood not for Christopher, or Colin, or Clive, or anything of that ilk, but Catherine. He had believed her immediately. It was too preposterous to be a wind-up. Did that mean he would have to call her Ma'am? Or Miss? No wedding ring he noticed, sensible shoes, neat, a bit straight up-and-down for his taste but wearing make-up and .... he looked at her legs as she walked through the door he held open for her, were they tights or stockings?

Her boss, Detective Chief Inspector Derek Martin, could not care less. He had seen it all. Started as a rookie, on the beat, all weathers, day and night; worked his way through the streets then off them, out of uniform into tan cords, scuffed brogues and a blue M&S anorak with a hood under which he wore hand-knitted jumpers. He had come up the hard way: the right way, through the ranks, with dogged progression. Had done it by the book. Procedure mattered. He was a proper copper, even if he only just met the regulation height. Now he was going grey in the pursuit of criminals, his pension was on the horizon and even his moustache seemed to have lost enthusiasm for the chase. It was his habit to stroke it with forefinger and thumb, as if to console, but over time this seemed to have dragged the corners of his mouth closer to the ground than the rest of his face and had given him the jowls of a bloodhound.

Unlike everyone else in the section, neither Martin nor Catherine smoked. He never had; his wife had asthma.

Catherine would have loved to, but had given up in order to pay her mortgage. She had all but given up drinking as well, but knew that there would be times when she would have to be one of the lads, so could still down a pint.

"Morning Scott", the DCI's moustache breezed as he walked it into the open office. Catherine was already at her desk. As fast as the others were being occupied, the room was fugging up with cigarette smoke, aftershave and the aroma of instant coffee. It was noticeable how the levels of aftershave seemed to have increased and levels of B.O. dropped after Catherine's arrival. Even Martin had to admit that that might be a good thing. The cigarette smoke persisted undeterred however, soaking itself into carpet, files, hair and clothes like a bad mood.

"Tea, Boss? Milk, two sugars?"

She did not mind offering to put the kettle on. It was when people – men - assumed that that was all she did, that was so infuriating. The Detective Chief Inspector was sitting at his desk, eclipsed by its bulk, listening to the phone receiver and comforting his facial hair. His jowls were trying to reach the top of the desk. Yeah, he nodded, and she headed off to the kitchenette.

"Good morning, Group Captain." Sister Cullum stood at the head of her posse, as tightly arranged as her own hair tied into a twisted plait that seemed determined to suck her face back into itself. She had a scraped look; even her body seemed thinly spread over her bones so that her rigid uniform skimmed over her body, rather than fitting it. When she walked, thin-legged, briskly, without hip movement or pleasure, the starched cap on her head seemed to cut through the air like a knife. She led with her nose: sharp, narrow and accusatory. Everything moved out of her way.

Her ward was ready for inspection. Every patient capable of independent movement and able to sit upright, had been placed in the chair allotted to each bed and now sat, poised, awaiting the Group Captain's ward round. If spoken to, they must address him as 'Sir' and answer his questions, quickly and efficiently. This was not a social visit; he was a busy man. All breakfast trays had been removed, beds were made, sheets straightened, hospital corners sharpened, blue bed covers smoothed, all beyond reproach. Every iron bedstead stood erect and attentive, the clip boards at their bottom ends pert, up-to-date and anxious to be correct.

Behind Sister Cullum stood with her staff, no less intimidated than the furniture. The House Officer was a disgrace but, sadly, there was little she could do about that. He was beyond her remit and if he was content to wear a grubby, white coat without shame or remorse, then there was nothing she could do for him. She frowned at the image of his stethoscope hanging out of one pocket and his British National Formulary leering from the other. His hair was too long, his coat was too short, he needed a bath and his shoes needed a jolly good polish. Only his name badge shone with any sense of pride and decorum, but that was because it had been bought for him by proud parents - who would undoubtably be shocked at the current appearance of their son. Jenny Cullum was married to her career and, obviously, had no children, but she knew that any respectable parent would share her displeasure.

She noticed with irritation that Staff Nurse Melissa Sharp had positioned herself too close to the scruffy HO. Something would have to be said. It was unseemly behaviour and not to be tolerated on her ward. Fraternisation between nursing staff and doctors in the workplace was unprofessional, despite what went on outside it, especially in the nurses' home. Miss Sharp was, unfortunately, extremely pretty and had one of those in-and-out figures that could be so attractive. Consequently, she was no better than she should be and required careful watching, especially around patients. As if there wasn't enough to do. At least her senior staff nurse, Glenda, could be relied upon. Every ward should have a Glenda O'Keeffe. Single, dedicated, mid-30s and determined to win promotion, however long it took, she was sturdy in mind and body, well-starched, crisp and diligent. Always on time, always there, always willing and a mine of information about the other staff, as well as patients. Glenda was an excellent deputy and although Sister Cullum could manage perfectly well without her help, it was still extremely useful. A selection of student nurses hovered in the background, identifiable by blue gingham dresses and stripes on their hats, marking their levels of training. With them was the SEN and a domestic in her green tunic standing alongside the porter in navy blue trousers and a blue shirt. It was not strictly necessary for the last two to be present, but Sister Cullum liked to include them; it increased their sense of value as well as the size of her team.

She ran Upper Gastrointestinal like a military operation. Group Captain Potts OBE would find nothing to complain about in her domain. She knew that he had recently returned from active service in Northern Ireland and, after time at the RAF hospital at Halton, he was on secondment to Birmingham Central to develop his specialisation in all things liver-related. Rumour had it, so Glenda said, that this was his reward after a particularly difficult posting – the RAF equivalent of R&R. His dog was something of a nuisance, of course. Animals really should not be on hospital premises but, as long as it stayed in the office with the Group Captain's secretary, Sister Cullum could tolerate its existence. He was, after all, a very senior officer and doctor and he had an OBE. Nobody was perfect.

Chapter Two

"We look ridiculous."

"Nonsense. You look very smart in your uniform."

Kings Cross. Two girls stood on the station platform, one swamped in an over-sized, bottle-green duffel coat, the other, the elder, strapped into another of the same size but at least two sizes too small. She could hardly move. The box pleats of her skirt hung down below the hem of the coat like a pelmet. Below, a pair of knees stared miserably out onto the world, exposed and pale.

"I'm seventeen. Why do I have to wear knee length socks?"

"Tights are too expensive, so socks are better for you."

Not for me, the knees glared.

"Why can't I go to a normal school?"

Ruth Youde pretended not to have heard. She had no intention of engaging in warfare with her eldest daughter, not when they had a train to catch. David her husband was away on detachment, again, and here she was despatching her offspring off to North Yorkshire, again.

"Dad didn't get posted. I could've done my A levels here, without any disruption. And even if we did move, I could've stayed with someone and finished them here. I'm nearly eighteen. Old enough to vote. Get married... Not wear knee length socks."

Ruth took no notice. She turned to the smaller girl.

"Have you got everything, Nicola, darling? Sue's got the tickets and she'll look after you. She's also got money for something to drink from the buffet car. Now, remember to count. Coat, overnight bag, sandwiches, comic for the train. As long as you've got four things you haven't forgotten anything."

It was nonsense of course, but Nicola said nothing. Better just to let things slide and then do what you wanted when Mum was out of the way. Honestly, Sue was meant to be intelligent but she could be so stupid. Still, that meant that she as the younger sister could do pretty much what she liked and no one noticed. Sue would keep the money for cigarettes but the other girls would let her share their drinks. There would be a whole coach of them travelling from King's Cross to York, where they would be met by one of the nuns then escorted across the Moors to Colditz on the coast. So, she smiled, extended her fingers from inside the sleeve of Sue's hand-me-down coat and took her mother's hand, as they went out of the front door.

"Stay together, won't you?" Ruth said to Sue.

Ruth and the other mothers watched the train pull out of the station. Some, like her, wore sunglasses but most were dry-eyed. Ruth hated seeing her girls go off; it never got any easier. They did not seem to mind and David said it was good for them: character building. He was a leader of men and they had to learn to do the same. Independence and resourcefulness, as well as a good education. Nothing better. Wished he'd had their opportunities and advantages he had said as he disappeared through the door on his way to work.

"Here we go, again."

It was Joan, whose daughter, Janet, was in the same class as Sue. The girls were sometimes friends when there was no one else.

"The school are sending a coach for them at York. They'll all be sick once they start over the moors, of course, after the rubbish they've eaten, but they'll be fine by tomorrow morning. Coffee?"

Yes, Ruth nodded, unable to speak. On the train, they had already been forgotten. Sue had lit up, abandoned her coat, hitched up her skirt, rolled down her socks and belted her tie around her waist. Damn. She would need to buy more cigarettes at York.

The train arrived in York on time, although Sue knew that it would be late leaving, by the time they had all unloaded themselves onto the cold platform. If she made sure she was first off, she would have just enough time to get to the kiosk and buy a pack of twenty before the coach left. Sister Sarah-Louise, known as Sloppy, had come to meet them, so it would take ages to get organised. Sloppy taught music and did everything lento. She was also tiny – no taller than Nicola – and relied heavily on horn-rimmed, pebble glasses, so it would be easy to slip off unnoticed amidst the fray. What would be the collective noun for a group of pubescent school girls, Sue wondered as she fled. A quiver? A catch? Of what? Maybe an STD. Depends what you were looking for she thought, as green box pleats flapped over bare thighs.

"Is everybody here? Good. Thank you, driver, we can go."

The coach lumbered off into the city traffic. Sloppy held onto the back of one of the front seats as she took a final look along the length of the coach. A hand was up – finger tips just evident at the end of a bottle-green arm.

"Yes Nicola? What is it? If you want the toilet, you should have gone before we left."

"No, it's not that. My sister's not on the coach.

Chapter Three

So much blood. Clearing up was going to be difficult and tedious. Never mind, it had to be done. Next time things like that would have to be checked more carefully. Small details, but significant.

She was looking upwards. The eyes were fixed and unfocused, wide shut, filming over already like egg white exposed to heat. Except that she was cold.

It was, in fact, very cold. That was good. The low temperature helped, although it had become a nuisance after a while, reducing feeling and flexibility. The work would have to be done more quickly in the future, but then they had always had to work faster.

It was all about the extraction. It had to be done properly if it was to get better.

Be objective. Analytical. Stand back. Study it with a critical eye.

Improve.

Chapter Four

DCI Martin put the phone down and grimaced. His moustache drooped sympathetically. Without bothering to comfort it, he strode out into the noisy, smoky open area.

"We've got a body," he said and everything stopped.

"Sex?"

"Don't mind if I do."

No one laughed. Then, voices from all over the room.

"Where?"

"When?"

"Is it him?

"On the game?"

"Christ."

Martin held up his hand and the noise stopped.

"I don't know, not yet. The body's been damaged – but I don't know how."

"Where is it, Boss?"

"The Gorge."

The Gorge. An unruly, steep-sided cleft in an otherwise tame landscape, close to the A64, the main road from Leeds and York.

Leeds. Where prostitutes were being murdered: hammered and stabbed into a pulp; beyond recognition. It had shocked them, even though the woman probably had it coming.

DCI Derek Martin and Mags, his asthmatic other half, did not have children but not for want of trying.

"Just wasn't meant to be" he would tell people and move on. He could only imagine the pain felt by parents who lost children but that was bad enough. Mags had found comfort in budgerigars, which she bred in the back bedroom. They had tried a cat, but the fur made Mags wheeze so he had bought her a budgie, then two and then, one thing had led to another, as it were. New born budgies were the ugliest things Martin had ever seen. Rough red jellies, all limp and helpless with lumpy, blind, black eyes, huge heads and see-through limbs. They repulsed him, even as they started to develop and became less livid in colour. The jelly sprouted spikes where the feathers would be and the beaks were sharp, insistent pincers. The eyes became narrow black slits before they opened, as the body became bruise coloured and grew in size to match the head. And the noise! From the moment they hatched they squealed and screamed. It never stopped. But it kept Mags happy and the back bedroom had become a sort of nursery, after all. So many half-formed bodies in little boxes, just like all those babies they had lost.

"Right. You all know what to do. Scott, with me. The rest of you, get on with it. Well? Whaddya waiting for?"

As if on cue, every phone began to ring, the cigarette smoke cleared and the kitchenette was deserted.

Catherine drove, and Martin thought. Neither spoke much. Occasionally, the DCI gave directions but only when he sensed that his DS did not know her way. She was a foreigner, after all, from down south, wherever that was. He was a Yorkshireman born and bred, although not from around here, not originally anyway. But now North Yorkshire was home, his patch; this was where he would die – hopefully in Whitby, to the sound of seagulls instead of budgerigars.

Uniform had sealed off the area and were now irregularly standing around on the uneven ground. The Gorge was an ugly grin in the landscape. Caused by glaciation, apparently, it was steep-sided and narrow. A path threaded across its narrow bottom, stretched thin, as if desperate to reach the end and escape and it was always dark, either by shade or by night. Cool in summer and cold in winter. Snow was a rarity, kept out by the trees on both slopes that shaded and hid.

"Hell of a place to put a body", Martin said to no one in particular, as Catherine parked the car at the top of one of the slopes. They would have to clamber down to the site, which was identifiable only by the white tape around it. It was thickly forested and the tape was roped around tree trunks, against some of which uniformed officers were leaning for balance. Catherine grieved for her tights and vowed to wear trousers in future, whatever they said about her bum. At least she had sensible shoes, lace ups, low-heeled and unfashionably platformless: regulation issue in all but colour. It had not escaped her notice that the Boss had sneaked a look at her feet when they got out of the car.

He had given nothing away but she had sensed his relief. Perhaps footwear was something they had in common? He was short for a copper, just tall enough, but had not succumbed to the temptation to wear platform shoes like so many of his colleagues, who generally towered above him. His feet and hands were actually quite dainty, Catherine saw, but his shoes needed cleaning and his nails were bitten down at the sides where the skin had been nibbled, just a little. He must do that in private she thought. I've never seen him do anything except stroke that ridiculous moustache.

They stooped under the tape and stepped into the arena. The DCI went first and Catherine followed. Uniform watched her bend and dip below the tape with interest – not much to look at, but she might be wearing stockings. Another reason to wear trousers, Catherine decided. And wellingtons. With thick socks. She would keep some in the office as well as her car.

The body was not what they expected, nor what they had most feared. It was impossible to decide whether it had been a man or a woman: decomposition was so advanced that gender had ceased to be relevant. The forensic lads would have to work that out. The hair was surprisingly luxuriant in comparison to the face, which was more skull than flesh. No eyes, just sockets and the mouth all teeth and jawbone: yellow, muddy, closed zip-tight. The hair was straggly, but quite long - shoulder length - not that that meant anything. Everyone had long hair these days.

What was unusual was the positioning of the body. It was so neat. Orderly and organised. Especially in such a hostile environment. Someone had worked extremely hard to achieve that effect and, both the DCI and Catherine, were struck by the care with which it had been placed. Laid to rest, literally. It was sepulchral. Straight-limbed legs lay side by side down to the feet, which were touching. The arms had been folded across the chest and hands lay calmly upon it, reaching towards the shoulders. All that was missing was the coffin.

"Bloody weird." Martin said eventually.

Catherine agreed. It all seemed so ... peaceful.

They both knew it was wrong to feel so relieved.

"Not the prostitute killer, then?" Catherine asked.

"Doesn't look like it. All wrong for that. No bashed in head for starters."

"Not killed here, though," she suggested.

Martin raised an eyebrow and stroked his moustache.

"Oh yeah?" Smartarse.

"Look at the grave."

They looked. It was shallow but even-sided, measured and straight-edged. Clearly it had been prepared, rather than dug in haste. Had it not been for the tree roots and confined space, it would probably have been deeper and then the body might never have been found. It was astonishing that it had been found at all; no one willingly clambered up and down these slopes; everyone there would testify to that. The body had obviously been placed there, naked, but how anyone had managed to get it there was a mystery, never mind prepare such a careful bed for it.

"It'd have to be a man. A woman couldn't do it."

"Not necessarily," Catherine murmured.

"Someone strong and fit," her boss mused.

"And determined. It could be a woman." Catherine spoke more loudly this time.

"Maybe. Who found it?" Martin yelled at one of those in uniform.

"Man walking his dog. Well, the dog. Not the man. Ran after a squirrel or summat and the man had to go after it. Found the dog digging and saw bones so reported it."

"Telephone?"

"Aye. At a farm, over there." He waved somewhere towards the trees beside him.

"Well," the moustache finally decided. "I'll let you deal with that, Scott. Go and talk to the chap who found it. Who, when, how and all that? Wouldn't hurt to have a chat with them at the farm too; see if they remember anything. Don't s'pose they will, of course, but ask anyway."

He's going to ask me to take a statement from the dog in a minute she thought. And how is anyone supposed to remember anything over a time scale that even we don't know? It could be years.

"Yes, Boss."

"I'll get back then. Uniform'll take me; you can use the car."

"Thanks, Boss."

It's my car.

They left the site and began the ascent upward as the police photographer and his gear were on the way down. Only Catherine was not wheezing with the exertion, but her tights were wrecked. She hoped the concealer beneath had held as she followed her boss; at least he was looking ahead. She need not have worried. Her legs were the last thing on Martin's mind.

The man who had found the body had plenty to say, but nothing of any significance. No, he'd never walked there before and had found it a bit creepy, y'know? But he was on his way to Leeds and had the dog in the car, so decided to let him out for a run. He'd parked at the top and had no intention of going anywhere near The Gorge, but the dog had run off and he'd had to follow. Damn dog. Never did as it was told. It'd been a right palaver to get down that slope - it was that steep, he'd thought he might slip and who'd've found him? Maybe that's what'd happened to the poor sod he'd found - fell, died and left to rot. Yes, another cup of tea would be lovely – ta – two sugars, aye. Nice farm. Had they been there long? Hard way to earn a living. He was in sales himself and liked to take the dog for company on long drives. He was a Manchester man – wrong side of the Pennines, eh? Ha ha. Travelled all over. But no, here he eyed Catherine with sudden suspicion and intense sincerity. He wasn't no murderer. The dog proved that.

Quite why was not clear, but no one argued. Catherine made notes and arranged for him to come into the station and make a statement. No, no tea for her, thank you, but if the farmer or his wife did remember anything, however small, from the last year or so, that seemed odd or unusual, please would they get in touch with her? She gave them a number to ring and headed back to the station, downhearted. What now lay ahead was a long day of desk work, checking missing persons once the forensics came through and writing reports. She should have had that cup of tea.

Chapter Five

Catherine was wrong. No sooner had she parked and walked into the office when she found that everyone else was on their way out.

"Missing girl. Call's just come in. Gotta find her."

No need to explain why. No, she wasn't a prozzie in the Leeds red-light district but she was female, young – seventeen – on her own, scantily dressed by all accounts and had just vanished. Silly bint was supposed to be on a school coach, apparently, and had only been missed when the coach was halfway to Whitby. She had got off the London-Edinburgh train with the other pupils and then disappeared. No, no one knew why or where, but it was a concern. Short skirt, school uniform – she was asking for it. Hadn't even taken a coat. God only knows what might have happened.

Catherine listened to her colleagues, silently, until the point when they said the missing girl had been on her way to a convent boarding school. Unable to bear the grunts of speculation and sexual analysis of the convent-educated, she asked who had reported the girl missing. She wished she hadn't.

"A bloody nun!"

"What's that got to do with anything?"

The men stared at her, then laughed. Stupid cow. No point in talking to women. They just didn't understand.

"I'll drive. Keep death off the roads," one of the lads announced.

Catherine felt the heat in her face and hoped it would not dislodge her make-up. Unknown to himself, the DCI came to the rescue.

"You stay here and answer the phones ... co-ordinate. Someone sensible. The boys'll handle this."

She was not sure if it was salvation, a vote of confidence or an insult, so nodded and went to her desk. Phones were ringing all around the room, which had now more or less emptied. Only she, the admin staff and a couple of desk-bound coppers remained. The missing persons would have to wait; the body in The Gorge could stay there for all anyone cared.

The ward round was going well enough for even Sister Cullum to have a stab at a smile. It pleased her to see that the patients, despite them being civilian, had fallen into line and were being drilled into the military precision with which she ran the ward. The dishevelled House Officer continued to be unfortunate, but she would speak to the Group Captain about him. If necessary, her complaint could be taken to Matron, or even the Chairman of the Consultants' Committee. As a serving member of the Armed Forces, it might not be politic for Potts to deal with an NHS doctor. Staff Nurse Sharp was altogether easier – in every sense of the word, apparently - to deal with, and would be taken on one side later that day and reminded about the standard of conduct required for one in her position, especially if she wished to stay in it.

Sister Cullum smiled, evenly, and listened to the Group Captain talking to his patients. He had arrived on time, of course, with his entourage. There were always two consultants but the second, more junior on this occasion, quite properly kept quiet and let the maestro conduct. If only the SHO, the Senior House Officer - had as much sense. Better turned out, (not difficult) than the HO making eyes at Melissa Sharp, this SHO was determined to be noticed. Well, he was. His questions were earnest, smart and appropriate but, alas, invited investigation by Potts. Regrettably, his answers were not always correct but the man had neither the wit nor sense to shut up. So embarrassing. Everyone felt it, except him. The Senior Registrar, Registrar and other HO with the second consultant winced and flushed on his behalf, but to no avail. The Group Captain however was unfazed; his face a mask. Unflappable. Sister Cullum could not decide whether he minded the frequent SHO intrusions or had simply not noticed them.

Patients who had had very recent surgery were permitted to lie tidily on their beds with their wounds undressed and covered with sterile paper sheets, which were swiftly whisked away when the consultant arrived. He would inspect them, bending stiffly over for a closer look, checking for any signs of infection or impairment. She wondered how it felt to survey the effects of your handiwork bed by bed, day after day. Did he remember each one? Probably not, but to do him credit he always made a good show of remembering that the incisions were part of a real person. Sometimes he was even quite chatty, in a professional way.

How were they feeling? Not too painful, he hoped– they could help manage that if necessary? Any other discomfort? What were their bowel movements? That was good/not good/would improve/needed to be recorded so please inform one of the nurses. Likewise breaking wind, which was an excellent sign; certainly nothing to be embarrassed about. Were they eating? This was always an unsettling topic of conversation. For herself, Sister Cullum thought that the hospital food, although bland, was perfectly adequate and nourishing. However, there were always those who disagreed, usually the over indulged sort who were under the impression that they were in a hotel. Most of them were sensible enough to keep quiet but, occasionally, someone would break ranks and complain about the menu. She had noticed that it was very often the least expected. Public school sorts reared in boarding schools and the deprived ate everything put in front of them, without demur. It was those in between who could be so problematic, the ones that fancied themselves middle class but called lavatories, toilets, and held their knives the wrong way. Of course, she knew she should not judge, but they were so demanding, so pernickety. All fur and no knickers, as her father had once said to her mother when he had not known that Jenny was listening.

The Group Captain was talking to one such now. The woman had been an emergency admission, suffering from acute pancreatitis brought on by gallstones and she had done nothing but complain from the moment she had arrived. Pancreatitis was extremely painful, they recognised that, but really, the song and dance that she had made was almost embarrassing. So disruptive, so selfish. And she was just the sort to complain about hospital food. It was not what she was used to, tasted disgusting, was overcooked, undercooked, too dry, too boring, too little of it. At which point the remark had been made that perhaps that was a good thing and had she eaten less elsewhere, she might not now be suffering from the complications of the gallstones that had put her in hospital.

Fortunately, no one was listening to her complaining. The Group Captain studied her notes while the minions shuffled and fidgeted so as not to hear. The House Officer and that minx Sharp were naïve enough to think that she, Jenny Cullum, did not see their winks and nods but they would soon know better. Potts was keen to move on to the next patient, a particularly interesting case. It was a kidney patient, a relatively young man with a wife and family. A nice man, softly spoken, unobtrusive, uncomplaining and amenable. No trouble at all. He was very unwell but, fortunately for him, had not reached the landmark age of fifty, beyond which renal failure was not treated and invariably resulted in death. He had been diagnosed with glomerulonephritis – inflammation of the kidney filtering system, which had seriously impaired his ability to clear waste from his body and had damaged his kidneys – both of them. There was no doubt about his diagnosis; he had had a biopsy to prove it. That in itself had been a dangerous journey; a kidney biopsy was a tricky and risky procedure but it had been unavoidable and it was to both his credit, and Potts', that he had survived.

What he needed was a new kidney. Now he was teetering on the edge of dialysis, hospital bound, his fluid intake restricted to 1.5 litres a day. Careful monitoring, daily blood tests, a low protein diet and treatment for high potassium levels had combined with pain and illness to exhaust him. He looked worn out, tinged with yellow, anaemic, uraemic and lethargic. Everything was too much trouble – eating, thinking, speaking; living. The daily struggle to stand and be weighed to check for fluid retention was almost more than he could bear.

Potts had a particular interest in this case. This was what excited him; thrilled him. He would have loved to have been able to open up the man, remove one of the diseased organs and replace it with a healthy one. Restore him to life and energy and, this he had to admit excited him more, become a pioneering transplant surgeon in the process. A true leader of men. It had started in 1956 when he was stationed at the military hospital at RAF Halton where the then Wing Commander, Ralph Jackson, had established a renal failure unit. Potts had been a very junior medic at the time, who had come through officer training without distinction. He was a steady, reliable sort of chap; the salt of the earth; a good egg but he wanted to be so much more. Not for him honours and awards as an officer cadet but he planned to make his mark nevertheless; to matter; to be noticed and applauded. Maybe even knighted, like Sir Ralph. Perhaps that was why he tolerated the intolerable SHO with his interminable questions – another anxious-to-be-noticed wannabe.

After a brutal tour in Northern Ireland, where he had patched up and repaired too many bodies broken by conflict, (they were not allowed to call it war but the wounds were the same), Potts had been able to exert some influence over his current posting. That happened after you had been on active service: unspoken recognition of the trauma experienced led to a sort of kindness. He had also been awarded an OBE for his services to medicine. The man still had a job to do, of course, but let him do it where he wanted, rather than where we want, seemed to be the policy of those that made such decisions.

So, he found himself, here, in Birmingham, working with civvies, with a special interest in the Renal Unit.

The patient was much the same. Quiet, yellow-tinged, languid and accommodating. His stomach was slightly bloated which was a concern: any fluid retention was dangerous. The taut belly protruded roundly from the bony pelvis and ribs, as Potts gently felt it through the flannel pyjama jacket. He lowered the pyjama trousers down over the man's pelvis to examine the extent of the bloating, noting the thinness of his legs with their wasted muscles. The man would need to tighten the drawstring of the pyjamas, yet again, if they were not to fall down the next time he had to stand up. It was doubtful if he would be able to walk to the weighing scales now; they would have to put him in a wheelchair.

No one spoke. There was no point in asking how he felt. Potts thought of the split and ravaged bodies he had witnessed in Northern Ireland. So many. So many perfectly good organs exposed and wasted. And even away from the conflict, people were dying on the roads and in accidents every day. Tragic.

Chapter Six

"The police were very understanding," Sister Sarah-Louise told Reverend Mother when they finally arrived in Whitby. "At least that's what the chief policeman said. At first, I didn't know whether to believe him or not: he was wearing an anorak, but everyone seemed to defer to him so I suppose he must have been in charge. He said it was a good outcome and that's what mattered, but I can't help thinking they were being polite. Some of them looked rather cross."

Reverend Mother removed her glasses and ran a finger under the top of her wimple then over her whiskery chin. Sloppy – yes, the girls had got it right – really could not be relied upon. All she had had to do was collect a group of pupils from a train and put them on a coach, en masse, yet she had still managed to lose one.

"Where was she found?" she asked eventually.

"Outside the station, wandering around, half frozen. She wasn't even wearing a coat."

The Head of the Order brightened and the struggling moustache unfolded itself from the indentations above her mouth.

"So, she couldn't be identified as one of ours?"

"Oh no, I don't think so. Her tie was round her waist and well, she had made her skirt terribly short. She looked awfully ... disreputable."

"Her parents will have to be told of course. I can't imagine how they will take it. He's one of our Service parents and they're always most supportive. Did you get the name of the officer in charge of the investigation? ... No. Never mind, I am sure I can find out. I shall call the Chief Constable and thank him – and apologise for the inconvenience caused. I'm sure he will respect our privacy and keep the matter confidential – out of the Press."

"What will happen to Sue?"

"That will have to be discussed. Thank you, Sister. You may go."

In the sixth form common room, the atmosphere was less civilised. Sue had pinned Janet up against the radiator which, for once, was working and she was becoming uncomfortably hot.

"Why the hell did you let the coach go without me? I told you not to."

Janet wriggled, pulled up her socks against the heat scorching her calves and narrowed her eyes. This was really gross. It wasn't her fault that the fathead had gone off for cigarettes and disappeared. What was she supposed to have done? Told Sloppy that Sue Youde had gone off to buy a packet of fags and wouldn't be long, so please could they hold the coach? She was just lucky that she, Janet, blameless and now being picked on, had managed to carry all her luggage to the coach as well as Sue's. She noticed that Sue had a spot developing on her chin – a really big one – and rejoiced. Serves her bloody well right. And I hope she gets expelled. Suspended at least. Her parents'll go mental. Suddenly, the heat against her legs did not seem so hot.

Sue had released her and stormed off to sulk somewhere – or to have a quiet smoke, probably both. Janet decided to ring her mother and tell her what had happened. Joan would be delighted. She had a pretty good idea who had revealed to their compatriots on the RAF station that 'their place in the south of France' was, in fact, a static caravan.

The forensic results on the body from The Gorge came in at much the same time as the DCI and his boys arrived back at base, in a nicotine fog that comforted them for their disappointment. They were pleased that the lass was okay – of course they were – a nice girl like that. Other girls, like those on the game in areas like Chapeltown in Leeds, were a different matter and knew the risks. They had it coming really. Tarts.

The body had been in the ground for some time – months rather than years by the look of it, but it was difficult to be exact. Although it had deteriorated beyond anything recognisable, it had been identified as male in spite of the strings of hair on the shoulder blades. t couldn't be the work of the Leeds killer then, that was clear, and the nicotine fog grew thicker. There was no evidence of violence other than post mortem animal interference – and the peaceful demeanour of the body as if laid out on an undertaker's slab, was baffling. Fascinating. DCI Martin had never seen anything like it. Putrefaction had destroyed any effective analysis of the organs and flesh but they were looking for a relatively young Caucasian male, probably in his late twenties or early thirties. His only interesting feature appeared to be the traces of his AB negative blood group, not that it was of much use to him now. He had been healthy according to the length and condition of his bones, about 5′ 10″ tall, no fibres found on the body, nothing under the finger nails that belonged to anybody else, fit and quite strong, so the chances were that he had met his end by a male hand. Well, of course he had. The boys howled with derision when they heard and the nicotine curtain briefly opened with their exhaling laughter. Bloody forensics. Everyone knew that women were weird, unfathomable, mardy bints but tidy murder wasn't their usual *modus operandi*. Not of fit blokes anyway. Wasn't possible. Might've lashed out at someone with a knife – an erring husband maybe, but couldn't have dug a grave like that, never mind got the body there. Might have been able to lure some soppy git into a wood, but halfway down The Gorge? No chance.

They brewed up, lit up and sat down at their desks to tackle paperwork; the lucky ones got to go through missing persons.

"Just gated?"

"Until the sixth form exeat weekend."

"But that's only a few weeks."

"I know!" Sue could not believe it. She had expected to be expelled or at least suspended but being gated was meaningless. There was nothing to leave school grounds for anyway, not on the North Yorkshire coast, where there was nothing between the school grounds and Norway except a lumpy hockey pitch. Even the trees lining the stone walls were stunted and streamed inland, like wind-blown hair. What she did not know was that her father had been on the phone to Reverend Mother and that undertakings had been given; a contract had been made. What Sue had done was most regrettable and The School could not tolerate any such further behaviour. Here an ominous silence interposed. Wing Commander Youde knew better than to interrupt. Let the nun have her moment.

However, Sue was a most promising student, Reverend Mother went on. She recognised her pupil's potential and did not want to disrupt or jeopardise what might yet be a very promising academic career. A place at Oxford or Cambridge was a valuable asset to any young woman. It was also an excellent advertisement for the school, but neither of them mentioned this. If Wing Commander and Mrs Youde could guarantee that Sue would never again behave in such an irresponsible and, it had to be admitted, uncharacteristic manner, then she, Reverend Mother, would be prepared to overlook the incident. Just this once. So that the young lady could complete her studies and go out into the world unblemished.

Chapter Seven

How can time pass so quickly and yet take so long?

The man dying of kidney failure in Sister Cullum's ward was living in two worlds. On the outside he was part of a real world, time regulated, recognisable and measured. Bells rang, meals came and went, lights went on and off with the day and the night. Ward rounds, bed inspections and being washed marked the mornings; visiting strangers told him it was later. And there was always the drug's trolley, dividing his life into bearable and less bearable sections. Because it was the world inside him that mattered. Pain went so slowly. Time no longer had meaning; it was only a question of how much pain he had and how long it would last. What was the difference between a second and an hour when pain was unendurable? He had learned only to expect nothing, unless the drug's trolley was in sight. Life was measured in terms of temporary relief, when he could breathe properly and touch the other world around him. Everything else hurt and crawled, slower and slower, as the pain increased. Was it wrong to want it over?

That surgeon, the senior one, the Group Captain they called him, seemed to understand. He had taken to moving away from the others, who followed him around like dogs, when he came to the dying man's bed. Leaving them standing silently in a group in the middle of the room, Potts would come right up to the bed and bend over, speaking quietly, looking the patient in the eye, hardly ever touching him but just studying the distended abdomen and changing colour. Now he was cholera yellow, spread against the white sheets, at odds with the blue of the bedspread and the curtains that would be drawn around him for his twice weekly dialysis. They wheeled him in his bed to the large machine these days. He would slump, semi-sitting, propped up against pillows, motionless, fascinated by the process of seeing his own blood travelling in and out of the plastic tubes. He hardly noticed the large central line in his neck except when he turned his head and heard it bumping against his skin. Did that happen when women wore earrings, those long pendulum ones? He wondered, but could not be bothered to find an answer. The fistula on his wrist at the point of connection for the dialysis was uncomfortable but, in some ways, had become a friend. It gave him something upon which to focus his pain; something to visualize and confront, to combat and resist. He knew that the end when it came would probably be sudden. Swift. Something to look forward to.

Two weeks is a long time to a dying man. Was it really just two weeks ago Potts wondered, that he and Scampton had gone away for the weekend? As he had sat in a line of traffic slowly negotiating road works, being squeezed from two lanes into one only to crawl past the deserted blocked off lanes, he had mused that a dialysis machine would have been quicker. That reminded him of his dying patient.

"There must be a way," he had told Scampton, who winked at him with sympathy from his foetal curl on the front passenger seat. Not until he smelled the air beyond the car fumes would he bother sitting up and taking notice. They would go for a long walk and then sit together. Potts would read and he would doze.

In Birmingham another chair of the Group Captain's was occupied, but rather more energetically.

"Lean back more," Staff Nurse Sharp was telling the scruffy HO. "I can't get my legs up."

"I don't think it'll go back much further"

The chair creaked, too racked to say more.

"Mind my stockings."

"I'll get you a new pair," the HO breathed into her ear, now pressed against his left nostril. She smelled delicious; edible. All sort of starchy clean and scented soap, healthy, fleshy and antiseptic. Her hair, tied back tightly off her face in a knot to help support her high cap was smooth and glossy against his eye. He hoped the metal hair clips would hold, but it was not the headwear he feared for.

Now she was on the move again, hoisting herself properly up onto his lap, legs on either side, knees up to his armpits. Her feet stuck out into the air towards the ceiling and she was able to lean back slightly so that they could see each other's faces. Just. A bit blurry because they were so close, but at least now he wouldn't get a hair clip in the eye. The HO grinned and grabbed her buttocks. Fingerprint hard. He slid his fingers underneath the suspenders and squeezed, as much to keep her from falling off, as to show pleasure. Ownership, if just for one, brief, shining moment. He knew she did this with everyone but who cared? It was his turn now.

"Oooh," she said, reaching down into his unzipped trousers. High waisted and previously belted, demure and modest in the face of the world, they now lay open and welcoming.

He thanked God he was not wearing a pair of the large, 'so that they can breathe' cotton underpants that his mother always bought him. Leaving home had given him the freedom to choose his own underwear. Today he was not ashamed of his tight purple briefs, although Melissa did seem to be struggling to get into them, even with her deft fingers.

"Ooh".

She was in.

The chair groaned.

The HO leant back. The staff nurse leant forward, wiggled her buttocks, settled herself and pointed her stockinged feet further towards the ceiling. As they bounced with increasing fervour, her skirt rode gloriously upwards to meet the top of her apron, fixed over her chest. The fob watch pinned to it picked up the rhythm enthusiastically, her cap shifted ... but held; her Peter Pan collar clung to her neck as a dying man to life.

The HO had begun to sweat. He hoped she would not notice. Her hands were holding onto his head, clutching his hair and he wished he had washed it this week. But she seemed fully occupied elsewhere and ... ooh ... he understood why. He hoped she would not realise this was his first time – and not just on a chair.

Which was struggling. Designed only for one, however substantial, the dimensions of two engaged in such consummate exercise was proving a challenge. It really did not have much more to give. It held its breath, as the HO held his, and then they both exhaled together, as one. He released into the Staff Nurse at the same time as the chair released itself onto the floor. The leather howled, the back gave way and the HO followed it down to meet the ground, still clutching the nurse's buttocks as she sank into him with a gasp.

They lay there, all three of them, exhausted and spent. Fortunately for the HO, the caring hands of the nurse had cushioned the blow to his head as it met the linoleum floor and she in turn had fallen further into him, so no harm had been done. Indeed, it had turned out to be an unexpectedly pleasurable development.

"This floor's filthy," the Staff Nurse commented as she lay on top of the now much scruffier HO. "There're dog hairs everywhere"; she sneezed, lifting her head a little for a better view of the lino. I bet Sister Cullum never comes in here."

"Not like me."

"Or me."

They giggled.

She levered herself up into a sitting position, straightened her legs and began to examine them.

"You owe me a pair of stockings," she said.

Chapter Eight

If the Group Captain had noticed anything untoward about his chair on his return to duties, he had said nothing. Staff Nurse Sharp had arranged for the broken seat to be replaced with another shabbier version of the same type. The scruffy HO chose not to ask how, but accepted Melissa's assurance that one of the porters, "owed her a favour", and left it at that. What the Group Captain did notice on his return, was that his office appeared to have been cleaned; the floor had obviously been swept and mopped. There were less dog hairs clustering against the skirting board and there was a new smell – less dog and more disinfectant.

He put it down to the efficiency of Sister Cullum. Standards of cleanliness in civilian institutions left a great deal to be desired. Not so the Services, of course. Everyone was trained in minute attention to detail. Even during his own officer training, he and the other cadets had been required to clean their bed springs with toothbrushes. Surprise inspections were the norm; failure to pass muster was unthinkable. Civilians did not understand the mindset behind such discipline, which went so far beyond mere cleanliness. It was all about self-discipline and obedience to orders, in any circumstances. A time might come when instead of a toothbrush he would be holding a firearm. Orders must be obeyed.

It had been an eventful two weeks. His male kidney patient had died. A sudden spike in the man's potassium levels had triggered a cardiac arrythmia and death. It had, at least, been quick. In spite of everything they had done – the meticulous monitoring, low protein diet, restriction of fluids and treatment for hyperkalaemia, his leg had continued to swell, he had lost his appetite and had become more and more confused. What irked Potts more than his own sense of failure, was the knowledge that even though the man was viable for all the renal treatment they could give him, it was lack of knowledge, research and resources that had sealed his fate.

Always sombre and austere, except when alone with Scampton, the Group Captain seemed no different than usual. Naturally, he was disappointed when a patient died – who wasn't? But, as Sister Cullum reminded her nurses, not every outcome was positive. It was all part of the job; death was a fact of life and their job was to nurse. Doctors healed; they helped. That was why it was so important that they did as they were told – here she eyed Staff Nurse Sharp – at all times. Rules were there for a reason; standards must be maintained. Which was why hospital corners on sheets had to be perfect, the wheels of the beds must all face forward, (you never knew when a patient might have to be moved quickly) and personal appearance, (she frowned at the mental image of the scruffy HO) must always be neat, clean, tidy and exact.

"There's something else going on," Melissa said to one of the student nurses in the sluice room afterwards. "She always does this when she's got things on her mind. Lecturing us makes her feel better."

Melissa was right.

Senior Staff Nurse, Glenda O'Keeffe, always so redoubtable, had something to report to Sister Cullum, that was of a most concerning nature she had said. Something so serious that the reputation of the hospital itself might be at stake. This had caught the Sister's attention, exactly as Glenda anticipated. She had, of course, come to Sister Cullum in the first instance, as her immediate superior. No one respected rank and authority like Glenda, patiently waiting for the promotion that she knew would, one day, come her way.

Would Staff Nurse O'Keeffe like to tell her about it? Jenny Cullum braced herself for the complaint about one of her team that she was certain was about to come. It would probably be Staff Nurse Sharp, again. Yes, somewhere private was a good idea. Her office?

She was glad she was sitting down when she heard.

"Are you sure?"

Glenda O'Keeffe was a thorough, obedient nurse. Sturdy cannon fodder. Pedantic - but that had its merits. Nevertheless, she did get things wrong. Perhaps she was mistaken? It would be an easy mistake to make; understandable. Sister Cullum would be the first to acknowledge the stress under which they so often worked.

No, Glenda was a Senior Staff Nurse and absolutely certain – even offended by the suggestion. She had checked several times. It was her job; she took her responsibilities extremely seriously. There were definitely drugs missing. There were discrepancies in diazepam and haloperidol: the amount in the dispensary did not correlate with the amount that she, herself, had ordered. And it had happened more than once. She had checked. It was unfortunate that as they were not controlled drugs, accurate records were not required to be kept, but she was absolutely certain, (dramatic pause) that there were discrepancies. Small, admittedly, but very noticeable to someone as sharp-eyed and conscientious as herself.

It was not so much the nature of the drugs that had gone missing, as the fact, that was so worrying. Both could be found in most households branded as Valium and Haldol – mild sedatives for everything from psychosis to hallucinations in alcohol withdrawal. Sister Cullum could hazard a guess as to any number of likely thieves. Everyone helped themselves to the occasional aspirin or paracetamol from time to time. If it kept them on their feet and at work, no one cared, if they even noticed. It was, of course, strictly against the regulations but even she had done it when a student nurse. Never since though, and even then, it had only been the odd aspirin when she was having one of her painful monthlies. It was common knowledge that bandages, antiseptic swabs and gauze found their way into pockets and handbags and left the premises for home use, but drugs? That was different. Staff Nurse O'Keeffe had been right to draw it to her attention. The situation was to be monitored but not publicised. Sister Cullum would deal with it. However, she wished to emphasise that nothing about the ... incident, was to be said. To anyone. Was that clear? She did not need to add that if it became common knowledge, she would know immediately from where it had come.

Left alone, Jenny Cullum was preoccupied. She had her suspicions. It wasn't just the restless nights she had experienced, or the beads of sweat that prickled her upper lip when the girl was close. She had seen the way that she behaved, her too-tight uniform and strained apron bib across her chest; the way she flaunted herself in the presence of men and the fineness of her hair when it strayed from beneath her cap. It was disgusting. She was ashamed for her. Even though she already knew most of what was written in Melissa Sharp's file, she pulled it from the filing cabinet and began reading.

Chapter Nine

The exeat weekend had not been a success. In fact, Sue wondered why she had bothered to go home at all. School was bad, but this was appalling. She had thought when she caught the train south with Janet, that it would be okay; her father was away, God knows where and cared even less. He would not be there to lecture, sigh, roll his eyes and criticize her clothes, make-up, what she ate or didn't, when she got up, when she went to bed - and that was just for starters. But it would be such a relief to get out of the convent.

However, she had underestimated her mother. Ruth simply did not speak to her. At all. Throughout the whole weekend, from the time she collected her daughter and Janet at King's Cross. The silence began as soon as Janet had been delivered to her front door, as carefully as a gift. The smiles and greetings shared with Joan died the second Ruth turned to walk back to the car. It was as if Sue did not exist.

She was left pretty much on her own all weekend, gated at home. It would have been better if there had been a scene, a row, even just an expression of disapproval or anger. Anything rather than the sense that she was there, but invisible. It was only the scent of her, like a bad smell, that had come home. Her mother might spray air freshener at any moment and she would evaporate; fade away; disappear without trace. Even when she sneaked off into town and got her ears pierced, which really hurt and cost far more than she had wanted to pay, no one said a word. She knew her mother had noticed; how could you miss the red swollen lobes with the tiny studs like full stops in the middle? And the smell of TCP she had to use to keep them clean. It was a relief when the time came to return north, which in itself was horrifying beyond belief. There was none of the fond farewell routine on the station platform this time. Sue and Janet loaded themselves onto the train with hardly any luggage and absolutely no school duffel coats. Janet, of course, was showing off about what she had done over the weekend. She had been to a party, been shopping and look, was wearing the coat she had bought. Wasn't it great?

It was, but Sue would die rather than say so. It was also exactly the same coat that she had coveted since she had seen it in Miss Selfridge, as well Janet knew. As she sat there, slightly too warm but determined to flaunt the triumph of her wide lapelled tapestry maxi-coat, Sue wanted to kill her. It wasn't fair. The whole world was out to get her. Just because she had made one little mistake. It wasn't even as if she smoked a lot; she actually didn't enjoy it and resented the money it cost. But now she was a marked woman. Whenever anything happened, people automatically assumed that it was her fault, and it made her rage. There were girls at school who smoked far more than she did, sneaked out at night, drank, never turned up for breakfast because they preferred to lie in and sometimes even brought boys back to their rooms. But no one said a word; they never got caught and it was so bloody unfair.

The plan was that they were to be met at York station by another girl in their form, whose parents would drive them all back to school. Both Ruth and Joan were happy with the arrangement: it meant that they would not have to worry. Their girls would be safe and arrive back at school on time, chaperoned and monitored in the nicest possible way. It wasn't that they did not trust them, not really. Even Sue. But there were some strange people around and you just never knew. Better safe than sorry.

As the train pulled into York, Sue informed Janet that she was going to make her own way across the moors back to school. Yes, her mother knew; it was all agreed. Not that it was any of Janet's business. Sue liked her independence; it would be such an asset at university and, by the way, had she told Janet she was thinking of taking a year out before she went to Oxford? Or Cambridge. She hadn't decided yet. Oh, yes. To travel. See the world. A convent boarding school was so limited; there was so much more to life than new clothes and parties.

It was an easy enough journey by bus. Sue caught a bus to Malton almost immediately, where she could pick up the stopping service all the way to Whitby. This would be a slow, ambling journey along the narrow moor roads through the cold-stone villages. There would even be enough time at Malton to get a cup of tea and a smoke. And when the packet was empty, she was giving up. That would show them.

When she got off the bus at Malton it was late afternoon, dark and cold. She actually wished she had her school coat for protection, but there was a café was just around the corner where it would be warm. She lit a cigarette and imagined herself in its glow. The café was stuffy, smoky and Formica, with red plastic tomato sauce bottles on the tables. That made Sue like it; her mother would have refused even to enter. She paid at the counter and sat herself with a cup of tea at a table in a corner near the window. There was no ashtray, so she used her saucer.

"May I join you?"

He was softly spoken, not bad looking but middle aged. Much too old. No backbreaking Yorkshire accent though, which was a plus and nice eyes.

She said yes, and he sat down, opposite, with a coffee from which he took a sip.

"Ugh. You made the right choice."

She looked at him.

"Tea. The coffee here's always disgusting. You'd think I'd know by now."

He smiled and she smiled back. What was she doing in a dive like this, he wanted to know? Could he get her something to eat before she caught her bus? It would be ages before she got to Whitby. Did she live there? It was a lovely part of the world, especially in the summer, one of his favourite places. Did she know the Magpie Café? Best fish and chips in the world. She did! He was going that way himself later and would have offered her a lift, if he had not known that she would refuse. A sensible girl would never accept a lift from a stranger.

But perhaps he could walk her to the bus stop? It was getting dark and, well, you just never knew, not these days.

The café was almost empty and there was nobody behind the counter, so he left his money beside the cash register where it would be sure to be found.

"Allow me"

He held the door open, stood back, then followed her out into the street.

“It’s cold. You should have a thicker coat,” he said. “Here. Have my jacket.”

Sue’s refusal was pathetic so he put it around her shoulders.

“Ow! I’ve been stung!” she said and stumbled. She put her fingers on her neck against the pain but could not find it. The hands held her tighter and the street lamps danced. They seemed to reach out to catch her, as she felt herself falling and had gone out by the time she hit the ground.

Chapter Ten

Cold like steel. Grey. Unforgiving. Breath hanging in the air, unable to move, gasping. Freezing where it hung. Visible. White against encroaching night.

The moors were quiet. The forms in the distance, hard to make out at first against the cold air and rigid white ground, were people, wrapped in subdued colours, blending in with the winter world around them. They huddled close to the glacial earth which forced itself up against their soled feet like bitter rising sap, claiming and clawing at their legs. Come to me; stay. Be mine.

The circle tightened. Gloved and mittened hands were tightly gripped, even those of the woman leaning on the walking sticks who had to reach up her arms towards her neighbours so as not to break the link. Whatever happened, no matter how cold it became, the connection must be held. Spirit would warm them. The Gods must be appeased.

At the same time, far away in Birmingham, the light pushed itself out of the un-curtained windows, yellow and heavy, spilling itself onto the tussocky lawn that surrounded the nurses' home. Beyond the narrow grass moat, the shrubs in their frozen beds drooped with the cold and the wet, longing for the arrival of spring. The trees gazed with envy at the rows of glass, heralding light, colour, warmth and life. The day shift was over but the night was young.

No one saw the slight, dark figure in the trees. Standing so still, whoever it was, could have been a loose branch or a sapling. Even the light on the grass did not reach as far as the rigid body, staring at a window on the ground floor.

Catherine was in the bath when the phone rang. She dripped onto the lino floor as she spoke into it; her hair needed rinsing, there was a draught from under the door grabbing her ankles and melting the towel around her shoulders, but she did not feel the cold.

"The same girl? Are we sure? It's not like last time?"

No. Definitely not. At least they already had her details on file. Her parents had been informed – well, her mother. The father was off somewhere but was being located by the RAF. The last thing they needed though, was the parents on the scene while they co-ordinated a search. Yes, dogs, the lot. Catherine needed to get there now.

Chapter Eleven

June 1977. Six months later.

"Nothing."

"How hard have you looked?"

"Very. There's nothing. We haven't a clue who he is. It doesn't help that we don't know exactly how long he's been in The Gorge. There's nothing in missing persons at all ... even for months before the estimated date of death." Catherine shrugged her shoulders and DCI Martin tugged at the wiry ends of his moustache.

"What about his blood group? I thought it was unusual."

"It is. It's AB negative but still, we've got nowhere. We don't keep records of missing persons' blood groups. Maybe we should."

"What about other police forces?"

"Not a thing." Catherine's irritation showed itself as she uncrossed her trousered legs and placed both feet steadily on the floor, side by side, in solidarity. She had spent hours – days – weeks, it seemed, trying to identify the body in The Gorge but had got nowhere. Even as she dealt with the case of Sue Youde and every bloody thing else, she would return to this one, annoyed by her failure to find an answer, her lack of results. It was all about results the lads kept reminding her, especially if she was going to wear trousers and play by their rules. They had consigned the dead man to the files of the unsolved long ago; poor sod and all that, but other things to do now. Life went on.

Not in Leeds, however. Not if you were a tart. The killer had struck in February and then again in April. It was the same *modus operandi* – a woman of the night would be hammered over the head then furiously, repeatedly stabbed and maimed in the stomach and abdomen with a knife, before being dumped nearby. The West Yorkshire police were all over it; they knew the perpetrator was a man, with a car, a kerb crawler, with some sort of violent grudge against sex workers. But they also knew that the prozzies knew the risks – they were whores - it was a part of the job. A little frisson, some over-enthusiastic horse-play – the girls knew what might happen every time they went with a fella, but the sex was consensual. It was a business transaction, all part of the deal and, more often than not, there was a tidy profit for the woman in a little rough and tumble. But murder was different, even for tarts. The police had told them to stay off the streets but they took no notice. Needed the work they said: families to support, bills to pay, kids to feed. Well, couldn't they work in pairs or something? If they had to walk the streets, they shouldn't be doing it alone. That at least made the girls laugh. Try telling that to their customers.

The news of the murder of a sixteen-year-old shop assistant who had been mistaken for a prostitute, hammered over the head, stabbed twenty times, carved up internally and left with a broken, glass screw top bottle embedded in her chest hit the headlines and changed everything. What had previously been confined to Yorkshire suddenly became national news. This was no prostitute killing. She was an innocent victim. Young, pretty and pure; no lady of the night or the streets, and the outrage that followed was heralded throughout the land. The public were up in arms. Suddenly it could be one of them, their daughter or sister or mother. Now no one was safe. Then the national media came up with a label – The Yorkshire Ripper - and the legend was born.

In the station the pressure was really on and everyone was asking questions, especially about Sue Youde. Her killer had not been found and, what was worse, they still had nothing to go on. No one had seen anything. The woman who owned the café remembered Sue sitting in the corner with a cup of tea; she had noticed her because the lass was smoking but didn't use an ashtray. She'd seemed like a nice girl – nicely spoken, posh southern sort – so it had been a surprise to see her using her saucer for the cigarette ash. There had been a man with her but nothing out of the ordinary; it was a busy café. No, she really couldn't give them any details about him. Middle-aged maybe, average height, same sort of clothes as everyone else at this time of year – warm trousers and jacket, perhaps a flat cap. She really couldn't remember. They all looked the same when they came up to the counter and ordered. He might have been the one who'd had a coffee and nothing else – she only knew that 'cos she'd had to go into the back and on her return, she'd found the exact money for one coffee beside the till. No tip included. Now, her regulars would always leave her a bit extra so, yes, she could definitely say she didn't know him. Had never seen him before. As to being able to identify him if she saw him again, she very much doubted it and, as she'd already given them as much of a description as she could, would they mind if she got on with her work? It was her own business and she ran it herself, very well. How she could be expected to remember every one of her customers was beyond her.

Apart from the killer, the woman in the café had been the last person to see Sue alive and could not even accurately say when she had left, or with whom. Nothing of her had been seen again before she had been found, in an abandoned farm building. Her torso had been neatly sliced open and sealed up again. She had also been drained of her blood. All of it.

DCI Martin's team briefing had descended into a free-for-all but he let it run. It might lead somewhere. Anywhere would be good.

"It could've been the Ripper. A schoolgirl, same age, similar appearance. He must've had a car to get her to the crime scene and we're not that far from Leeds. He must've been disturbed or he'd have got rid of everything. And then he used the car to get away."

"Yeah. It was dark when it happened – not as late as the lass in Leeds but still night time."

"But not the same MO. Or blood group. Forensics said there was AB negative blood at the scene, which is rare."

"That's right. And she wasn't bashed on the head or stabbed. The cuts were really careful – precise. Clean and planned. Whoever did it seemed to know what they were doing. They sewed her up afterwards, like tidying up, or trying to make her look normal."

"Why the hell would anyone do that?"

No one knew.

"But what about the missing organs? The Ripper does that. Don't forget the tarts in Chapeltown. They were really messed up."

"The Youde girl was drugged first. She was knocked out and drained. Then sliced."

"That Press embargo didn't help. More publicity might've helped us find who did it."

"Yeah. Why wasn't it made public? The papers would've loved it."

"That was down to the Chief Constable." DCI Martin was annoyed. He had strenuously opposed the decision at the time, but it had come from the top, so there was nothing he could do. The girl's death had been reported but downplayed; no details about the case had been released and certainly nothing about the way she had died. It was unprecedented but Martin had not been consulted. He never was. And he knew why. Perhaps if he had joined a Lodge at the start of his career and learned how to shake hands the Masonic way it might have been different, but it was too late now. He would never know for sure which of his colleagues had taken the Masonic oath but it wasn't hard to guess. Something to do with the way they assumed a stance in a room, or looked at each other. Complacent. Superior. Hidden in plain sight.

"We were lucky to find her."

"We've got nothing to go on. No shoe size, no tyre tracks, blood stains. Nothing."

"Except time, place and mode of execution - and that's our way forward." DCI Martin's moustache was in danger of being rubbed out. “The way that girl was carved up was so organised. We need expert help. Scott. Get onto it.”

Catherine slid out of the briefing and headed to her desk, not sure where to start. The DCI and his moustache were still talking.

“It looks to me like Yorkshire’s got not just one killer, but two.”

It was a lovely evening: warm, as mellow and sweet as dessert wine. The grass outside the nurses’ home was turning brown for want of rain. Bare dry earth was beginning to break through where the grassy tussocks had been shaved bald by the lawnmower. Rectangles of flattened grass showed where the sunbathers had laid on their towels. In the flower beds the upright, burgeoning shrubs were fighting for space with the proliferating weeds and litter. The only promise of shade could be found in the trees beyond, but even here the sun was stretching out its arms to find a way through the darkness.

Melissa’s room was hot. She had opened the window but the air outside was as stifling as that inside, yet she felt cold. Shivery. As if she was being watched. She looked out of the window but there was nobody there - not a soul.

No one saw the figure standing behind the first line of the trees, utterly still, silent as the shadows.

Chapter Twelve

Catherine started with the BMA, who were not helpful. We are the British Medical Association they told her, not a police force. She should contact the Chairman of her Regional Health Authority. This proved more fruitful and she found herself being passed down to a medical staffing officer, who not only seemed prepared to give her time but also information. The more junior they were, the more human they seemed to become she thought, as she explained to the man at the other end of the phone what she wanted.

"Someone with medical knowledge who can throw some light on the nature of the procedures. A surgeon probably."

She forbore to quote her DCI: "Not a quack but a sawbones, a proper one."

The man on the phone was intrigued. Was this connected to the Yorkshire Ripper case? Oh, well, never mind. Yes, he did know someone who would fit the bill. He was an Upper GI consultant with a great deal of experience and a particular interest in the liver. Upper GI? Upper Gastrointestinal – abdomen, stomach, that sort of thing, which would cover the sort of injuries Catherine had described. He was a military man who had served in Northern Ireland and was now working in Birmingham, in a civilian hospital. Was it a problem for Catherine that he was from out of area? He was definitely the man she needed, but there were other options closer by, if necessary.

No, Catherine would like to contact him. Should she do that direct? Great, let me have the details. Yes, she had got pen and paper. She tried not to sound impatient, especially when she had finished taking down the information and wanted to hang up, but the medical staffing officer wanted to talk about the Ripper case. Everyone did. If there was anything he could do to help she was to contact him, immediately, direct, and he gave her his extension number. He wished her the best of luck and offered to keep in touch in case Group Captain Leonard Potts was not able to help. His name was Pete; could he have her number?

Catherine gave him the general station number and beat a hasty retreat. She decided to contact the consultant before she reported back to the Boss. In her shoes, it was always better to have some sort of result than just the possibility of one. There might also be financial implications from bringing in someone from out of area, so it would be better to deliver the goods then sort out the cost, rather than the other way round.

A woman answered the phone - the consultant's secretary she said. The Group Captain was in theatre but she would ask him to call back as soon as it was convenient. Yes. Immediately. Anything to help an investigation in Yorkshire. Wasn't it awful what had happened to that poor girl? For a moment Catherine was thrown – how did the woman know so much about Sue Youde, but then realised that it was the most recent Ripper victim to whom she was referring. It was ghastly, but there might be some advantages to being associated, even remotely, with what was happening in Leeds.

The consultant did ring back, quickly. Catherine was on another phone when the call came in, so cut short her conversation in order to speak to him. Having no experience of anyone in the military, she was not sure what to expect. A cross between a Hollywood sergeant major and General Kitchener perhaps. What she got was a surprise – perfectly ordinary, evenly spoken, with not a trace of a barked order. He was very polite and listened intently. When she had finished, he paused for a moment, then said that he thought he could help and would be delighted to do so – to assist in any way he could. Did they need him at the station or could the information be sent to him for analysis? He would need all the photographs, reports, forensic information – everything to do with the girl's death, about which he knew very little; he didn't remember seeing anything in the Press about it at the time. DS Scott must understand however, that he was only a surgeon. There was a limit to his abilities and he could not possibly comment on anything other than the actual injuries inflicted on the young lady.

That was perfect; exactly what they wanted, Catherine said. It would be better if he could pay them a visit rather than sending him the information, in the first instance. They would like to meet him, to get to know him better and it would be easier to give him a full briefing on site, if that was possible. He must understand that the case was technically an unsolved, older one and they were anxious to establish whether or not it had any connection with the ongoing Yorkshire Ripper investigation.

The Group Captain said he would see what he could do. Some rearrangement and reorganisation at his end would be required, but he hoped to be able to pay them a visit very soon – within the week. How did the constabulary feel about dogs on their premises?

Sister Cullum tried not to let her irritation show – so unprofessional. But what was the point of having an expert on secondment from the RAF, if he was not going to be there? No doubt these were extraordinary circumstances and, yes, of course, one should always do one's best to assist the police with their investigations. She also understood that it was a murder enquiry, but did that stop patients coming into her ward in urgent need of specialist care and attention? Perhaps, if he had spoken to her first, instead of letting her hear it from his secretary as his schedule was being rearranged, it would have been less ... mortifying.

The atmosphere was particularly chilly the following morning when Potts and his entourage arrived for the ward round. In Jenny Cullum's world everything was wrong; nothing was clean enough; right-angled hospital corners were found to be off-centre; the patients were untidy and one of the student nurses was discovered sobbing her heart out over a bed pan in the sluice room. How much cleaner was she supposed to make it?

However, Sister Cullum's concerns were not confined to the temporary loss of a senior surgeon. Since the appalling discovery of drugs going AWOL from the ward dispensary, Staff Nurse O'Keeffe had been set to watch, monitor and report back on any untoward activity whatsoever. Just before the ward round began, she had requested a quiet word at the Sister's earliest convenience, which augured extremely badly. Nothing good would come of it, that was for certain and, Jenny Cullum was ashamed to admit, her mind was not fully on her patients as she escorted the medics through her realm. As soon as they had been despatched and the student nurse who kept sniffing had been told her fortune about not cleaning bed pans properly, a rather tetchy Sister Cullum closeted herself in the office with her Senior Staff Nurse.

"Well? What is it?"

Glenda O'Keeffe took a deep breath.

"Missing instruments."

They looked at each other. "Go on," said Sister Cullum's eyebrows. Only then did she notice that the woman was holding a piece of paper in her hand to which she now referred. Dear God, the woman had a list! How many were there?

"Syringes, needles, scalpel holders and blades, speculums, artery forceps, Rampley sponge holding forceps and at least one sigmoidoscope."

Sister Cullum's eyebrows seemed to have got stuck halfway up her forehead.

"Anything else?"

Again, Glenda O'Keeffe looked at her list.

"Only amyl nitrites and some Bells, Three Barrels and Harvey's Bristol Cream."

"Some?"

"A couple of bottles ... of each."

The loss of the alcohol was not really a surprise but, nevertheless, on the back of everything else, was very annoying. Patients could be given a 'wee dram' or modest nightcap at night to help them sleep; many of them waited all day for the arrival of the bottles on the drugs trolley in the evening. The disappearance of a bottle or two was generally overlooked, especially at Christmas, but there was an unspoken agreement as to the limit of the amount that went missing. Much of it was believed to end up in the nurses' home or consumed at one of the many parties that medics attended. Harmless enough, although reprehensible, but the loss of medical equipment was a different matter altogether.

"But who would take such things? And why?" Sister Cullum was genuinely perplexed.

Could she really not know? The Staff Nurse was equally puzzled. Jenny Cullum had been a trainee once and lived in a nurses' home. Surely things could not have changed that much?

"I don't know, Sister. What do you want me to do?"

"Leave it with me for the moment. And, as before, not a word to anybody. But keep a close eye on things and let me know immediately if anything else goes missing ... or if you hear anything. Anything at all."

Chapter Thirteen

"It was him. I know it was."

"We don't know that."

"I do." Ruth Youde had had enough. "I know it in here." She thumped her chest but it did not ease the pain. "I never wanted them to go away to school. There was no need; we weren't going abroad again. If they hadn't gone to that bloody place, Sue would still be here. This is all your fault."

David Youde had given up arguing. The woman was beyond reason. He knew it was no more his fault than hers, but what upset him most was that he missed Sue more than he had ever thought possible. She had always been his favourite. He had enjoyed their discussions, which had become heated debates, as she had grown up and seemed to disagree with him about everything. Yet, strangely, he had liked that. She was sharp-witted and clever – cleverer than him and more academic. Nicola, he hardly noticed. She did not show much promise and seemed unlikely to go to university – not a decent one. So, he understood his wife's pain. It was always there, tight and hard, like being short of breath but unable to inhale or breathe properly. Sometimes it faded when he was busy and his mind was elsewhere, but those were the times he dreaded most because he knew that, eventually, he would have to remember and then it would hurt twice as much. Obviously, there was no point in talking to his wife; there never had been and now that she was so irrational – well, thank God for work. The padre and the station commander had paid them a formal visit, offering support, condolences and compassionate leave, all of which he had declined. The fact that his brother officer's daughter was Sue's classmate and the travelling companion who had abandoned her had not helped. Neither he nor Ruth believed, for one moment, that Sue had left York to travel alone of her own volition. There would have been a row, one of those silly teenage girl fallings-out that happened all the time and Sue would have been forced to make her own way back to school. Janet had not told the truth. She was probably too scared, so was sticking to her story. She was adamant that it had been Sue's decision.

"It was nothing to do with me. She said you knew all about it so I didn't argue."

His daughter could be stubborn David knew, but she wasn't stupid. She would never have accepted a lift or consorted with a stranger, especially someone like the Yorkshire Ripper. She wasn't even in the right place. No, something had happened and she had been abducted, kidnapped, set upon... something. It had been a relief at the time that the case had been kept discreet, that the Press had not been allowed to walk all over it and the public to feast over every ghastly detail. The Chief Constable had turned out to be one of them. He belonged to a different Lodge to David but that didn't matter; they were Brothers, bound by the same beliefs and they looked after their own. But now, seeing the response to the death of the young girl in Leeds, David had begun to wonder about the wisdom of the decision. It had seemed right at the time but, well, perhaps, if there had been more publicity, the killer might have been found. Then they would know if it had been the work of this Yorkshire Ripper.

There was, however, one thing upon which he and Ruth agreed. Nicola was coming home. Now. They would go and get her together. The school had been told and her trunk had been packed, along with her bed linen, text books and cutlery. It was not much but, in the circumstances, Reverend Mother had even agreed to waive the fees in lieu of one term's notice.

Chapter Fourteen

As Nicola Youde was on her way south, Len Potts and Scampton were on their way north. Scampton was pleased. This was an unexpected break in routine and, much as he enjoyed the company of the nice lady secretary in the funny smelling office, he would much prefer to be with Him.

When the engine died, they were somewhere that smelled different. It was busy with lots of cars but there was a whiff of open fields in the air and they were together, so Scampton was happy to get out of the car, relieve himself and stand patiently while the boot was opened. Today the Service Dress hat was coming out; it must be important. He was wearing his Number One uniform and, suddenly, Scampton was anxious. Did this mean a long wait in a strange confined space? He would rather be in the car. Summoned, he followed, at heel, on a slack and unnecessary lead. It was all for show and he knew the form: submissive demeanour, wagging tail, lashings of canine *bonhomie*, no dribble.

There was a salute when they reached the top of the steps where they met another pair of trousers but these were non-uniform, which made a nice change. He wagged his tail with as much interest as politeness, especially when the legs developed arms that reached down and scrunched his ears. Lots of other differently-uniformed legs appeared and went as they marched through doorways, down corridors and finally, into a large smoke-filled room that made his eyes sting and momentarily blurred his vision. After they had threaded their way across the room – for once he was glad of the lead – he found himself required to lie down on a dirty lino floor beside an ash-filled waste paper basket, which he sniffed with suspicion. The ear-scrunching arms apparently belonged to someone with whom He would be working closely. They seemed to be getting on well, so the dog relaxed, leant against the bin and went to sleep.

Potts was pleased to have been met by the Detective Sergeant at the entrance to the station. It felt proper and organised, and she seemed the same. He understood that it was unusual for a woman to be a Detective Sergeant on a serious incident squad and had wondered what to expect. Something between Hattie Jacques in *Carry on Constable* and Miss Marple perhaps? What he found was a relief, and he would have been amused to know that Catherine was feeling much the same way about him. Both taller than expected, slimmer, one less posh and the other less Yorkshire, both observant and shrewd, quietly assessing the other under the cover of polite introductions and small talk. Potts noticed that the DS was wearing make-up but trousers, not a skirt; her hair was brushed not styled and he liked her sensible footwear. Her shoulder bag swung rhythmically as she walked, following her body much as Scampton followed his. She in turn had been surprised by the gentleness of the dog which offset the man's cold demeanour and austere face. He was obviously fit, with a chiselled face that suggested more than it said. She wondered what had happened to make him like that. But clearly, he could not be completely devoid of feelings and kindness, otherwise why the dog?

"The head of the investigation, Detective Chief Inspector Martin - Group Captain Potts."

"Derek"

"Len."

"Glad to have you on board, Len. DS Scott will look after you but tell me if there's anything I can do. I'm looking forward to your analysis. We're under pressure with this one."

They were indeed. The murder team in Leeds were getting nowhere with the Yorkshire Ripper case and were anxious to know whether or not he might have widened his activity beyond the Leeds red-light district. If it transpired that Sue Youde was one of his victims, it would substantially add to their problems and while they believed DCI Martin's assessment of two killers not one, they needed to know for sure. And if there were two, that was at least one more than they needed to worry about – over to you DCI Martin. The Leeds team had enough to deal with. Ironically however, money was no object. The Chief Constable himself had authorised whatever expenditure was required; the Ripper had to be found so, of course, DCI Martin could bring in outside expert assistance. Anything. Whatever it took. Just get a result.

Consequently, the meeting of the two bosses was remarkably cordial, although Martin rather resented the height of the Group Captain who towered over him. He was not sure about the dog either, but it seemed inoffensive enough and there had been no complaints, so he decided it could stay. At least it wasn't a budgie and it didn't squawk.

"What should I call you? Detective Sergeant might be very time consuming."

"Most people here call me Scott."

"Fine. Well, Scott, let's get started."

Catherine had prepared all the material which was piled on the desk where Scampton was asleep. Potts unbuttoned and unbelted his jacket, carefully removed it and looked at the woman.

"Do you have a coat hanger?"

She was astounded.

"I'll find one, sir," but I can't guarantee it she thought as she headed towards the Chief Constable's PA on the floor above. Her only hope.

When she returned, complete with wooden hanger, pursued by instructions to return it as soon as possible, she found that Potts had very carefully folded the jacket and laid it over the back of an adjoining chair. He was bent over the desk, examining the files, studying the photographs, completely unaware of her. She hung up the jacket, reverently, shaking out the non-existent creases and fastening the belt with the buckle in line with the buttons. But where to hang it? The lads flung their clothes over the backs of their chairs or on the floor, all the easier to grab. The DCI never even seemed to take his anorak off. Finally, she hung the jacket from the stationery cupboard door handle and hoped that anybody looking for paper would notice it was there.

Would the Group Captain like a cup of coffee? Tea? No, he would not, thank you, but perhaps some water for Scampton ... the dog.

"This is very interesting. Fascinating, from a medical point of view." He was looking at the images of Sue Youde's torso, before the pathologist had been at work. “Look at the way the wounds have been stitched. It’s untidy, very amateur. Not like the work of a proper surgeon at all. I could show you some of mine and you would see what I mean. The incisions are also too long – much longer than they need to be. It’s as if someone was exploring the body, finding out about the organs, rather than just removing them. You say they weren’t found? ... I wonder why. You are also correct about the care with which the incisions have been made. This isn’t the work of a deranged or angry man – or woman. Whoever did it, has a reasonable knowledge of the human body, but lacks training. A medical student? Maybe even a butcher, or a vet. Anyone with access to sharp knives and an advanced biology textbook but,” here he hesitated, “this is just speculation, but the fact that all the blood was drained from the body suggests that whoever it was, wanted to see what they were doing.”

Silence.

“I can see why you wanted an Upper GI specialist. The liver and pancreas have been removed with the right kidney. The heart hasn’t been touched. Not a crime of passion then eh?”

Was he being flippant? Catherine did not know what to say.

“The way the liver has been removed is very interesting. Look – you can see that the peritoneal reflection has been carefully divided, and the inferior Vena Cava has been divided above the entry of the hepatic veins, making sure to preserve them with the liver, but above the renal veins, making sure the blood supply to the kidney was not damaged.”

She did not have a clue what he was talking about but leant closer to him over the image, following his finger on the photo as his enthusiasm grew. He smelled earthy but clean, like Wright's Coal Tar soap. His fingers were long and slender like those of a musician, with deep, square set nails. They were short, no-nonsense nails, practical and short, clipped not filed and antiseptic clean, yet - she was surprised at herself - they were peculiarly attractive. Soft pink, with high half-moons at the base, she found herself mesmerised by the moving hand, oblivious to what was being said.

She pulled herself together, stood back and remembered her vitiligo.

He was thoughtful. "It's almost as if the killer wanted to see what a healthy liver looked like. She was young, fit, slim and didn't drink at a guess.... It makes no difference if it's a male or female organ except in size. A healthy liver is a healthy liver."

Now he raised his head and looked Catherine in the eye.

"I must admit that I find this fascinating. As a surgeon I usually only ever see inside diseased bodies. What was the victim's blood group?"

Catherine rummaged through the mound of papers. "B" she said eventually, "according to her mother."

"But the only blood found on the scene were minute traces of AB negative? That might be significant."

Neither of them spoke. Potts bent down to stroke Scampton before continuing.

"There was no evidence of any sexual interference you say? That would suggest that this was very clinical, like an exercise in dissection. The victim was drugged? What with? . . . Valium. Yes, of course. Injected presumably as none was found in her stomach. Hmm. A common enough sedative and easily obtained. Dead before all this started," he said, waving his hand over the photographs, "which is a mercy."

He was quiet again for a moment.

"Who was she?"

Catherine told him what they knew.

"Her father's in the RAF?" Now the Group Captain was looking at the DS, loud in disbelief. Scampton awoke and lifted his head.

"Good God. Not David Youde?"

Chapter Fifteen

Potts was a wing commander and Youde a squadron leader in 1973, but they were both in Northern Ireland at the same time, living in the Mess at RAF Aldergrove. Despite this, they saw relatively little of each other. Potts was assigned to the Field Hospital and Belfast's Royal Victoria while Youde flew helicopters. All the time. Helicopter pilots did not seem to have any limits to hours or assignments. The world around them had learned to ignore the constant thrum in the sky and even the local dogs no longer bothered barking at them. Occasionally, the two men would meet in the bar or over a meal in the dining room, where they would chat. Their Masonic bond was never mentioned. They were in different Lodges but it was enough to know that they belonged to the Brotherhood. That much had been established when they first met: an imperceptible sleight of the hand to all but those who were looking for it, followed by a glance, then complete understanding. Subsequently their conversation was usually work related. Like most of the married men on unaccompanied detachment, Youde preferred not to discuss home and family – out of sight was out of mind – and Potts had no one to discuss.

Potts spent much of his time working with medics. He had helped to train a small team of NCOs to act as medics out in the field, or, more accurately, the Fall's Road. These lads accompanied the foot patrols that went out, every day and every night. The medics might have the back-up of an armoured jeep but where the soldiers went, they went too.

Their training had evolved with the nature of the injuries they had to deal with. Starting with the effects of stones, bricks, bottles and whatever came to urban hand, they had graduated through the ranks of harm to the world of 1973: bombings, explosions, shrapnel, sniper fire and even the soldiers' own ricocheting bullets.

Potts had formed a close working relationship with the team. His own skills and surgical ingenuity had been tested by the injuries that these medics treated. Together they discussed the most effective ways of patching up the ever-changing nature and severity of the carnage they encountered. One of them, a lance corporal known as Vinnie, Potts found particularly interesting. Vinnie had joined the army at sixteen, straight from school but wanted to be a doctor. Or if not a doctor, a nurse. Something. Anything, in a hospital. His passion made his colleagues laugh but appealed to the wing commander, who realised that he felt the same way. It was more than just wanting to heal, treat or care. The desire to take something that was broken, beyond hope, and put it back together again was irresistible. An addiction. Power – not for itself but for what it could do for others.

That was why it seemed so unfair that Vinnie did not make it. He had been through Bloody Sunday and then Bloody Friday. Twenty bombs in thirty minutes all over the city. Vinnie had been one of the army of medics, RUC men, ambulance drivers, doctors, nurses, passers-by, ordinary people and the only slightly injured who had picked up the pieces that afternoon. It had been hell, caught on camera for the world to witness, but Vinnie and the team of medics had survived. That was why it had seemed so cruel that while tending to an injured soldier a short time later, Vinnie had been shot. Slap bang in the belly by a sniper. The worst possible place. He had started to bleed out at once and knew what it meant. They managed to get him to the RV but the damage was done; as much blood as they could put in, the more it seemed to come out. Both Potts and Vinnie knew that there was nothing that could be done and he died, in a cloud of morphine and blood, before he even got to an operating theatre.

It was David Youde who had listened as Potts talked. Ruth Youde would have been astonished. Her husband? The emotionally immature father of daughters, about whom he had no understanding whatsoever? Who always had an answer, even if he had not heard the question?

Potts talked for a long time and David Youde listened. He kept the drinks coming and then stopped them when Potts had had enough. In the morning he checked that Potts was up, dressed and ready for action. Not a word was said between the two men about the night before, but Potts never forgot. He could hardly remember what he had said but he knew that David Youde had heard, and, what mattered more, that it would never be repeated or referred to. The man that Potts had become that night would never be exposed. So, when one of the medics who had worked with Vinnie asked Potts how he made sense of death, how he coped, it was easy to answer.

"Think of them as meat," Potts had said.

Catherine and Potts were in the open office in the police station. Now it was she who was listening.

"David Youde and I were in Northern Ireland at the same time but I wouldn't say I knew him well. He flew helicopters. We really depended on people like him – the helicopters never stopped. In fact, I couldn't sleep without their noise when I first came back."

Catherine smiled and let him continue.

"He didn't talk much about his family but I knew he had a daughter of whom he was rather proud. Wasn't she rather academic?" Potts asked Catherine. "I seem to remember he was hoping she would go to Oxford or Cambridge."

Catherine did not know, but could certainly vouch for the distress of the whole family. The younger daughter was apparently being removed from boarding school, so that they could all be together. Potts turned his head to stare at her. She noticed that he had hazel brown eyes, flecked around the edge with green. Goldfish in a pool on a sunny day.

"He's got another child? I didn't know that."

He was looking at the photos before him, laid out on the desk with his hands pressed hard upon it, pointing away from them, as if afraid to touch what he could see.

"Is everything alright, Sir?"

"Yes. Fine." There was a brief pause, then, "It's so much worse when you know the victim."

Catherine wondered what had happened to him in Northern Ireland.

"I'd like to see the scene of the crime, if that's possible."

Now he was the Group Captain again, back to normal.

"It might help to build a picture of the killer, a sort of profile. Assuming of course, that it's not this Ripper fellow and I think we can safely say that it isn't. That's what you wanted to know but if I can help to catch the person who did this to the daughter of one my colleagues, then I'll do whatever I can."

Catherine would arrange it at once. She would take him herself.

So it was that they were out of the office when the news came in that another body had been found. It was not that of a young girl but an older woman, still recognisable despite having been out on the moor in a shallow grave for some time. She had been found by a gamekeeper who was making an annual inspection of the remote area around the Fylingdales' radar station. The weather was kind; the sun and the midges were out. The man had set off early to trudge across the springy ground with his dog, checking out its grouse population and the notoriously boggy lower areas. They had fallen, literally, across one, sodden indentation in which the woman lay, submerged in brackish water. Her colourless face had been exposed and she lay, eyes closed, at peace, just below the surface of the peaty water as if wearing a dark veil to preserve her modesty. Like the body in The Gorge, she was naked, her arms neatly folded across her chest with her hands flat against her clavicles. Her legs were chastely closed, in line with her body. No longer youthful and slim, her waist had thickened and her slack breasts swayed and shivered when the water moved – the only part of her that showed any sign of life.

Her bed was as measured and precise as that of the man in The Gorge but, unlike him, her torso was a trellis of cuts. It was like fretwork, as if someone had used her flesh as a block upon which to sharpen knives.

Chapter Sixteen

It had to be there, somewhere. This was ridiculous! She had put it, as always, on the top of her chest of drawers with her cap and hairclips, ready for the morning. It was always the last thing she put on, pinning it to the top of her apron and checking the time. Untidy she might be, but not disorganized. Contrary to what beastly Sister Cullum said, there was a difference, and Melissa had it nailed. Her morning routine was always the same, timed to the second, tried, tested and proved beyond all reasonable doubt. But now her nurse's fob watch with the upside-down face was missing. She distinctly remembered putting it there, yesterday evening, before she went out. There had been a greasy smudge on the glass that she had wiped off with the pair of clean knickers she was putting on. Damn. She glanced at the alarm clock beside her bed. If she did not go now, she would be late and Sister would go spare.

"Glenda! Thank God!"

Staff Nurse O'Keeffe was surprised. It was not often that Melissa even noticed her. She must want something.

"Glenda. I can't find my fob watch. I don't know where it is. I put it out ready like I always do but it's gone. Are there any on the ward? Sister'll go mad if I haven't got one."

Melissa seemed really concerned. Glenda was again surprised, this time into sympathy. She thought there might be one in the bottom drawer at the nurses' station she said, "but I don't know if it works," she shouted after her vanishing colleague.

"Doesn't matter!" Melissa shouted back.

That was the thing that most annoyed Sister Cullum when Glenda told her what had happened.

Now Melissa and the scruffy House Officer were in the laundry cupboard. He had followed her from the ward and into what was more of a room than a closet, warm and smelling of starch, a little like Melissa herself, but less accessible. They were talking.

"Pott's room?" he suggested, fixated by the sight of her legs as she stretched up to a top shelf in search of sheets. The crisp, gathered skirt of her uniform had risen well above her knees and he could almost see the top of her stockings. Anticipation was making him feel a little sweaty. He wiped his hands on his white coat. It was already unbuttoned and needed washing, sagging sadly under the weight of his stethoscope, BNF handbook, a packet of mints and an unopened condom in the pockets.

"No more chairs," she said into the shelf as she stretched a little further and her stocking tops came into view.

"Can I help?" he offered, without moving.

She shook her head and seemed to find what she was looking for. As she descended, she had an idea.

"What about going back to the nurses' home, where all the stuff is? We could have a party! There's enough for everyone if they bring a bottle."

"I'd rather it was just us."

"Oh, it'd be fun. The more the merrier," Melissa argued, a little too keenly. She was beginning to get bored with this one. What had seemed to be attractive anti-establishment, non-conformity now just seemed to be scruffiness and lack of attention to detail. However, there were still options; perhaps the privacy of her room would be better for some of those. The amyl nitrites would be a good way to start and would set the right mood. Go out with a bang, she mused, thinking about the Senior Registrar who had just arrived on the ward. He was a little older and thinning on top, but was very clean and had completed all his exams. He was also recently divorced, much to the indignation of Sister Cullum. Two birds with one stone as it were, Melissa thought and smiled. Unfortunately, the HO interpreted this as consent and immediately began to run a hand up one of her legs in search of flesh.

"Not now," she hissed as she batted him away with her bundle of sheets and headed for the door.

"When?"

"Tonight," she sighed. "Bring something to drink. I don't like sherry or whisky."

Catherine, Potts and Scampton stood inside the abandoned farm building where Sue Youde had been found. The dog was on his lead, even more unnecessarily than usual. There was no way he would have ventured off to investigate, never mind contaminate a crime scene, old as it was. The place smelled of death. He did not need to be told that something bad had happened here, it was in the air. As the three of them walked slowly around the shady interior Potts asked question after question, as much for himself as to break the atmosphere. Catherine listened intently. He had a pleasantly deep, yet soothing, voice. Where was the body placed? When Catherine told him that it had been found on plastic sheeting spread out on the ground, he bent down and touched the floor with the ends of his fingers, as if testing the temperature. Even our field facilities in Northern Ireland were better than this, he remarked, looking up at Catherine, hinting at a rueful smile.

The track they had driven along to the building was hardly passable by day in the dry, never mind on an inclement winter night, Potts observed. The killer must have had some sturdy form of transport otherwise how could he have moved an inert body? Catherine explained that no one had noticed anything unusual; the building was isolated and the windows had been blacked out. Nobody had seen or heard anything. Potts said that he would very much like to see all the photographs that had been taken of the scene when the poor girl was found. He was also curious to know why the body had not been buried. Had the killer been disturbed? He, or she, seemed to be careful and organised. It seemed uncharacteristic that the job would have been left unfinished unless there was a very good reason. A female killer was unlikely but ought not to be ruled out. There were hardly any female surgeons practicing in the NHS but that did not mean that a woman might not want to try and the work on Sue Youde had been messy and amateur. Any 'she' would have had to be very strong though, so the indications pointed to a male perpetrator.

Would Catherine mind if he had a quick look around on his own – to get a greater sense of the place? Thank you. Yes, he was sure Scampton would like to stretch his legs.

"Go with Scott," he told the dog, handing over the lead. He would only be a few minutes.

Catherine returned with relief to the outside world, fresh air, sunshine and *sang froid*. She did not understand why she felt so unsettled. Everyone had been shocked by what they had found when the girl was discovered by the searchers, but that was months ago. The smell had haunted her for days but here, today, the sun was shining, it was warm and the only smells were outdoor, natural, green and alive.

"Come on Scampton," she said, walking away from the building towards open ground. "Don't run off," she said, releasing him.

Inside the outbuilding, where the dust floated in the few mean streaks of sunlight that slithered through the grimy black windows, Potts walked slowly across the floor, backwards and forwards. At one point he stopped, bent down and rubbed in the dust with his finger. Then he stood up and went briskly to the door which he pulled shut behind him, rubbing the dust from his hands as he walked away.

Chapter Seventeen

"Where is everybody?"

Catherine, Potts and Scampton had arrived back at base and walked into an almost empty room. Phones were ringing on every desk.

"Incident. The Golf Balls. You're to go there. Boss's orders."

Resisting the temptation to answer one of the howling telephones, Catherine immediately turned around and headed out of the door through which she had just come. Potts and Scampton hesitated, then followed. As he headed for the green Volvo and Catherine towards her car, Potts called out.

"Do you know the way?"

"Not really."

"I do. There's an RAF station there... if I may accompany you?"

She nodded. His input might be helpful and it would certainly be useful if he knew the way. It did not take long to leave behind the tamed fields of the farmed, natural world and reach the open moor. As they ascended up onto the high land, the landscape changed. Boundaries no longer existed; everything rolled out before them at will. At the moment it was more yellow ochre than green; dry, rusty heathland pitted with dark troughs and deep shadows where the land dipped and rose like the moving sea. The combined camouflage colours of the Volvo and Morris Marina almost blended into the landscape as they travelled along the grey line of the road. It was all new to Catherine and as they rounded the Devil's Elbow up onto the high moor, she gasped. It was beautiful and terrible. Even the sunshine could not hide its hostility, its insidious power. And over it all, like resting Gods, the Golf Balls dominated the skyline.

The Golf Balls. The three huge, white symbols of the man-made world of the Ballistic Missile Early Warning Station of RAF Fylingdales. Visible for miles, a tourist landmark, known and seen by thousands yet ever secluded, secretive and unknown. Catherine had heard about them of course. Who hadn't? You could even turn on the car radio as you drove past the site and hear the interference caused by the radars. Coach tour drivers did it for the entertainment of their passengers *en route* to the seaside at Whitby, but Catherine did not. Her eyes were fixed on the activity visible some way from the perimeter fence of the high security station, where the body had been found. She gave thanks for the wellingtons in the back of her car and hoped she would not sweat too much as she ploughed her way through the coarse, twisted undergrowth; there would be nowhere to touch up her make up.

She stopped the car at the side of the road where the other police vehicles were clustered. Potts had pulled in ahead of her, but kept his engine running and did not get out of the car. She walked up to the driver window which he had wound down to speak to her. He was looking at her closely, his eyes caught the sun and scattered gold. She noticed that Scampton was in the front passenger seat and smiled; they were like an old married couple. She wouldn't have been surprised if the dog gave directions or poured coffee from a thermos for the Group Captain.

She had had misgivings during the drive about the propriety of Potts at the crime scene. “I’m sorry, but …” she began.

“Don’t apologise. This is police business. I’m going to go on to the station. They’re not expecting me but it won’t matter and I may be able to help from there – with telephones, communications, that sort of thing. Tell DCI Martin what I’m doing and that if he needs anything to send someone – you perhaps? – to let me know. I’ll warn the guard room and liaise with the station commander.”

It was not easy to trudge over the low, rough growth and scabby ground to the huddle of tape, uniform, non-uniform, photographer and forensics. It was also quite a long way, well outside the security area of the radar station and beyond any possibility of surveillance or vision. As she gave thanks for her wellingtons and trousers, Catherine learned how easy it would be to get lost in this landscape, especially in the dark. At the moment the days were long and the nights Arctic short – sometimes you could even see the Northern Lights – but in winter it would be so much more treacherous. It was more tripping and stumbling than walking: horizontal climbing. The dips and troughs obscured her view like high waves, as she sank down into the land then rose up again to refocus on her destination. It was also slow. Whoever had come this way with a dead body had to be very strong, very determined and very familiar with the area. It had to be someone local, surely? That would narrow their search and almost certainly rule out a female killer.

She fixed on her boss's blue anorak as a marker and threaded her way over to the crime scene. As she arrived, out of breath, hot and sweating but resisting the temptation to wipe her face, Martin was deep in conversation with one of the forensic lads. No, there was no chance that the woman, whoever she was, had been killed here the man was saying. She had been moved and was definitely dead when she was buried. The grave was shallow, like that in The Gorge, and had been carefully prepared in the sense that its sides were straight and it was an exact fit for the body. Also, the cadaver had been laid to rest in a similar way, as if in church or somewhere sacred. There was no question of her simply being dumped. Time had been taken. She had been concealed, yes, but ... here the analyst hesitated ... it was almost as if she had been tucked up in bed. Apart from the wounds over her torso, of course, which varied in depth and length. The deepest cuts were over her liver and abdomen, but they would not know the full extent of the damage until they got her back to the lab and had a proper look. Yes, they would analyse any traces of blood and identify the blood groups. He sounded resigned. They were all too well aware of the significance of an AB negative connection; there really was no need for DCI Martin to be so insistent, or impatient. They could only go as fast as they could go, couldn't they? He could tell them one thing though. She had pierced ears – look – puncture marks in the lobes. But no earrings and yes, of course they had looked all around the site. Whoever had dumped her here had taken great care to cover their tracks.

"Didn't the schoolgirl, Sue Youde, have pierced ears?"

Catherine had interrupted, as much to let her boss know that she was there, as to contribute. He looked at her, quizzically. Catherine went on.

"I'm sure she did. Her ear lobes were sore, as if she'd just had them done."

"Check. Find out. Anything else?"

Catherine shook her head. She had nothing to add about the body, but Group Captain Potts was at the RAF station and could assist with communications, which might be helpful. However, she had had some thoughts about the possible identity of the killer.

Martin looked at her.

"Well?"

"It has to be a man, strong, fit with some sort of medical background or interest, who knows this area well. That suggests that he's local, maybe a GP or working in a hospital in some capacity – even an orderly or a porter with access to medical procedures and equipment. No woman would be able to get a body here, like this unless ..."

"Go on."

"There's more than one killer. Maybe two or three - a team. Working together."

"Bloody hell."

Potts had been as good as his word. When she arrived at the fortified, outer gate and was stopped at the barrier by an armed man in RAF uniform, Catherine found that she was expected. She was identified, checked and searched, then permitted to enter and escorted through an inner gate into the guard room. There she found Scampton and they waited together for the Group Captain. At no time was she ever left alone. Everyone was very polite and courteous but there was no conversation or familiarity of any sort. Even Scampton seemed subdued and on duty. He wagged his tail but kept a respectful distance. When Potts arrived at the guard room, he explained that the discovery of a dead body in the environs had placed the base on high alert as a matter of security protocol. Most people did not understand the strategic importance of the station. They regarded the Golf Balls as some sort of eccentric local landmark without realising that they were a key part of shared UK/USA intelligence. Not only would they give notice of an impending ballistic attack, but they also tracked foreign spy satellites and were an integral part of the USA Space Surveillance Network. It was understandable, therefore, that tension was high and would remain so until any connection with the nearby crime had been ruled out. In the meantime, he would change into something less formal then meet her back at police headquarters to be of whatever assistance he could.

"How do we know it's not him?"

"Group Captain Potts?"

"Yeah. He fits a lot of the criteria."

"But it can't be."

"You don't know until you've checked."

Catherine had wondered, at first, if her boss was joking but it had become very clear that he was not. Nor anything like it. Perhaps things were getting to him she thought. Three bodies; no suspect; virtually nothing to go on and what he needed was results. That must be why he was so jumpy and irrational. How on earth could the Group Captain be a suspect? We – they - the police had approached him! He had agreed to help, seconded from work to which he was devoted in Birmingham but now motivated, not just by an innate sense of justice, but a desire to find the killer of the child of a brother officer.

"Check him out, Scott. Find out his blood group."

The briefing was terse and direct. DCI Martin was feeling the pressure and his moustache was bearing the brunt of it. He had not slept much the previous night, even before the body was found on the moor. Mags had been up most of it, tending to some avian post-natal crisis in the back bedroom and Martin had been worrying about the case. It was fortunate, if that was the right word, that national attention was focused further west in Leeds, on the Ripper. Senior officers were preoccupied with that at the moment, but another mass murderer, in the same county? At the same time? It was unprecedented. It had also clearly been going on for some time and they did not even know if the human remains found in The Gorge were the first. God only knew what else was out there, waiting to be discovered.

Now they had three bodies but only one had been identified. What disturbed him most was the fact that the bodies differed in age and sex. How were they being chosen? Why were they so different? Two had pierced ears

– Scott had checked, but no earrings and it had been impossible to tell if Gorge man had or not. Their killer was methodical, careful and deliberate, yet his victims appeared to be random. It did not follow. What was worse, they had absolutely no idea who might be next.

All this was conveyed to his team by a salvo of rapid-fire questions that felt like death by firing squad. Catherine noticed that he was wearing a different hand-knitted jumper, clearly one of his wife's less successful attempts. It was bobbly with wear, the cuffs had stretched and frilled out over his slender wrists and it hung forlornly too far down his body. It was a rather unpleasant shade of tan, on the wrong side of orange. Only after the briefing was the significance of his choice of attire revealed to her.

"It's his major incident sweater," she was told. "He doesn't take it off until the case is solved."

She looked again at the state of the jumper and felt discouraged.

"We're looking for a fit, healthy, strong person, probably male, with AB negative blood who has transport big enough to carry a body, lighting and equipment. Our killer has access to knives, cutting tools and basic medical instruments. He knows the area. Maybe he moves around for work. There might be an accomplice but generally, from what we know of this kind of killer, they work alone. We'll keep an open mind about that while we focus on finding this bastard. Oh, and he might be targeting women with pierced ears. Well, what are you waiting for?"

Thus, they had been dismissed to their desks, to trawl missing persons, to check out every GP, butcher, undertaker, hospital employee or anyone else they could think of who met any of the criteria. They were to go back to Malton and question everybody – yes, again – who had had anything to say about the disappearance of Sue Youde and they were to do another door-to-door. Somebody, somewhere, must have seen or heard something.

Chapter Eighteen

"You're early. I'm not ready."

Melissa was annoyed. Who had let him into the nurses' home she would like to know? Honestly, anyone could get in. There had been rumours of someone wandering around at night, a perve or Peeping Tom probably. They had been told to keep their curtains closed at night and even during the day if they were getting changed. Her room was on the ground floor which, generally, in all other circumstances, was considered a big advantage: easy access, no long drop for departing guests, no stairs to climb if you were exhausted or drunk and even a convenient patch of garden for sunbathing when the weather was fine. She also liked to have her window open all the year round, so having to lock it at night was a real pain. Perhaps she would get one of the porters to put a bolt or something on it so that she could open it, at least a little, without fear of intrusion.

"I couldn't wait. You look nice." The HO had come straight from the ward and it showed. Melissa looked at his unwashed hair and his exhausted coat hanging dejectedly from his sloping shoulders. He even still had his BNF in one pocket, although it was doing its best to escape, lurching perilously out of the lower edge as if about to throw itself out. Beneath the once white coat he was wearing an ancient pair of cords, balding over the knees and the front of the thighs where he had repeatedly rubbed his hands. His shirt was checked, flannel-soft from a lifetime of his mother's laundry; his polyester tie, wide, bright and fashionable was too short and too heavily knotted to sit with anything but reproach at his neck. It was also holding the ends of his collar together in the absence of a button. His name badge hung down from the coat with shame, hiding itself and all form of identification.

"You need a bath." Melissa had had enough. She gave him a towel, her wash bag and her dressing gown. "It's down the corridor."

The HO beamed. "Great idea. Let's go."

Melissa suddenly smiled. This was more like it. Perhaps he had possibilities.

"I'll get the stuff and join you," she said.

She went straight to the chest of drawers and crouched down beside the bottom drawer, the deepest and the heaviest to pull out. A layer of hearty winter jumpers and cardigans faced her, consigned to oblivion for the summer. She lifted out a couple to put on the floor, and gasped. Her head swam. There, perched on top of a long-sleeved shirt was her fob watch, with its face the right way up, as if to make itself more identifiable.

"How the hell?" She spoke aloud and stared at it. Yes, it was definitely hers – there was her name engraved on the bar above the chain, from which it hung and bounced on her chest day in, day out. Or had done, until it went missing. Perhaps it had got caught up with the stuff raided from the ward dispensary, but, if that was the case, why wasn't it underneath with the rest? Could she have dropped it in the drawer? So carefully? On its own?

Should she touch it?

Of course, she should. It was her fob watch. She picked it up, very slowly, between forefinger and thumb, least it bite ... or explode ... or something. It hung from her grip, passive, happy to be restored to its rightful upside-down position.

Weird. She shook her head and placed it, deliberately, on top of the jumpers she had removed from the drawer. Then she looked at it – made a mental record of its exact whereabouts and returned to the contents of the drawer. Shoving aside the rest of the garments, she found the stash of instruments and amyl nitrite beneath. Or what was left of it.

Most of the syringes, needles, scalpel holders and blades were there but not all. It was impossible to know how many had gone, but what was very clear was that the little glass bottles of amyl nitrite had been substantially depleted, along with the artery forceps and speculums. And where was the Rampley sponge holding forceps and the sigmoidoscope? She had had big plans for those and their potential for sexual gratification. There was no way, no way on this earth that she could have mislaid them.

"I bet it was that bitch down the corridor," she hissed aloud. "How dare she?" At least the bottles of booze were secure. The HO had taken them into custody for safekeeping and even some of the sherry was left.

Grabbing a couple of the little glass bottles she stuffed everything else, except the watch, back into the drawer and slammed it shut so hard that the chest of drawers shuddered. She would deal with the bitch down the corridor later. First, she had some serious pleasure to get on with.

"Come on. It's nice and warm."

He was already in the bath, lying back, arms crossed behind his head like a pillow as he had practised in the mirror at home. It made his shoulders look broader and expanded his chest, which he was sticking out as far as his sucked in stomach would allow. The taps were still running and he was counting on the water level rising above the level of his pelvis so that his genitalia would stop floating quite so half-heartedly. If she concentrated on his chest, Melissa might not notice, but he need not have worried. She had plans of her own.

She was stripping. He could not believe it. For him! Very slowly and all wiggly and twisty, like in the films he had seen. Now she was pinging her bra straps before shimmying down to his level and turning her back to him, so that he could undo it. That was more difficult than he anticipated as he had to uncross his arms and lean over. His hands were wet and the hook and eye thingies were very fiddly, but eventually he did it and as she wriggled her shoulders and the bra came off, she turned back to face him. Nipples at his fingertips! Joy! But before he could touch and taste, she had moved herself upwards. Now she was standing, one leg bent at the knee resting on the side of the bath, as the other stood straight, firm and flexed. As he hoped to be. Perhaps he should turn the temperature of the water down? But that would mean leaning away from her crotch and her panties and the suspenders and her stocking tops. So, he stayed where he was as she began to stroke herself. Her back was arched and her head thrown back, just like in the films she had watched, as she used her adept nurses' fingers to manipulate, unfasten, tickle and treat. Such caring, loving hands. He was mesmerised, and so close. Right up against her.

"Are those the stockings I bought?" he murmured out of the side of his mouth that still had access to fresh air.

"Hm"

"Good." And he tugged at them hard until the suspender fastenings gave way and they descended to her ankles in a shredded rush. "I'll buy you a new pair," he said, grabbing her panties with both hands and pulling them down. Unfortunately, they stopped just below the point of entry due to the leg bent on the side of the bath, but Melissa rose to the occasion, reacted swiftly, lowered her leg and the recalcitrant underwear was no more.

Oh God, the water was so warm. Would he be able to get it up? She was sitting directly over his uncooperative organ. And he wanted to, so much.

"Try this."

From nowhere, she had produced one of those small glass bottles of amyl nitrite that he had seen before in the dispensary. With those ever-adept fingers she popped off the top. The air and his nostrils filled with the smell of dirty socks.

"Don't swallow it," she said as she held it right under his nose. "Just sniff".

The rush was instant. He heard his heart, clamouring to get out his body which could not keep up with its speed and power. The room seemed to be inside his head, which was enormous. He could do anything. Fly, swim, breathe underwater, stop the water flowing from the taps with a look, a thought or a sign. Melissa was a sensation across his body, inside his head and, now, he was eating her up. He felt her bouncing up and down on him. Higher and higher; harder and harder. As he plunged, she sank, further and further into him, just like that glorious moment when they fell off Pott's chair and he had thought they were one person. Falling forever, together, down into the warm watery arms that held, caressed and enfolded. The running water roared in his ears; every drop falling from her was a rainbow, shrieking with joy and shouting colour. He had never felt so alive. So strong. So full. All around him the world was on fire, turning red and shouting out loud.

"It's all over me."

Melissa was floating above him, ascending, rushing to meet the ceiling, which seemed to be shouting at them:

"Turn the taps off!"

The door was shouting too.

"What's going on in there?"

Then Melissa was all crimson, glistening and streaky, smelling of dirty socks and iron. Why was she covered in blood?

"Your nose is bleeding. Oh my God, it's everywhere."

It was. All over the bath, the floor, Melissa, her dressing gown, her underwear, his underwear, his trousers and shirt, inside her wash bag, outside the door, flowing unrestrained into the corridor in all directions; it was pooling around the feet of the person on the other side of the door who was asking if they needed any help. Only the kipper tie, synthetic and garish seemed to have survived; or perhaps the watery runaway liquid had decided it was already colourful enough. His white doctor's coat lay at the centre of the increasing flood, unable to absorb any more of the colour while his name badge, once so proud and bright, was lost to sight.

“Come in. It’s not locked.”

The door opened against the torrent. Melissa had turned off the taps, but water was still cascading joyously over the side of the bath.

“What’s happened?” The nurse in the doorway really was not sure. She had worked in A&E but never seen anything quite like this. The blood yes, but not combined with that amount of water and nude bodies. She sniffed.

“Poppers?”

Melissa nodded and they looked at the recumbent HO.

“He’s had a reaction?”

Melissa nodded again and lifted herself out of the bath. The water lurched about her. It tried to escape but was kept at bay as the level dropped, despite the influx of blood flowing from the nose just above it.

The other nurse vanished and by the time she returned, Melissa was standing beside the bath, paddling in the cast-off clothes, as if treading grapes. In the newcomer’s hands was a toilet roll.

“We need to pack it,” she said and began to stuff toilet paper up the HO’s nose. “It’s a good thing I’m on ENT”.

As she stuffed, Melissa pulled out the bath plug and the water began sadly to drain away, all hope of escape over. But it had been fun, although the HO appeared to be suffering considerable discomfort from the toilet roll shoved up his nostrils, as well as his stubbornly erect manhood.

"We need to get him back to my room," Melissa panted, lifting his feet. "Careful or it'll snap," she added as the other nurse tackled his shoulders and they bent him over the side of the bath onto the floor.

"Who is he?"

"HO. Upper GI," Melissa answered.

"Maybe what they say is true," said the nurse, looking from the protruding organ to the HO's face. "He's got a big nose. And big feet," she added.

"He's got potential," Melissa said, critically. They both studied the engorged appendage before them.

"Seems a pity to waste it." The nurse glanced at Melissa.

"Help yourself ... See if you can get him to wash his hair."

Then they were dragging him down the corridor to Melissa's room, using the water as a slide.

"One, two, three, lift."

He was on the bed. The bleeding had stopped and he was drying off. So was Melissa but she was shivering with cold. As her dressing gown was still on the bathroom floor, she wrapped herself in a dry towel and contemplated the body in front of her.

"It must have been his first time," the other nurse said and bent over the patient to examine the damage.

"I love you," announced the invalid with his eyes still closed and grabbed the nurse. He pulled her on top of him, his hands clasped around her buttocks in a vice-like grip. "I'll never let you go."

By now the news had spread, the bathroom had become something of a celebrity and everyone on the corridor wanted to join in. Melissa was relieved to find that she had sufficient amyl nitrite, although she doubted if she would ever get rid of the smell in her room. However, it was the artery clamps that proved to be the unexpected stars of the show. Everyone wanted a go so they had to ration them; it meant that only one nipple out of every two would be very sore the next day, but the sensation was delicious and generally agreed to be well worth the pain.

The HO was exhausted. He had no idea of the time but the bed was comfortable, he had never felt so fulfilled and it was all thanks to the wonderful woman beside him. Disregarding the metalwork clinging to his chest, he turned over to face her.

"Who are you?" He felt cold. Where was he? What had happened? This wasn't Melissa.

"I'm Louise," the naked body said, snuggling into him. He had nice eyes. "And you're Tim?"

"No. Paul," the HO replied, liking the closeness of her body.

"Oh! Melissa said you were called Tim."

"My head hurts," he moaned before they fell asleep.

Chapter Nineteen

Potts and Catherine were back at the police station.

"It's a little awkward but there's something we need to establish before we can move forward." Catherine blushed. That was not the way it was meant to come out. Whatever would he think of her?

"In the case, I mean," she added, lamely, and bent down to scrumple one of Scampton's ears.

"How can I help?"

She waited until her face had cooled before she stood up again, and looked at him.

"We need to eliminate you from our enquiries."

He was on it like a scotch bonnet.

"I understand. Of course, you do. I'm sorry, I should have thought of it and saved you the embarrassment. Obviously, I meet some of the criteria of your suspect."

She said nothing, only smiled gratefully and let him continue. He was making this so easy for her. How could the boss ever have doubted him? But she took the stars out of her eyes and looked at the gold flecks in his. Everyone had to be considered, however improbable.

There would be any number of people who could vouch for him in Birmingham he said, and he felt sure he could account for his whereabouts at the time of the Youde murder. He would have to check his diary; his secretary would have the details but the most significant thing was that he was of the wrong blood group. He was a universal donor and could prove it. He loosened his tie and undid his top buttons, then reached into the gap that appeared close to his neck. Catherine again noticed his slender fingers. His shirt was double cuffed and fastened with discreet cuff links, exactly as she would have expected. His neck was smooth beneath his close, shaven chin which was stretched upwards as he reached into the hidden space. A muscular neck, the tendons ridged out above the collarbone making a furrow into his shirt, from which he pulled a set of metal dog tags on a chain. They must still be warm, Catherine thought, wanting to touch them.

"Here". He was pulling himself towards her at the end of the chain around his neck, holding one of the tags upon which his blood group was clearly marked. "See?"

There it was. Blood group O negative. Proof positive. He would not even need to do a blood test for them.

"The other one's my service number. For identification. We wear them all the time, even if we're not on active service."

Lingering too long over the dog tags she looked into his face.

"Thanks," she said and smiled. He smiled back.

DCI Martin was still wearing the unpleasant major incident hand-knitted sweater. Never elegant, it was now beginning to need washing. He had appeared from his office, stroking his moustache, which was also beginning to resemble the sweater in all but colour. His jowls sank ever lower, as if trying to find refuge in his knitwear.

"Forensics report is in. Gather round." He did not bother to wait for them before he began.

"I'm not reading the whole thing, just the bits that matter. Listen up."

The woman on the moor had been in her late thirties/early forties and healthy. There was no evidence of sexual interference but, unlike Sue Youde, she had not been a virgin. On the contrary, she appeared to have given birth to at least one child. She had stretch marks, a thickened waist but wasn't overweight and didn't appear to have smoked. Here he peered through the nicotine fog in the room.

"Not Farrah Fawcett then?" one of the lads smirked.

"Nothing wrong with the older woman," someone else offered and sniggered. "Experienced. Know what I mean?"

Catherine glared but kept quiet. Martin took no notice.

Apart from the slashes across her torso, which were many and varied in length and depth, she appeared intact. However, it was not the wounds that had killed her. Like Sue Youde, she had been drugged and exsanguinated; the injuries were inflicted after death. The body had been moved to the moor from the place of death. A sharp knife had been used – possibly several, with different blades. The woman's liver and kidneys had been penetrated but not removed. It was almost as if the killer was testing the water, for depth and obstacles; he had sliced around the organs, like cakes in a baking tin, but had not removed them. However, here DCI Martin looked up at the room and his moustache quivered. Forensics had found traces of AB negative blood.

There was a silence. Always the blood.

"What we don't have is a motive."

More silence.

"Our killer seems random. He chooses men, women, girls and God knows what else. It doesn't fit the profile of this type of killer; even the Ripper has a pattern, a type of victim." DCI Martin was speaking quietly for once; everyone was listening.

"Scott. Where's that sawbones? I can't see his dog."

"On his way back to Birmingham, sir. To the hospital."

"You've checked him out?"

"Yes, sir."

"Well call him. Tell him about the forensics. Find out what he thinks."

He turned back to the room.

"I want a list of all possible suspects on my desk by the end of today. Anyone who might have a connection, however small. And I want to know who the dead woman is. Where she's come from. She's had children. Someone must have missed her."

"And I want a motive," he flung at them as he disappeared into his office.

Chapter Twenty

"I was under the impression that they had mirrors in the nurses' home, Staff Nurse. Or perhaps you're too important to use them?"

Melissa winced. She wanted to gag and her head was banging against her hair. One of her nipples was chafing against her uniform under the apron pinned to her chest, against which her watch bumped when she moved. She had tried sliding rather than stepping to avoid the movement but it only made her feel more floaty, as if she would take off. At least that would have been quiet. Oh, to be able just to disappear into the air, to vaporise out of sight and sound of Sister Cullum.

"Go and straighten your cap and sort yourself out. Ward round begins in," Jenny Cullum consulted the timepiece hanging attentively on her own discreet chest, "two minutes."

"Where is that scruffy House Officer?" she hissed as the consultants appeared ahead of schedule and Melissa made a run for it.

Sister Cullum pressed her thighs together as tight as her lips and greeted the consultants. Thank heavens the Group Captain was back. She would deal with Melissa Sharp later.

Although it was probably just coincidence, it felt as if the hospital was going to hell in a handcart since the Group Captain had gone away. Not her ward, of course, but she had heard the rumours about the goings on in the nurse's home. Judging by the appearance of Melissa Sharp and the disappearance of the slovenly House Officer, the stories were to be taken seriously. What happened off-shift and in the privacy of their own homes was beyond her remit, obviously, but anything that impinged on the honour and running of her ward was to be taken extremely seriously. She had no intention of compromising her standards for the sake of an immoral minx who could not keep her legs closed. It was women like that who gave them all a bad name. Men always took advantage; it was their nature but, well, she sucked in her breath so far that her stomach met her spine, if it was offered to them on a plate, why wouldn't they?

It was different with women. More loving; softer and kinder. More metaphysical. All men wanted to do was to penetrate and gobble you up; take you over; own you. She remembered her one attempt at love making with a male medic when she was a student nurse and shivered. Her stomach heaved. Never again. It had been uncomfortable, sticky and absurd. She had been left with only a chafed vagina and a damp patch on her bed. Since then, men had been consigned to bitter experience. After a period of celibate R & R during which she had qualified and begun work at Reading, she had come to the realization that she preferred woman. Then there had been someone special, whom she had met when she moved to Birmingham. Jenny had been ready to commit but her partner was not willing. She was damaged: had been trapped in an unhappy marriage with a man she loathed and only wanted to be free - from everyone. So, she and Jenny had gone their separate ways and since then Jenny had been alone. No one, then, was more surprised to witness the warmth of her greeting for the Group Captain than herself. But mean it she did. Perhaps, because he so clearly did not want to sleep with her; possibly because he did not even seem to like her very much.

He had arrived back and immediately sought her out for an update: so professional and gratifying. Just as it should be, she had told herself and put Melissa Sharp to the back of her mind. Of particular interest was a patient, Helen Lofthouse, who had just been admitted. She was relatively young, in her early forties, with a husband and three children still at school. The pain in her upper quadrant had been there some time, apparently, but she had only very recently said anything. She had been "too busy," to bother about it she said, "until it got that bad, I couldn't hardly breathe." Then she had told her husband who had panicked and brought her into A&E. Now he was desperate to get her home again as his mother-in-law had moved in to take care of the kids, but Sister Cullum and the other medics were adamant that she was going nowhere until she had been seen by Group Captain Potts. Yes, the lady had had an ultrasound he was told, and the results were 'interesting'. She had gallstones but, in addition and of more concern, what appeared to be a mass close to the gall bladder.

Potts was intrigued; really quite animated Sister Cullum thought, as she watched him scrutinising the ultrasound report. He went straight to the patient, striding down the ward as on a parade ground, eyes fixed ahead, arms swinging in perfect time with his left-right, left-right legs. He doesn't even know he's doing it, Jenny Cullum thought. Yet with the patients he's gentle, almost tender. That's why they believe in him and do whatever he tells them. Even this patient, who blushed when he asked if he could examine her and asked if it was really necessary. It was, he had answered, but he would not hurt her. Oh, it wasn't that she had replied … and fell silent. Consultant and patient had looked at each other for a moment then Potts had asked, very quietly, what was worrying her. Without any hesitation she had confided in him.

"I'm fat," she had whispered with shame. "I used to be thin but after three children I just seemed to put it on and now, well, I don't want people to see." His kindness then reduced her to tears. No one would see her but himself and he thought that the human form, however it was shaped, was a miracle of nature. He would examine her in the utmost privacy – just Sister Cullum would be there to hold her hand. It would only take a moment and then it would all be over. And, he had added, she was in pain, wasn't she? That could not go on, could it? So, let's get the examination over and done with, then we can talk about the right treatment to get rid of it. How did that sound? Very good, she had replied and lifted up her nightdress.

"I need to operate, as soon as possible," Potts told Sister Cullum when they had re-opened the curtains around the woman's bed and were walking away. "The gall bladder needs to come out but it's the unidentified mass that really concerns me. I won't know what it is until I open her up and if it's what I think, it needs to come out too. Let's get her on today's list if we can, or first thing tomorrow morning."

"First on the list tomorrow might be best." Jenny threw it out there like a gauntlet. Over to you, sir, but I do know what I am talking about. Wondering how he would react, she deliberately avoided his gaze.

"Yes. That works for me."

Quietly satisfied she watched him go to the end of the ward and leave through the double doors. He never looked back.

It was the last straw. Melissa had had enough. She knew – was absolutely certain – that the underwear had been in the top, left-hand drawer. She had put it there. It was new, a matching bra and panty set, bought specifically with the Senior Registrar in mind. The underwear was an investment in her future; she did not splash out like that for anyone. Pale blue, the bra was sheer and silky smooth, with a tiny flower in the centre. The briefs were very brief indeed, just pinpoints at the side. They barely reached her hip bones; the most substantial thing about them was probably the lace trim at the top. She had bought them with her blue suspenders in mind, teamed with a pair of translucent white stockings. Black seemed too obvious, even a little tacky for an SR, to start with at least. No matter that the stockings had been bought by that scruffy HO, (she was sure he said his name was Tim). Louise was welcome to him.

There was no doubt about it. The underwear had gone. Someone had been in her room, invading her privacy, violating her possessions. She had been burgled. Robbed. Again. It was an outrage. Everyone in the nurses' home, including that bitch down the corridor, had sworn innocence about the watch and the stuff nicked from the ward dispensary, but this was different and she was going to get to the bottom of it.

Chapter Twenty-one

In Yorkshire DCI Martin's jumper and moustache were having a hard time of it. Over-stretched, over-stroked and badly in need of cleansing, they were both clinging to the hope that someone, somewhere would come up with a name or an explanation or, at the very least, some sort of motive. Anything to relieve the pressure. No new information had come from the house-to-house enquiries in Malton; no-one had seen anything; it was so long ago; they'd already told the police everything. Besides, everyone knew it was the Ripper and he was in Leeds, not Malton.

At about three in the afternoon, Martin exerted his rights as the Boss and summoned his troops.

"Well? What have you got?"

He was standing in front of the large pin board in the main office, pen in hand, armed and ready for action. Behind him were photographs of the three bodies but only one name. Aggressive question marks dominated a network of lines leading from each of the bodies, going nowhere.

"Scott. You start."

"Nothing on the Moor woman's identity as yet, sir, but," here she indicated the team of weary deskbound coppers, "we have come up with a list of close-fit suspects for the killer."

"How many?"

"Four or five, sir. We narrowed it down to age, occupation, locality, transport and gender". She deliberately avoided using the word sex. Her colleagues would think she was tight-arsed and frigid but it just wasn't worth their jeering and innuendoes.

"Who's at the top?"

"A mortician. Wilfred Black, thirty-eight. Works at the coroner's court in Scarborough but lives in Whitby. Sometimes he drives the coroner's van to ferry bodies between the coroner's and post mortems and, this is the interesting bit, he has a van of his own, registered in his name. He's unmarried and lives with his mother; his father died when he was in his teens. No previous, squeaky clean on paper, he's never even had a parking fine."

Somehow DCI Martin suddenly seemed less exhausted. His moustache had lifted but only at the ends. There was still a long way to go. Nevertheless,

"It's a start. But I want something I can bring him in on. Find out where he was when Sue Youde disappeared; what he was doing that night. Pay him a call; get onto the coroner's court. Ask questions – the neighbours, his mother, his bloody chiropodist for all I care. I want you to be hammering on my door first thing tomorrow asking for a search warrant because we've got something to go on. Well? What are you waiting for? And the rest of you, keep searching. Find out who this woman is." He jabbed his pen at the photograph of the corpse on the moor. "Even if it means contacting every police force in the country and if that doesn't work, Interpol. I hate this jumper as much as you do," he said, plucking at one frilly-edged sleeve.

Chapter Twenty-two

It was a perfect morning; the best of an English summer. Just the day for surgery, Potts said to himself as he route-marched Scampton and himself through their early morning schedule. A brisk walk/semi-jog with measured stops for press ups - for him, not the dog, followed by a high protein breakfast: poached eggs, not fried. He liked a slice or two of bacon, just on the edge of well done, but they had a tendency to make him thirsty which had to be avoided in theatre.

"Just eggs today, thank you, on brown toast. Nothing for Scampton." In the dining room doorway, steward and dog exchanged regretful glances.

Jenny Cullum was up early and on duty betimes. Glenda O'Keeffe had been entrusted with the preparation of Mrs Lofthouse but, capable Staff Nurse as she was, Jenny wanted to make sure that everything ran with the military precision that the Group Captain was used to. Other wards might be found wanting, but not hers. The patient was a model of complicity; the Group Captain had her completely in his thrall. There was none of the usual objection to being nil-by-mouth, which invariably seemed to upset patients more than any type of surgical procedure. Mrs Lofthouse even welcomed the food deprivation. Good for her figure, she said; something she'd have to get used to when she was dieting, properly. Seriously. As soon as she was better.

The procedure had been explained, consent given, forms signed. Now she was sitting up in bed, bathed, starved, raring to go. No less keen was Mr Lofthouse; the sooner his Helen was operated on, the sooner she would be home and her mother would be gone. Neither husband nor wife seemed in the least perturbed by the nature of the procedure, nor the presence of the unidentified mass that was to be investigated. Really, Jenny Cullum thought, it was as if the Group Captain had put them under a spell. What a gift he had. As she watched the porters unlock the wheels, (all facing forward) of the bed and steer the patient out of the ward, she marvelled, yet again, at the surgeon.

The moment was lost. Staff Nurse O'Keeffe would like a word with her. Yes, now, if it was convenient. It was about Staff Nurse Sharp.

In theatre, Potts was awaiting the arrival of his patient with pleasure. His team, all of them, were there, prepared and pumped. One could not line them up like troops and run an inspection as in the RAF, but that had not stopped him from discreetly assessing each one: appearance, demeanour, readiness for action. He was satisfied; they were in position; he had confidently greeted his patient and had a few words with her before they put her under. Now the real work could begin.

There she was. Flat on her back on the table, arms by her side, intubated, ventilated, neatly tucked in with a sheet. Potts felt a tingle, a thrill. Virgin territory lay before him, his to uncover and explore. It was exciting and daunting at the same time but the sense of power outweighed the responsibility; no one did this better than him, not after what he had been through. Helen Lofthouse was a lucky woman.

Removing some of the green sheeting, he exposed the area for invasion, streaky brown with iodine like mud. Seeing it alongside the green cotton sheet reminded him of camouflage and the broken men he had patched up in Northern Ireland. Everything washable and reusable, except the men. In the background he could hear the Little Susan autoclave puffing away in the prep room as it finished sterilising the instruments, like a steamy *hors d'oeuvres*. He was positioned to the right of their unconscious host, as befitted the most important guest, supported by the second assistant. Opposite stood his first assistant, alongside the scrub nurse. Were they ready? Yes. Very well. Let battle commence.

His opening gambit was a dose of antibiotics from the anaesthetist – Metronidazole and Cefuroxime. There was a silence. He looked at his first assistant, who nodded and then the second assistant, whose perplexed eyebrows were furrowed above his mask.

"They're new. Do try to keep up. A good surgeon is always *au fait* with the latest drug research and development. Right. Let's go. Kocher's first."

He made the slanted, vertical incision just under the right ribs, down to the right side. The flesh parted smoothly, silently and swiftly, exposing the yellow omentum, friable, greasy and fatty, welded over the gall bladder, stuck to the liver and the right colon. Very gently he inserted one gloved finger into the gluey softness and began to ease it off the abdominal wall. It was messy; omentum bled to the touch and was now beginning to ooze. It was difficult to see, but the finger knew its way and pressed on, finding a foothold for the retractor to be inserted by the second assistant who had shimmied his way to the left of Potts, anxious to get something right. Holding his breath, he fixed the crevice open for the dissection of the blubbery cover.

It was slow going. It had to be. At last, the gall bladder came into view, like a plant sprouting from the pancreas. Except that this plant was not so much grape green and fertile but decayed and necrotic, black and red like charred raw meat. Pus leaked from it and with that, a handful of stones: small, dark, hard pebbles that spilled out of the festering sac. Nestling beside the same, partner in crime, lay the mass that was the source of so much speculation. It was substantial, inflamed and fixed. It was also very successfully concealing the hepatic porta - bile duct, hepatic artery and portal vein. Potts did not realise that he was sweating until he felt the scrub nurse wiping his brow, which he resented, but stood still to let her finish and said nothing. She had a job to do.

Unlike some surgeons, he did not keep a running commentary of his actions. A few well-chosen words or comments at strategic moments was all he felt was required. He was a surgeon and teacher, not an entertainer. He expected his assistants to be informed and capable; they were there to consolidate and improve, not to start from scratch. Well might the second assistant feel ashamed about his failure to keep up with the newest drugs. It would have to be recorded of course, but was not personal. Nothing with Potts was ever personal. Everything was about the best possible outcomes.

Sweat-free, Potts applied himself again to the problem in hand. Literally. He managed to locate the hepatic porta, but finding much more than that within the tangled inflammatory mass was almost impossible. They would have to do it the hard way.

"Pledget!" he demanded. He began to use it to gently brush the tissue. "This is going to put today's list back but it can't be helped." It was a slow, painstaking, speck by speck process of scraping away the tissue, like archaeological dust, to expose the elusive structures within. Only then could he tie off the blood supply, deftly and securely with 2/0 silk.

Time for a breather but not a break. Potts never slacked. He might sometimes ease the pace but he never stopped, and today was no different. And if he never stopped, neither did his team. Lead from the front; set an example; standards must be maintained. He turned his attention to the slabbed mass at his fingertips.

What was it? Cancer? It was certainly stuck like hell to the gall bladder. What to do? Leave or remove? The gall bladder had to come out, there was no question about that, but with or without its sidekick? He gazed into the cavity as if looking for an answer somewhere in the wet darkness or hidden in the slippery layers of yellow fat. Only he could make this decision and it had to be the right one. The mass stared defiantly back at him, challenging and stubborn. The patient continued to lie unconscious on the table while Potts debated with her innards.

"We'll resect the mass and part of the liver," he eventually announced, "but it might get tricky." The anaesthetist looked over to him from the top of Helen Lofthouse's oblivious body with concern.

"Don't forget, I can stop this procedure at any time if I think the patient is in danger," her eyes said. Potts knew perfectly well, thank you. He knew what he was doing.

"Crush clamp with diathermy".

The second assistant resisted the temptation to groan and prepared for hard labour. He clamped and pulled, hard. Without him, no one would be able to see what they were doing. Potts marked out the dissection plan, his map of campaign. Smoke covered the hole in the green sheet; the smell of cooking flesh – roast pork at Sunday lunch – filled the theatre as Potts took a seven-inch clip and slowly crushed small pieces of the liver. Close behind, the first assistant brought up the rear, using forceps and diathermy to seal the small vessels to reduce the risk of bleeding. Meanwhile the second assistant continued his vigil, arms aching, brow sweating, pulling like hell to maintain a view. So far, so good, even if he was already knackered.

Then the bleeding began. And did not stop. It was as if the body had been quietly amassing reinforcements behind the lines and had now released the hordes onto the invading army. The barrage was ferocious – constant, full-bodied and defiant. As the second assistant pulled, Potts crushed, the first assistant burned and the theatre sister brandished the sucker against the flood; she sucked and sucked and sucked, yet still the blood flowed.

"I'm going to pack it".

Taking a deep breath, Potts stuffed a pack into the wound to push the sides of the liver together. He held hard, the pack pressed, absorbed and, slowly, the bleeding slackened. Then ceased. He exhaled.

Too soon.

The moment the pressure on the pack eased, there was a cloudburst of blood, ever-more determined to repel the aggressors. It was a torrent. The anaesthetist's eyes were wide-open over the top of her mask, which was sucked into the gaping hole of her mouth as she inhaled with horror. The call for more blood had gone out; the runner had sprinted to answer the call, then sprinted back again, even faster, to confer with the anaesthetist. The blood continued to flow.

"Keep going. We've got to get them out."

It was almost impossible to tell what was happening amidst the pumping blood, the packing, the sucking, the fingers and the forceps, not to mention the sweat, panting and tension in the rest of the room. Time seemed to have stopped, replaced by pulsating blood. The smell of iron now overwhelmed that of roasting pork and everything was wet. After an eternity, Potts lifted a slippery, dark lump up in triumph from the quagmire. He held it up, dripping, sloppy and soft with pus. It tried to slide through his fingers, snotty and sly, but he held it tight.

"Got it."

As a Roman General he held the gall bladder and attached mass aloft, a tribute to the Gods for a successful campaign. A moment of thanks and achievement, then back to reality and the aftermath. Slopped into a metal dish the heart of the enemy was gone, soon to be whisked away for analysis, but the blood, even more infuriated and determined, had to be brought to heel.

"Push the liver together."

So much easier said than done. If only they could see it. The second assistant was still toiling valiantly with the clamp; the wound was open but vision within was almost impossible through the deep, dark, venous pools of blood. Thick, black puddles filling every crevice of the cavity contrived to hide the liver: guerrilla warfare behind the lines.

“Pack it... Press... Harder.”

Usually cool and pleasant, Pott’s voice had now become a bark. Somehow, between the packs and the pressure, he was managing to individually tie off the bleeding veins. The silk sutures were instantly soaked but they held, lost within the blood swimming over them even as they were created.

“BP unstable and dropping.” It was the first time the anaesthetist had actually spoken but it was the last thing anyone wanted to hear. As Potts exerted the first assistant to apply more pressure to the packing, the anaesthetist was replenishing the emptying body with large quantities of fluid and blood. She looked concerned and fixed a look on the lead surgeon.

“You’re using fresh frozen plasma?” Potts asked her. She shook her head.

“No. It’s on order from the regional blood service. There’s none of her blood type in house.”

“Good God. What type?”

““AB.”

Potts stopped mid-suture and stared at her.

“Right,” he said eventually, addressing the whole room. “We’ll pack the liver and take a break.”

It was their turn to stare. Potts never took a break.

"You've worked hard. If we pack the liver tightly the bleeding will stop and you can get something to eat. I understand that lunch is available," he looked to the theatre sister who nodded in confirmation. It would only be soup, sandwiches and a sausage roll but at least it was free and nearby. God knows they needed some sort of reinforcement. The second assistant was close to collapse; the first assistant looked as if he had been marinaded in tomato sauce; Potts had blood dripping from his elbows as he lifted his arms up out of the chasm. All of them felt bruised and weary. They had not noticed it until he had suggested they take a break, and then it had washed over them like rain. Only the anaesthetist would remain to monitor the patient until they returned in clean gowns, scrubbed, refreshed and for those who smoked, fortified with nicotine.

Twenty minutes later they were back, suffused with caffeine, relief and scotch egg in place of sausage roll. In the unforgiving theatre light, the heavily packed wound, although bloody, had calmed down and seemed less menacing. Potts went back to his internal stitching and the first assistant put in a Robinson drain to remove the swill of pus and blood.

"Close please," Potts told the first assistant who had never been so happy to oblige. "Prolene suture then silk to skin".

The only person not to feel overwhelming relief was Helen Lofthouse, who would never know what she had been through.

Chapter Twenty-three

"I hope this is important, Staff Nurse Sharp. We are very busy."

They were in Sister Cullum's office. Glenda O'Keeffe was there, as a witness, just in case. Jenny Cullum did not trust Melissa Sharp. Yet today her uniform was straight, her hair in place and her cap properly pinned. She appeared to be wearing her own watch. Yes, that was definitely her name engraved on the bar. Even her hosiery looked relatively demure.

"Staff Nurse O'Keeffe says that you wish to make a complaint?"

"Yes. I do. Someone's been in my room. When I'm not there."

"Uninvited?"

"Yes."

"How do you know?"

"Things have gone missing."

"You've been burgled?"

"Yes."

"Are you sure? This is a very serious allegation and there are occasions, I have no doubt, when you have had people

– invited and uninvited – in your room for recreational purposes."

So, she does know about the party, Melissa thought. Probably just mad because she wasn't invited.

"This is different. This is when I'm not there and I don't know anything about it."

"What have you lost?"

Melissa noted the implication of lost and was livid. This was not her fault and she was going to prove it.

"Underwear."

"Underwear?" Glenda O'Keeffe squealed.

Sister Cullum indicated to her to be quiet. Her eyebrows alone registered surprise.

"What type of underwear?" she asked.

Melissa proceeded to describe the bra and panty set in great detail; she could make a drawing if they liked. Unfortunately, she did not have the receipt but she could show them the exact same in the shop where they had been bought. They were new; she hadn't even worn them except to try them on. It was an outrage. Who would do such a thing?

"Are you sure that you haven't lost them? Or mislaid them? Have you searched your room, properly?"

"Yes Sister. I have. I know exactly where I put them – in the top left-hand drawer of my chest of drawers. I distinctly remember putting them there because I thought how pretty they were. And now they've gone. Completely vanished."

"I'm more concerned about how someone could get into your room," Sister Cullum said. "Obviously, this has to be investigated. We need to find out if it was someone from inside the nurses' home or an intruder." She too had heard the rumours about someone watching the home and, although she preferred not to say anything to fuel the speculation, was well aware of the goings on in Yorkshire.

"Is there anything else missing?" she asked, eyebrows back in place, eyes fixed on her Staff Nurse.

Melissa hesitated, but only for the briefest moment. Obviously, she was not going to mention the contraband. And it probably was her own carelessness that had mislaid the fob watch.

"No," she said, fixing her eyes on her Ward Sister.

"Leave it with me, Staff Nurse Sharp. I will deal with this."

She paused.

"Nothing is to be said about it outside this room – by either of you. Is that clear? I'm sure there will be a very simple explanation but we don't want to cause panic, do we?" And if we do, I shall know precisely who has done it, her expression said. Class dismissed.

Chapter Twenty-four

"DS Scott! You might want to take this."

One of the admin staff was waving at Catherine from across the room and pointing to her phone. "Putting you through," she said and beamed in Catherine's direction. "It's about the woman on the moor," she announced, as Catherine picked up her receiver and began speaking.

The silence that fell over the whole toom was sudden and deep, broken only by Catherine's voice. In his office, DCI Martin became aware of the sudden hush and came out to see what had happened. Catherine was listening, intently, making notes, oblivious to everything except the voice at the end of the line.

"Well?" the DCI said when she had finished.

"We've got a possible ID for the Fylingdales body. A husband with a missing wife saw the appeal for information and got in touch with," she looked at her notes, "Stroud police. That was them just now. Do we want them to send the info or do we want to speak to the man in person?"

"Where in God's name is Stroud?" one of the team asked.

"I've no bloody idea," his boss replied, "but that's where we're going. Scott, you can drive."

Catherine was not afraid to put her foot down when she was driving the police pool car. It was not her engine or her petrol and if the car let them down, it was not her responsibility. The boss was navigating but the route was straightforward and she felt increasingly confident as they drove down the A1. As they headed away from the north, she wondered how the DCI felt. This was much more her comfort zone than his.

When they crossed into Nottinghamshire, he began talking.

"So, what really brought you to Yorkshire?" he asked. "Why did you move north?"

She thought for a moment. What to say? The truth, or the official version?

"I wanted a new challenge, sir. Something different. And the career opportunities were better, especially for a woman," she said, concentrating on the traffic ahead.

"Really?"

Silence.

Your move, Catherine thought, and kept looking ahead.

"I'd have thought it was better for a woman in London. More opportunities there. They're more open-minded than us northerners. What were you afraid of? The competition?"

"Oh no, sir, not all." Damn. She was cornered.

Another silence, while he awaited her counter-move.

"It was for personal reasons as well, sir. A new start."

"Ah."

Could she detect victory in his reply?

"Married, was he?"

"No! It was nothing like that, nothing like that at all." Anything but, she smouldered to herself, carefully avoiding his gaze.

"Ah," he said again, more kindly. "This skin condition of yours, isn't there anything they can do for it?"

She turned to stare at him and felt the heat creep into her face. How dare he?

"Have you always had it?"

"I was born with it."

"Don't worry. No one in the office knows except me. It's in your medical notes so I couldn't not."

The silence now was awkward.

"It must be inconvenient but, just so you know, I don't give a stuff." Was he trying to comfort her? she wondered. Where was this going? "You cover it well. Trousers, long-sleeved shirts, that sort of thing. None of the others have noticed. You're doing a good job."

"Thank you." She wasn't sure if she was grateful, or to what he was referring - her make-up or professional conduct.

They lapsed back into silence as the road unrolled ahead of them. She pressed the accelerator.

"So, this is what it looks like down south." DCI Martin was looking at the buildings as they drove through the market town, looking for the police station. Even the Cotswold stone was warmer, softer, soppier, he was thinking, but the people didn't look so very different. They spoke differently though, all sort of creamy and velvety, like buttermilk.

The Stroud police could not help enough. Coffee? Tea? Biscuits? The man they wanted to see was already in the interview room. They had made him welcome, looked after him and he was more than ready to talk to them. In fact, they could not shut him up. Was he a suspect? Did they think there was any connection with the Yorkshire Ripper? What a case that was! Did they know Chapeltown?

The man in the interview room was, indeed, more than willing to provide them with a voluntary witness statement. He wanted to be heard, he said. It needed to be said. As soon as they had sat down and introduced themselves, he began, and Catherine had to ask him to wait while she started the cassette recorder, before he began again.

He was tall, thin, dark haired and spotty. His face was mostly nose and eyebrows, which constituted most of his facial hair. His fringe was very short like the rest of his hair, which was all the same length and appeared to have been modelled on a pudding bowl. His name was Peter Gardiner, he was forty-five, a primary school head teacher, a father and most importantly, a Baptist, he said. With him on the table was a well-thumbed, portable-sized Bible which went everywhere with him, he told them earnestly, placing his right hand upon it as he began speaking.

"What I shall tell you is the truth, the whole truth and nothing but the truth," he announced.

"We're not in a court of law, Mr Gardiner," the DCI said. "We just have some questions we hope you can answer. It's information we're looking for."

"We're in the court of God," he said. "Searching for the Truth."

Perhaps he could tell them, then, why he had responded to the appeal for information about the identity of the woman found in Yorkshire.

His wife was called Linda, he told them. They had got married in 1961, the same year as their son, Samuel, was born, exactly nine months after their wedding. Everything had been fine to start with; they were God-fearing, ordinary people. Linda was his helpmeet, an excellent mother and obedient wife while he was the provider and head of the household, just as God decreed. Here he patted the Bible on the head like a friendly dog.

"The trouble started," he said, darkly, some years later, "when Linda began to get ideas." Women's Liberation and that sort of thing. Being a wife and mother wasn't good enough for her anymore; she wanted to get a job and be independent which, of course, he could not allow. "She said she was a Feminist and even went on a march. She had her ears pierced!" He sighed, sorrowfully. "Such vanity. The mutilation of a God-given body for vanity; how could she? But the real trouble started when..." here he paused, took a deep breath, glanced at the Bible and shook his head. "When I found out she was taking the contraceptive pill."

Catherine and the DCI exchanged looks.

"Yes," said Mr Gardiner. "I know. What was I to do? It's against God's law. She had to go. I had my son to think of."

"Did you kill her?"

"Me? Of course not. Thou shalt not kill is one of the Ten Commandments. But I had to protect my son, so I cast her out."

"When was this?"

"Four, five years ago. I don't remember exactly, but Samuel had just started at the grammar school. I remember because he had to take an entrance exam and I was worried that his mother's behaviour might impair his performance. It didn't though," he beamed. "He's doing very well there."

"Where did she go?"

"I don't know."

"Didn't she make any contact with you? With her son?"

"She tried. There were some letters, which I immediately destroyed, and I changed our telephone number. Samuel is better off without her."

"So, you have had no contact with her since about 1973?"

"That's right," he smiled. "But I hope she may be the woman you found. She fits the description. I did hear that she went to the Midlands looking for work. I think one of the letters might have had a Birmingham postmark. She was a receptionist before she married, so it's the sort of place where she'd find a job."

"You seem very keen to know if she is the woman we are looking for."

He looked surprised. Surely it was obvious?

"I need to know if she's dead or not. A divorce is out of the question but if I'm a widower, then I can re-marry in the sight of God."

The two interviewers stared at him. He smiled.

"I got rid of all the photographs of her, except one," he said. Here he reached into a pocket and pulled out a creased black and white passport photograph which he passed over to the DCI. It was impossible to identify as the dead woman.

"It's not a very good likeness," he apologised, "but our dentist will have a record of her teeth if that helps."

"Have you ever been to North Yorkshire, Mr Gardiner?"

"No. Never. I hear it's rather wild. I'm from Devon myself."

There was a knock at the door and one of the Stroud force appeared.

"Sorry to interrupt, sir, but there's a call for you," he said to the DCI. "It's urgent."

Five minutes later, Martin was back.

"Thank you, Mr Gardiner. The Stroud police will take your statement. Scott, in the car. Now." The DCI had not even bothered to enter the room but spoke from the doorway. Then he was gone.

Catherine threw an apologetic glance at the interviewee and left the room. What the hell had happened? Her boss could be abrupt, but this was ridiculous.

"They've found another one."

"Another body?"

"What else?" Then, slightly less tersely, the DCI filled her in as they headed for the car. He strode, she jogged.

"Male. Early thirties. But more recent. Much more recent."

"When?"

"Don't know yet. They're working on it. But within the last month or two."

"Where?"

"In a wood. Forestry Commission land. Just off the Scarborough/Whitby road."

"He's getting careless."

"I hope so. I'll drive."

Very little was said on the return journey. Catherine briefly wondered what Potts would be doing as they passed Birmingham, but kept silent. Martin was preoccupied and driving far too fast. At least if we get stopped, he'll be able to pull rank, she thought and looked out of the side window. The Stroud police would deal with Gardiner's voluntary witness statement which would then be faxed through to them. It seemed likely that the dead woman could be Linda Gardiner, but they would not know for certain until forensics did a dental records comparison. Then the problems started all over again, Catherine thought, and tried not to sigh. Someone – probably her – would be required to piece together the woman's movements between the time she left Stroud in 1973, until the discovery of her body on the moor. At least they would have a name, personal details and a physical description of her, although 'the Midlands' was not much to go on. Better than nothing though, and she felt they owed it to the boy to find his mother, not to mention the killer.

"Five minutes. We need to fill up and I want to make a call."

DCI Martin was swinging the car into the motorway services, too fast, and pulling up as close to the entrance of the building as he could. Fortunately, they were on the right side for the facilities so Catherine would not need to sprint across the walkway above the road to find a toilet..

Maybe, one day, we'll have phones in cars and there'll be service stations on both sides of the motorway, she mused as she washed her hands, peering critically into the mirror without time to repair any damage she found.

She was back at the car first and had to wait for the DCI, who had the keys. He arrived a few minutes after her and began speaking even as he was opening the driver door. Once inside, he leaned over and opened the passenger door, without pausing for breath.

"...not so much careless as desperate" Catherine picked up from the monologue as she sat down and reached for her seat belt. "It looks like our man – I'm sure it's a man, working on his own – is getting urges he can't resist. The dead man fits the MO in that he was drugged, drained and cut up. I've told them not to move anything until we get there but forensics have worked out quite a lot already, which makes a change. You fill, I'll pay."

A few minutes later they were back on the road again, heading north.

Chapter Twenty-five

The ground was dry and crunchy with pine needles, crisp on top but rotting quietly below into sponge. No need for her wellingtons this time, Catherine thought, which was good as there wasn't even time to put them on. The hems of her flared trousers left a thin trail through the needles and would need washing, as she picked up the pace to keep up with the DCI, who almost ran from the car to the where the body had been discovered. Forensics had looked for tyre tracks all over the area, but found nothing; whoever had done it had been clever. There was a rough road through the trees, which was used for access by the Forestry Commission, and the perpetrator had clearly followed the tracks made by their Land Rovers. It was the same road and tracks that the police had used to access the site and now it was impossible to distinguish between tyre marks. The body had been drugged, drained, mutilated and transported from elsewhere but no attempt had been made to dig a proper grave – no time presumably. It had been placed in a shallow indentation, hastily cleared, and covered with soft, dark, prickly earth.

"Blood?" DCI Martin gasped, slightly out of breath from the speed of his arrival.

"Not much," the man in the white overalls replied from his crouched position beside the corpse. "He was exsanguinated. Drained." He grinned. Catherine thought that Martin might implode.

"What type?" he hissed.

"The victim?"

The DCI glared and the grin died.

"Can't say. Traces of AB on the body. Maybe the killer cut himself when he was removing the organs."

"What's missing?"

"Liver and gall bladder. Maybe more, maybe not. We'll know after a closer look but, at a guess, I'd say he was in more of a hurry with this one. There are less cuts than the woman on the moor. It's almost as if,"

"What?"

"Well, this is just speculation, but it's almost as if the killer had more idea where they were going and what they were doing this time. They're getting better at it."

"When?"

"At a guess, seventy-two hours. No more than a week."

"Knives?"

"Yes. Very sharp. Thin bladed."

"Where are we with Wilfred Black?" Martin asked, turning to face a couple of his team huddled around cigarettes beside their parked cars.

"All over it, Boss. As soon as you called. They're bringing him in."

"On what grounds?"

"Helping with our enquiries."

"Have we got anything on him?"

"Not yet."

Wilfred Black was not what anyone was expecting but could have been made to fit the part. He was slim and wiry, rather than muscly, but clearly had strength enough to lift and move bodies. He also knew by both training and experience the most efficient way to transfer them. His hair was very dark brown, almost black, in stark contrast to the paleness of his complexion, which was almost white. It was as if so much time spent with corpses had begun to turn him into one, in appearance at least. In every other way, however, he was very much alive and extremely indignant about the attention that was being paid to him. He had done nothing wrong; they could not prove anything. It was all circumstantial and they had no right to bring him in like this. Just because he was a mortician. It was always the same. People didn't understand death, so they always assumed the worst and jumped to the wrong conclusions.

"He's playing games with us. He's trying to be psychological but it won't work." Martin said to Scott back at the station. "What it comes down to is old fashioned proof. Where was he at the time of the murder? I'd like to see him get out of that one."

"What if he does have an alibi?"

"He won't. Trust me. We'll interview him together but I'll do the talking. We'll make him wait first though. Make him sweat a bit."

"He's not under arrest."

"It's just a matter of time, Scott. Just a matter of time. I can feel it in my water."

While they examined the evidence, and Black waited, it began to look as if the DCI might be right. The mortician travelled the road past the scene of the crime almost daily. Not only did he know the area but he lived locally and always had. He had access to hospital equipment and instruments, was familiar with the human body, had suitable transport and,

"Get this," one of the lads announced with triumph. "He's a taxidermist."

"A what?"

"A bloke that stuffs dead animals."

"Bloody hell. And he looks like Dracula."

"Remember he's only helping with our enquiries, at the moment," Martin said before he and Catherine entered the room. It's not me who needs reminding, she thought, as they sat down opposite the mortician who did indeed, look like Dracula. How could anyone be that pale? Fear perhaps? He certainly seemed very uncomfortable; his feet tapped the floor and he had hunted-rabbit eyes. He started to speak as soon as they appeared in the doorway. Why was he there? He had nothing to hide? What would the coroner think? What business was it of theirs that his hobby was taxidermy? There was a surprisingly high demand for such craftsmanship, especially from bereaved pet owners. People should never underestimate the grief felt by bereaved pet owners.

He lived at home with his mother, just the two of them. Yes, they were close. They were mother and son, but they did not live in each other's pockets. His mother was as independent as she could be for someone with rheumatoid arthritis. That was why he had a van – for her wheelchair if they went out somewhere. She liked to go out into the country and meet friends. She couldn't walk far, especially on uneven ground. Yes, of course he knew the area. It was where he had been born and brought up. What did they expect?

Catherine noticed his defensiveness. So did the DCI. He slammed four images onto the desk in front of Black who looked not at them, but at the two detectives.

"What do you know about these photographs? Have a close look, Mr Black."

Nothing. He knew nothing. He did not know any of the people in the photographs. He had never seen them before. Clearly, they were dead; you did not need to be a mortician to see that but he had no idea who they were.

"Are they the people in the papers, the murdered ones?"

DCI Martin did not answer, just looked at the man on the other side of the table.

"It's not me! I'm not the Yorkshire Ripper! I've only ever been to Leeds once. Years ago. My mother'll tell you."

"Can you account for your movements, day and night, for the last two weeks?"

"Yes!" He was really indignant. "Working during the day – ask the court – it's all documented and at night I'm at home with mother."

"Will she be able to confirm that?"

"Of course."

Silence.

Catherine spoke. The DCI stared at her, but did not interrupt.

"Where do you do your taxidermy, Mr Black?"

Now he stared at her too.

"At home," he said. "I have a sort of studio, in the garage. It's too small for my van but perfect for my work. Mother doesn't like the smell of the chemicals."

"And is that where you are in the evening, when you're at home?" Catherine asked.

"Yes."

"Your mother is ...?"

"In the living room, watching telly."

"What time does she go to bed?"

"Not late. About 9.30."

"Before you?"

"Yes."

"Do you help her go to bed?"

"No! I'm her son. It wouldn't be appropriate. She's not that disabled, not around the house."

“So, is there anyone who can vouch for you being in your garage, then in bed, when you say you are?”

The white face had turned grey. DCI Martin picked up the baton.

“What blood group are you, Mr Black?

Chapter Twenty-six

Wilfred Black was still helping with their enquiries, voluntarily, without charge. Suspicion was not enough to arrest him, although that was more than enough as far as Derek Martin was concerned. But they had no evidence. His van had been seized and was being forensically taken apart but, so far, nothing; nothing at all to link him directly to the murders. Black said that he disposed of the animal insides by either burning or throwing them away with the household rubbish and he seemed to be telling the truth. When they had confirmed that Black was, without any doubt whatsoever, the proud possessor of type A blood, an air of despondency descended on the team. The DCI's moustache and jumper seemed to sag ever further.

"Perhaps we're approaching this from the wrong angle."

It was Catherine who had spoken and everyone started listening.

"What d'you mean?" said the boss.

"Well, we're assuming the AB blood is from the killer. But what if it's not? What if it's from the victims? Except for Sue Youde, we don't know what blood group they were because they were drained, but who's to say that what we found wasn't their blood? Maybe the victims were targeted for their AB blood type? It would give us a motive."

"How the hell would the killer know?"

"I don't know," Catherine had to admit. "But it might narrow down our list of suspects to people who had access to medical records or blood tests or something. Maybe they were all blood donors?"

"Which keeps Wilfred Black in the picture. He could have accessed court records, criminal charges, that sort of thing."

"Exactly."

The lads were speaking to Catherine as if she was one of them and seemed to have forgotten that she was female.

"So, Sue Youde was a mistake?" one of them asked.

They were listening to her; it felt good.

"Maybe. But I've had another look at her notes. There's nothing in her medical records that actually says what her blood group is. Her mother said it was B, but Sue hadn't been in hospital or had blood tests as far as I can see, so maybe her mother was wrong? It's possible."

"But how would the killer know she was AB?"

"I don't know," Catherine admitted. "But my point is, what if the killer doesn't have to have AB blood?"

"So, it could be Wilfred Black?"

Jenny Cullum was closeted in her office with Glenda O'Keeffe. The ward round had gone well and the Group Captain had congratulated her on the high standard of care in Upper GI, which she had taken personally. Indeed, she had to agree. There had never been any doubt about her regime, as far as she was concerned. Other people might not like it, but it worked. Standards must be maintained. The message seemed to be getting through, even to the likes of the scruffy house officer, who had started washing his hair and acquired a new pair of trousers. Even his name badge appeared to be brighter. He also no longer seemed to be quite so intimate with Melissa Sharp. All that ridiculous mooning around and standing too close to each other had come to an end. Ward rounds were polite and professional once more. No further items had gone missing from the ward dispensary and even the patients were being obedient. Jenny allowed herself the possibility of a brief half smile but her mouth could not remember which way to move.

"How is Staff Nurse Sharp?" the mouth said severely, back on familiar ground.

"Much the same," Glenda replied, equally severely. "But no new complaints."

"She seems less impertinent, or am I being over-indulgent?"

It was an interesting concept and Glenda was surprised into honesty.

"Her cap's straighter and she's still using her own watch," she said. "There're no new complaints that I know of. Perhaps the goings on at the nurses' home have had an effect."

Jenny Cullum certainly hoped so. In the light of Melissa's – unsubstantiated - allegations, the rules and security at the nurses' home had been reviewed and tightened to the point that Melissa was, without doubt, the single most unpopular resident. Men had to be signed in and out; visitor's curfew descended at 9.30 pm sharp when the outer doors were locked. External lights had been fitted up over the doors and cast their fluorescent fingers across the concrete path and bordering grass all night, so that legitimate residents, returning from equally legitimate assignations elsewhere, were required to find keys and indignantly fumble their way into their own home. At least there was plenty of light to see by. Those who had rooms near the doors could not sleep without black-out curtains which made their rooms hot and stuffy in the warm weather. And no one was allowed to fully open their windows, no matter how hot the night. The final straw was the ban on sunbathing – too provocative apparently. It would attract the wrong sort of attention and compromise general security, so it had to go.

Consequently, Melissa was not so much less impertinent as a pariah. Even the now-not-so-scruffy-HO declined to be associated with her. Besides, he was going out with Louise. Melissa herself was subdued. She could not care less about the other bitches on her corridor, or in the whole nurses' home. They could go to hell. No, what worried her was the unshakeable sense that she was being watched. Surveyed. Spied on. Someone was out to get her. Where they might be watching from was becoming an obsession. She kept her curtains shut, day and night and locked the door to her room, especially when she was inside. No one knocked on it but even if they had, she would have refused to let them in. The blue underwear had utterly vanished.

Chapter Twenty-seven

It looked like good news. The sleeves of the DCI's sweater had been rolled up above his elbows and his moustache had a perceptible lift. His jowls seemed less saggy, having followed the ends of the moustache on an upward trajectory towards the bags under his eyes.

He had manifested in the middle of the room and was waving a file in his hand.

"News on number four. Listen up."

The man did not yet have a formal ID but he was not unknown. He had been living on the streets of Scarborough and other east coast towns south of Whitby, for at least two years. No one was quite sure when he had arrived but he was a familiar local fixture, especially in the summer. Everyone knew him as Nippy on account of his pronounced limp. He had never been in trouble with the police, not even for begging. The theory was that he was a squatter in one of the once-elegant, but now almost derelict, seaside boarding houses behind the front line, 'all rooms with a sea-view' relics of a former glorious age. Having him identified as a local vagrant with no fixed abode was better than nothing, the DCI said. At least they knew he was local.

"Black must have known him," someone said.

"Looks like it," Martin replied, and pushed his sleeves further up arms. "But that's not all. Forensics have finally come up with something useful."

"Blood?" asked someone hopefully.

"No. That was drained out, like the others. But this time only the liver and gall bladder had been removed. It was neat; tidy. Well done. Quite a skilful extraction apparently, with a very sharp, fine bladed knife. He's been dead four days, so it must have happened at night."

"Which means the killer used lights?"

"Yes. No-one seems to have seen anything, but there's something else."

Dramatic pause. The moustache trembled before continuing.

"Nippy was healthy, especially for a vagrant. It looks like he's been very fit at one time; good muscle development, hard exercise, that sort of thing. As we know, he walked with a limp, which forensics say was the result of serious damage to his left leg. It's been really smashed up at some time and repaired with metal inserts – which are still there. For us to trace."

The ends of the moustache lifted with triumph and waited for a response. The lads all started to speak at the same time.

"Wilfred Black uses lights at night. He goes out hunting and trapping then says it's road kill."

"He's a weirdo."

"Nippy's a bloody stupid name for a cripple."

"The other hobos must know summat."

"Yeah, or saw him being abducted."

"How do we know he was abducted?"

"He was drugged."

"He could've known Black and got into the van himself."

"Someone must've seen lights in the dark. Even out there."

"Too many trees, dumbo."

"Okay that's enough. We don't know if it was Black yet, not for sure." At least they're thinking Martin thought. "Scott, you've been very quiet. What've you got to say for yourself? Any news on Linda Gardiner?"

"No, sir. Still working on it. But I think we need to find out how this dead man was injured and where he was treated. There's no evidence that he had piercings, in his ears or anywhere else; not even a tattoo, but we need see if there was any connection between him and Black. Maybe they were fellow taxidermists or something."

There was a howl of derisive laughter. Catherine blushed. Still the female despite the trousers.

"You can do that then, Scott. Your medical man might have some suggestions."

More laughter: less derisive, more raucous, serenaded by wolf whistles. "I don't know why you're laughing" Martin turned on the rest of the team. "You're the ones who're going to do door-to-door in Scarborough and talk to every vagrant between here and Bridlington. I'm going to pay a visit to Wilfred Black's mother."

The DCI took a young uniformed policewoman with him, 'just in case'.

"She's an old woman in a wheelchair; we don't know how she'll react," he told his companion. "Just smile, make tea and humour her."

Mrs Black was in a wheelchair, certainly, and took a few minutes to get to the front door which she did not open. Not until they had identified themselves and she had inspected their proof of identity through a narrow crack from behind a chain. Only then were they admitted, not into a fusty old-fashioned hall smelling of lavender and wee as Martin had expected, but a light, white, uncarpeted corridor. With Wilfred away, she was obliged to use the wheelchair, she told them, in case she fell. It was very inconvenient but she was still perfectly capable and independent. Rheumatoid arthritis was a disease of the joints, not the intellect.

"Better for the wheels," she said as they rubber-sole-squeaked their way across the wooden floor into an equally open, white living room coloured only with splashes of colour on the wall from the sort of art that Martin thought belonged in nursery school. The pictures weren't even framed. He thought with relief of his own loud wallpaper and soft patterned floor.

"You thought you'd find me dressed in black, sitting in a rocking chair, didn't you? With stuffed birds all over the place? Well, there are stuffed birds – excellent examples of my son's art, but this is real life and my son is not Norman Bates."

Martin had absolutely no idea what she was talking about. His gaze was fixed on a young lion in the corner of the room, snarling, with forever furious eyes.

"Ah. Yes. A young male – you can tell by the way his genitals haven't fully dropped and his mane is only half grown. Wonderful, isn't he? Inherited from my husband who was a collector but it's Wilfred who's the artist. He was so curious as a child – always had to know the how and why of everything. It wasn't enough for him just to see the specimens, he wanted to know how to make them and it went from there. There's quite a demand for big game but it's so difficult to get the raw materials. Wilfred has quite a reputation among the taxidermy society and is always being asked to travel abroad but never goes, bless him. Says he has to keep an eye on me."

By now Martin had moved his gaze from the lion and was taking in the rest of the room. The policewoman had shifted closer to the lion and was reaching out to stroke it.

"Don't touch! Please. It's been treated. For moths. Such a problem, especially if they get into the cases."

"Does your son have a girlfriend, Mrs Black?" Back to business. Martin tried to ignore the lion in the room.

"He's never said and I don't ask. It's none of my business. I'm not one of those interfering mothers, you know. Just because we live in the same house doesn't mean we we're attached at the hip."

"Does he have friends?"

"He goes to taxidermy meetings and conventions, has his work, looks after me and we attend church gatherings. How many friends do you have, Inspector?"

Martin began to think he might be in more need of the young policewoman's protection than Mrs Black.

"My son did not do it. You are looking in the wrong place. I've asked the Chaps and that's what they've told me."

"The Chaps?"

Mrs Black gave him a sad, long-suffering look. Another non-believer.

"Those on a higher plane, who have passed over."

"We are simply following all lines of enquiry and I'd like to talk to you about your son," Martin said, looking for a something to hang onto to prevent drowning.

"Have you charged him?"

No, they had not. Not as yet. Well, if they did, they were making a mistake she told them sweetly, smiling slightly. Which would come back to haunt them. And even if they did, they would never be able to find enough evidence to convict him. It would never even get to court. They were looking in completely the wrong place. Wilfred was a good man but different. He always had been, especially as a child, which was why he was picked on and bullied so withdrew into his own world. He understood that death was not the end but merely a step to another plane, another vibration. That was why he was such an excellent taxidermist. He worked with the spirit of the animal that had passed over. Did they have any idea how much comfort his work brought to those who had suffered the pain of loss and were grieving?

"Like you and your wife," she said to the DCI.

"I beg your pardon?"

"All those baby birds. She's in such pain."

He gaped.

She spoke. "You too, but you hide it better. Sometimes Spirit chooses a different path for us than the one we would like, but they have their reasons. You may search as much as you like, it makes no difference. I cannot prove that Wilfred was here when I was in bed but I know that he is innocent."

Either she was a genius or she was insane; maybe both. They would have to search the house, the garage and the garden; they already had her son's van and the coroner's court transport. They would take her statement but, he felt obliged to say this, she should be prepared for the possibility that she might be mistaken. She merely smiled and shook her head as she escorted them to the front door.

"Follow the young one, that's what they're telling me. Oh, and tell the police looking for the Yorkshire Ripper that they've found him, they just don't know it yet."

"No wonder Black's so creepy," Martin said as they were getting into the car. "She's not doing him any favours. Who's Norman Bates?"

The policewoman explained and suggested that he went to see *Psycho*. He refused. He and Mrs M. hardly ever went to the cinema and if they did, they would never watch something like that. Life was already weird enough.

Catherine was surprised to be put straight through to Potts. She had assumed that he would be in theatre, or on the ward, or doing what senior consultants did when they were being important and saving lives, so she was taken aback when the secretary announced that she would be transferred immediately. So surprised, that she was unsure what to say and stumbled over her words. He listened patiently and then attentively, once she was on safer ground, describing the latest development in the investigation. It would not be easy to trace the metal pins and rods, he said, but it could be done. He would need to see them but he really could not take another few days leave from the hospital. However, he was very keen to help. Perhaps they could meet halfway between Birmingham and the police station? She could bring all the visual evidence and reports, especially that of the pathologist. In fact, couldn't the pathologist extract the inserts from the leg? Then he could examine them properly. It would be really helpful. They could meet at a service station or something. How about somewhere near Nottingham?

Catherine would see what could be done. She doubted if such a meeting should take place in such a public place but maybe somewhere more discreet? Yes, why not? When would be convenient for him? Oh, he could arrange any time that was good for her, unless he had an emergency to deal with, but that was the story of his life. That apart, he was at her disposal. Scampton would be delighted to see her. They need not go into the service station at all but could talk privately in the car park. Scampton would prefer that. She would get back to him? Excellent. He would look forward to that.

After the call she found she needed to go and inspect her face, in the mirror over the sink, in the female toilets.

Chapter Twenty-eight

The search at the Black's was a challenge. Mrs Black insisted on being present so the searchers had to work around her, which was not ideal, but the whole process was rendered more difficult by the whiteness of the interior. It showed every mark. But search they did, thoroughly, throughout the whole house. Below floorboards, (at least no carpets to lift), behind pictures and wall-mounted animal heads, downstairs, upstairs, inside everything closed, under everything covered. The cases of animals and birds were peered into and probed, glass domes removed and their contents sniffed and viewed.

Nothing.

Wilfred's bedroom was a scene of particular fascination, piled high with the finished products of his taxidermist's art but nothing relating to any human remains whatsoever. The investigators were astonished by the number of candles, the lack of ornament and the whiteness of the house, but found nothing to incriminate the suspect, or his mother – until they got to the garage. Which was dark and windowless, harshly lit by a single, fluorescent, strip light across the centre of the ceiling, augmented only by a couple of angle-poise lamps over the workbench that ran down one side of the room. The bench was meticulously laid out with all the tools of the taxidermist's trade, immaculate, arranged in size order, lightly covered with grease-proof paper to keep off dust and dirt. There was a Belfast sink with a cold water tap in one corner, equally immaculate, although a little chipped. On the work bench were various projects – works in progress – hollowed out, lifeless animals ranging from a King Charles Spaniel to a ferret. They lay, stiffly, prone, side by side, staring at the intruders from empty eye sockets. Several more animal corpses were found, carefully plastic-wrapped and labelled, in the large chest freezer alongside the sink. Each parcel had a name and the details of their owners, all of whom would have to be contacted to verify that Nibblet, Thumper and Uggie were, indeed, their dearly beloved but now sadly deceased, domestic pets. Below the legal bodies lay a collection of so-called 'road kill', a motley collection of remarkably intact rabbits, a magpie, sparrows, moles, squirrels, a rat, two cats, a fox, an overweight corgi with a red collar and a muntjac. Packed in between the whole cadavers were organs and body parts, of all shapes and sizes, distorted and frozen, some in bags, some not, all open to suspicion. The floor had been swept but was black with the residue of years of footfall and dried blood. Filthy. Flooded.

"I want every single one of those body parts," the DCI told the search party. "Black told us he wrapped the organs and disposed of them but he was lying. Everything is to go to forensics for analysis. Take the whole bloody freezer if you have to. It looks to me like he's been keeping trophies from his victims. And every single speck of blood is to be analysed. I want to know where it came from – all of it. We've got enough to hold him on suspicion of illegal hunting and pet theft, at the very least. You're not telling me that that dog was roadkill. Look at the size of it. It'd have taken the bloody car out. Someone must have missed it. I also want every single chemical in here identified and checked and quantified. This place stinks. Well, what are you waiting for?"

Chapter Twenty-nine

It was safer to be at work Melissa had decided; where there was always someone, even if they were out of it, or unable to speak, or even complaining. Patients, nursing colleagues, porters, doctors, even Sister Cullum – anything was better than being alone in her semi-dark room. She never opened the curtains now. Opening them might mean looking out of the window and she could not bear the thought of what she might see, or, even worse, what she did not. Because she knew it was there. Whoever it was. Someone was there, hiding in the trees or the shrubs, watching. And waiting. All the time.

Even Jenny Cullum had noticed a change in the girl who, somehow, seemed smaller. She was pale and listless, with a glint in her eyes that seemed to ignite from nowhere, then extinguish itself once it had darted all around the ward. She looked haunted.

Glenda O'Keeffe was consulted. Was Staff Nurse Sharp on a diet? No, not that Glenda was aware, but she had heard that there had been a decline in Melissa's social life. Less parties and carrying on, (sniff of disapproval) with doctors and senior staff. Apparently, she had had her sights set on the newly divorced Senior Registrar, who had had a lucky escape. The girl was not a good influence. (Sorrowful shake of the head) Look how that scruffy HO had improved since he'd been going out with someone else. Really, Staff Nurse Sharp was something of a liability. No, not on the ward, as yet, but she, Glenda O'Keeffe, had her eye on the ball and would watch for lapses. After all, it was the welfare of the patients that mattered, wasn't it? Everything she did was in their best interests.

Emphatic silence.

However, she had heard...

"Yes?"

"Miss Sharp's rather partial to a drink". Not that Glenda could prove anything and no, she had not smelled alcohol on Melissa's breath, which always smelled of mints, not that that meant anything. "And she's asked to change her room in the nurses' home, to one on the top floor."

"More out of the way?"

Glenda nodded affirmatively. Case concluded. Of course, she would keep an eye on things and if there was anything to report, Sister would be the first to know. Was there anything else she could do to help, before she returned to her duties?

"I need to have a word with Staff Nurse Sharp. Ask her to come to the office. Now."

After Glenda had been despatched, Jenny Cullum was thoughtful. Then she smiled. Very briefly. But her face was as stone when there was a knock on the door and Melissa was invited to enter and to take a seat.

She really does look dreadful, Jenny thought, as she watched the noticeably thinner Staff Nurse look, hesitantly, for somewhere to sit, then deposit herself on a chair as rigid as herself. Jenny tried to look comforting.

"There's nothing to worry about, Staff Nurse Sharp. Melissa."

The name floated uncomfortably around the room, as if looking for a way out, then gave up and settled like stone on the desk between the two women.

"I just wanted to find out how you are."

Silence.

"How are things at the nurses' home?"

Melissa said nothing.

"No more intrusions or problems?"

Melissa shook her head uncertainly and focussed moist blue eyes on Jenny's face, which gazed back, as sympathetically as it could.

"You will tell me if there is anything that troubles you? I'm here to help. My door is always open."

They continued to look at each other for a moment before Melissa nodded and stood up.

"Thank you," she said in a voice that was more breath than sound. "Can I go now?"

"Yes, of course."

Only when the door had fully closed, did Jenny put her hand into her pocket, close her eyes and stroke the contents within.

While Catherine had the meeting with Potts to look forward to, her mind was preoccupied with the ongoing problem of filling in the missing pieces of Linda Gardiner's life. After she had left her husband, (Catherine could not blame her for that, but not her son) and moved from Stroud, the trail seemed to go cold. 'Somewhere in the Midlands' was not much to go on but it was something, and became much more once Linda's maiden name was entered into the equation. It made sense and Catherine was annoyed with herself for not thinking of it sooner. Once she had metaphorically stepped into Linda's shoes, it had become so obvious. A Linda Ruscombe with the same date of birth as Linda Gardiner was traced to a temp agency in central Birmingham. She had worked at a number of places around the city, eventually finding a longer-term contract as a receptionist at the city hospital. According to their Personnel Department, she had worked in A&E – Accident and Emergency, in case Catherine did not know what that was. Miss Ruscombe had started there as a temp - they always needed staff in A&E – in August 1975, and after a few months had been offered a twelve-month contract by the hospital. Temp agencies were so expensive; Catherine had no idea, the girl in the personnel department began to tell her. So, it was hospital policy to offer any half decent temp a longer contract and Linda had worked out well, at first. She was popular. Everyone called her Lyn. No, there wasn't much in the way of family history or personal information in her notes. She was married, but separated, and referred to herself as Miss Ruscombe. Her next of kin had been given as a Miss Jennifer Cullum. They shared the same address so, presumably, lived together.

Catherine listened with one half of her brain and made notes. The other half was focussed on the Group Captain. It was extraordinary. The same hospital as Potts; she would ask him about it at their meeting. He might even have known Lyn as she was called, unlikely though that was. At least there was still this Miss Cullum whom she could contact. It seemed that Lyn had fulfilled her contract but it had not been renewed. Nothing to do with them, the chatty personnel lady cheerfully offered. No, they would have loved her to stay but she had found the er, challenges of an A&E department too distressing. Well, there was a lot of blood; it was the first port of call after all, and some patients could be rather difficult. Sometimes people died; it was all part of the job. Unfortunately, they had nothing on Miss Ruscombe after she left at the end of 1976. No, there was no forwarding address other than the one on record and no information about her next employment. She seemed just to have disappeared.

Catherine asked for contact details for Miss Cullum. The personnel lady could do that, of course she could. Oh! How convenient. Jennifer Cullum worked at the hospital. Yes, she was a Sister on Upper GI - Gastrointestinal, in case Catherine didn't know what that was. Sister Cullum would probably be too busy to talk on the phone at the moment; a ward sister was always terribly busy. She had so much responsibility, but why didn't Catherine ring and make an appointment to speak to her when it was quieter? Perhaps personnel could do that for her? Anything to help the police, especially now. Weren't these Yorkshire Ripper killings terrible? It made one frightened to be a woman, even in Birmingham.

Melissa had been in her room for about an hour. She had changed out of her uniform as usual when she got back after her shift, and hung it up in the wardrobe. Her watch was on the top of the chest of drawers, right in the middle, where she could see it. But she made certain to glance at it every five minutes or so, just to be sure. She had, as usual, headed straight back to the nurses' home from the hospital, speaking to no one, carefully inspecting the garden area outside her window before entering through the main entrance. As she unlocked her own door she would glance furtively along the corridor, as if she was trying to break in to her own home. Once the coast was clear, she would sidle in through the door then shut it, hard, lock it from the inside and noisily slide the bolts into place. The more noise the better, so that whoever was listening would know that she was well protected. Impenetrable. The porter who had fitted the bolts, top and bottom, had thought it was hilarious. What! Melissa! The 'let's go for it don't mind if I do' party queen; the most popular nurse in the hospital and definitely the most obliging. The one who had needed him to replace the chair in the Group Captain's office? Now here she was, bolting her door against intruders. What was the world coming to?

Melissa had devised a routine which would keep her safe. She would check the bolts on the door, look at the closed curtains, count to five and then turn back to the door to re-check the bolts. Then she would go to the chest of drawers to touch her watch, turn it face down, count to five, then turn it back up the right way. If it was still there after she had gone back to the door to again inspect the bolts, then it was safe for her to sit down on her bed from where she could study the curtains. If they were fully drawn across with at least a two-inch overlap in the middle, then it was safe to undress. This was done, with difficulty, while sitting on the bed but it had to be so, in case someone could see through the curtains. They were heavily patterned and kept out the light but were only made of thick cotton. Wooden shutters would have been better but the porter had said that was impossible. He could get her another chair if she wanted but no, not shutters, or metal bars. Not for any number of favours. However, the window was firmly locked; he had done it himself and she had checked many, many times. She would have liked to check now, but did not dare to open the curtains.

She had removed her cap, dress and apron and was beginning to undo her suspenders when it started. A light tapping. On the window. On the other side of the curtains.

She froze, mid-motion, face fixed on the floor as she listened. Several light taps, like lazy hailstones against the glass. Then, nothing. Silence. She realised that she had stopped breathing.

The silence continued.

She breathed, hardly at all, without sound. The silence held.

She must have imagined it. Everything in her room was as she wanted it, so she must be safe. Lifting her head slightly she resumed the removal of her stockings and the tapping began again. Louder. More insistent. Now she knew it was real.

She waited. It stopped. She waited, again, for how long she had no idea. Only when the sound had not returned and dusk was falling, did she move from the bed, still half-dressed, and edge over towards the window. She almost crawled: it was too dangerous to stand upright; it was essential to remain below the level of the window sill. When she arrived at the point where the curtains overlapped, she took a deep breath, stood up to her full height and pulled them very slightly, very slowly, apart.

Pressed up against the window pane on the narrow outer sill was an upright body. Rigid. Leaning against the glass for balance. It had blonde hair, long bare legs, a tiny waist and huge breasts. Very blue eyes had been painted onto the rosebud-red-lipped, plastic face. The head was twisted to one side and was staring into the room, focused on Melissa. It was wearing a nurse's uniform.

Chapter Thirty

"This Jenny Cullum. She's at the same hospital as your medical man?"

"You mean the Group Captain? Yes, sir."

"Well, don't you think you'd better get down there and talk to her?"

The DCI absolutely refused to accompany her on the grounds that if he left Yorkshire again, another body would be found. Anyway, he wanted to keep an eye on the Wilfred Black angle.

"His mother has invited me to a séance." Martin waved a hand-written letter at Catherine. "Apparently they belong to the Spiritualist Church and they meet every week – on the moors whenever possible, to 'be closer to the Spirit World', but on this occasion at her house it seems, as there's no one to take her there."

Catherine stared. "The moors?"

Martin nodded.

"A séance, on the moors? Talking to the dead?"

"Makes Wilfred even more interesting, doesn't it?"

"Will you go?"

Now it was Martin's turn to stare. Catherine blushed. He changed the subject.

Forensics still had not come up with any results from his workshop and would have to be chased.

"Again" he said darkly, with his jumper sleeves rolled down over his wrists and his moustache drooping. So, Catherine had immediately called the hospital and left a message with Pott's secretary, rearranging the meeting for the next day at the hospital itself. She apologised for being so inconvenient but the secretary sounded quite pleased. Oh, it was no bother; it was always so much easier when the Group Captain was on the premises, in case of an emergency. She would pass on the message and put the meeting in the diary – would lunchtime suit? And she would try to keep the Group Captain out of the operating theatre so they had more time together. Scampton would like that, Catherine thought and could almost hear his tail wagging.

Also, she would like to arrange a meeting with Sister Jennifer Cullum from Upper GI. Could the secretary help her with that?

"With Sister Cullum?"

Yes, just a chat. Nothing formal. Just to help with our enquiries."

Catherine felt a chill descend at the other end of the phone. The secretary did not know; that was beyond her remit. She reported only to the Group Captain and another of his colleagues, a very senior consultant. She had nothing to do with the nursing staff and suggested that Detective Sergeant Scott contact Sister Cullum directly. She was a ward sister so had an office and an extension number, that was freely available from the switchboard. She could put the detective sergeant through to them if that helped, but as for any further communication between herself and Sister Cullum, that was out of the question.

What on earth was the issue with this Sister Cullum? Catherine mused, as she was connected and waited for someone to pick up.

It did not take long. Yes, she was Sister Jennifer Cullum. To whom was she speaking? A policewoman? Why?

Catherine explained who she was, where she was and what she wanted. Sister Cullum was reluctant. Did the Detective Sergeant realise how busy she was? Her time was not her own. However, if it really was just an information gathering exercise, she supposed she would be able to find a moment, but Miss Scott had to realise that she would have to fit in with the demands of an exceptionally busy and important ward. It had been some time since Linda Ruscombe had been in Birmingham and Jenny doubted that she would have much to say of any interest. She really could not understand why it was worth a trip all the way to Birmingham, especially with so many criminal goings on in the north, but no doubt the detective sergeant knew best. The news that Catherine had an appointment with Group Captain Potts on the same day was met with silence – heavy and hostile. It cracked apart when, finally, the nurse spoke. Then, of course, Sister Cullum would be happy to find time to speak to Miss Scott. She should have said. Anything to oblige the Group Captain.

So it was that Catherine found herself taking the road south again, this time on her own. She hoped her car would be up to the journey but anticipation outweighed apprehension as she set off early, ostensibly ahead of the traffic but, in truth, as insurance against breakdown and lack of acceleration. At least that was what she told herself. She would arrive in plenty of time to interview Jennifer Cullum, before her lunch with Potts. Quite when the elusive Sister would 'find a moment' for her, she had no idea, but she would be able to observe the hospital at work while she waited. This was Pott's world and she wanted to know more. Perhaps she might even see him. She carefully touched the foundation on her face at the thought and was glad she had washed her hair last night.

Chapter Thirty-one

Jenny Cullum had had time to think about her forthcoming encounter but had now put it aside, as she concentrated on work and the pending ward round. Melissa Sharp had not turned up for her shift which was extremely annoying, especially on such a busy day, but sadly, she felt it was indicative of the girl's mentality. No doubt she would pitch up later, when the pressure was off. 'Better late than never' written all over her face, wide-blue-eyed, wisps of hair trying to escape from hair grips, pleading some excuse or another. And she, Jenny Cullum, would have to be stern and severe. Just as she had had to be with Lyn.

Lyn. Not unlike Melissa but easier. So brittle and fragile when she had started work in A&E, that Jenny had wondered however she would cope, and, in the end, had been right. She sighed at the recollection. They had never stood a chance but she still felt the pain. Jenny had spotted and watched Lyn of course, well before their 'accidental' meeting in the staff canteen, over shepherd's pie. She had stood out from the succession of temps on hospital premises from the first, with her lovely eyes – blue like Melissa's but lighter, more rinsed out. Behind them, Jenny immediately saw the person that Lyn, with her help, should have been, even before she knew it herself. Mother and daughter, sisters, partners, equals and lovers. It should have been perfect and at first, it was. But then Lyn had rebelled and said she felt trapped. Jenny knew it was the pressure of working in such a demanding, distressing environment; A&E was not for everyone, especially if they were sensitive and impressionable. Even seasoned medics avoided it if they could. Those who stayed were a special breed: inured, hard-shelled, impervious. She had seen it so often and begged Lyn to change, to find something else, even if it wasn't in the hospital. They could still be together and it would probably be better, away from the gossip and speculation, their public façade, the deception and pretence. But Lyn had said it was all Jenny's fault. That she was being suffocated and just couldn't take any more: that she wanted to breathe. So, she was gone. And Jenny was on her own once more. She had destroyed all the things that spoke to her about what might have been: the photos, the clothes she had bought with such care, the silk underwear, the shoes, the bed linen, even the bed. She would have liked to eliminate the images in her head but, sadly, they lingered, although she had mastered how to conceal emotion, weakness and even some of the anger.

When Catherine had arrived and parked, checked her face in the rear-view mirror and decided to risk leaving the holdall containing what she had of the dead vagrant on the back seat, she took her handbag and briefcase and entered the hospital via the main entrance. It was busy but orderly. Well signed, it was easy enough to follow the sinuous, sterile corridors to the wards and then to locate Gastrointestinal, where she hesitated for a moment. Where was the ladies' toilet? It had been a long journey and should she put on some lipstick? Or would that be frivolous? This was work, after all, but too late.

"Can I help you?" A crisp, substantial woman in a uniform, topped by a cap, pushing a trolley loaded with notes and files was accosting her with undisguised antagonism. "Visiting hours aren't until this afternoon."

"I'm here to see Sister Jennifer Cullum."

"Oh. Is she expecting you? She didn't tell me anything about it."

Was this woman a matron or something? She would have made an excellent police sergeant, Catherine thought, as she read the name badge on the woman's chest: Staff Nurse Glenda O'Keeffe. She was annoyed with herself for not familiarising herself with medical ranks before her visit.

"Who shall I tell her is here?"

"Detective Sergeant Scott."

Another,

"Oh," but less hostile and more intrigued. "Wait here." She and the trolley then disappeared through noisy swing doors and Catherine was left, in limbo, wondering less about lipstick and more about hospital etiquette. It felt like the army or a police training college.

"Scott! How nice to see you!"

It was Potts, leading an assorted group of white coats and stethoscopes followed by a huddle of uncoated, anxious, earnest faces that could only belong to medical students. They stared as Potts came up to her and shook her hand; she half expected them to make notes.

"Ward round," he said. "Mustn't keep them waiting," but he was looking forward to seeing her later – in his office? They had lots to catch up on. Scampton would be delighted to see her. Did she have plenty to keep her occupied before then? He could not imagine that she had arrived that early to see him; there must be something else afoot. He was beginning to understand how these things worked. And he smiled, and everyone noticed but only Catherine saw the golden flecks in his eyes.

At that moment one of the doors swung open to reveal a sharp, angular woman in dark blue, with a face to match. The organza frill on her cap seemed oddly out of place, as if it lost its way from something altogether more tender and had been forced to attach itself to whatever it found first. It was Jenny Cullum. Potts introduced the two women, then led the way onto the ward. Catherine was told to wait, outside. Sister Cullum was sure she would understand. Perhaps she could find a cup of tea or something. There was a canteen – just follow the signs. If she returned in about an hour, it might be possible to talk but before then, it was absolutely impossible. By the time Catherine got round to speaking she found she was alone.

Fifty-five minutes later she found herself again on the wrong side of the double doors but this time, did not stay there. Pushing one of them aside, she entered yet another non-descript, disinfected corridor with the same unforgiving lino floor as all the others. Thank heavens for flat shoes. The corridor had suddenly developed limbs, reaching out on either side, stretching towards windows at their far ends as if trying to escape. Not so the inhabitants of the wards, confined to beds and barracks, patrolled by an astonishing array of diversely clad warders. White, blue, green, gingham and striped bodies dotted about, some at speed, some stationary, none of them smiling. Of Potts and his entourage there was no sign.

"Detective Sergeant Scott?" It was the starchy staff nurse again. Obviously briefed and prepared this time, she had her orders and the visitor was to be taken straight to

Sister's office, where she had been waiting for her. Catherine was not so much annoyed as intrigued by the implication. She was not late; if anything, she was on the early side of spot-on, but Jenny Cullum clearly liked to be in the ascendant. Her ward, her rules. Her time. This could be interesting.

Bidden to enter, she smiled as she sat down on the hard chair indicated opposite the desk, behind which sat the equally hard Sister Cullum. She was on the phone. Of course, she was, Catherine thought; she had to be making an important call for my benefit.

"Sorry," Jenny mouthed. "Important call. Yes," she enunciated with great clarity into the receiver. "Staff Nurse Melissa Sharp. She hasn't turned up for work this morning. It's possible that she has been taken ill ... she lives in the nurses' home."

Catherine said nothing. The receiver was put down and Sister Cullum turned her attention to her visitor. She understood that this was about her friendship with Linda Ruscombe, was that right? It was. Catherine simply wanted to find out more about the missing woman. There was no easy way of saying this and she hoped it would not be distressing for Sister Cullum, but they believed that Miss Ruscombe was the deceased woman who had been found in suspicious circumstances in North Yorkshire.

"The murder victim?"

So, she did know.

"Yes". They wanted to trace her movements from the time she had started working in the hospital until she had been found, Catherine said, quietly. She was very sorry. Miss

Cullum had been designated as Miss Ruscombe's next of kin so, naturally, they wished to talk to her. What could she tell them about Linda? Lyn, as she was known?

Not much, apparently. They had been friends; no more, no less. Lyn had come to work in the hospital, which is where they had met and found they had shared interests. They got on well, Lyn was in dreadful digs so Jenny suggested she move in with her and they share living expenses. Jenny had her own house and she and Lyn got on well. But Lyn had problems.

"She had baggage," Jenny said. She did not know all the details but she believed that there had been an appalling husband: "abusive and controlling." Lyn had been forced to escape and even had to abandon her child. "The man was clearly a monster. She wanted to get a divorce but he wouldn't let her on religious grounds or something equally ridiculous. I think he was just being difficult. Anyway, poor thing, she was very fragile. Vulnerable. I don't know what she would have done without me."

Catherine smiled sympathetically and waited for her to continue. She did not have to wait long.

"That was the problem, of course. Lyn couldn't cope. I told her not to work in A&E. She was far too sensitive and insecure for a job like that. You need to be tough to work there and that's the last thing Lyn was. Poor thing. It broke her."

"Is that when she left?"

"Yes. She finished her contract and then just disappeared. Packed up her stuff, not that there was much, and left. I came home from work one day to find she had simply upped and gone."

"When was that?"

"1976. Just before Christmas."

There was a silence as Jenny recalled the dreadful row they had had and how she had stormed off to the hospital ahead of Lyn, who said she would follow in her own time. She did not arrive and had never been seen again. Jenny remembered all the presents she had bought for her lover, chosen with more adoring care than she had any right to expect and which had all been discarded with the household rubbish before Christmas arrived. Even the earrings, that had cost so much money and taken so long to find. Linda had only plain gold studs to wear in her pierced ears, those ears that Jenny so loved to touch. The earrings she had found were perfect: as exquisite as Lyn herself. Without her to wear them they were useless, an offence. Unbearable. That year Jenny, who would never dream of piercing her own ears, had not even bothered with a tree, decorations or cards, except for the Group Captain. She had eaten baked beans for Christmas lunch but she had not cried, not once.

"And that was the last time you saw her?"

The phone on the desk started to shrill. Answer me, answer me, answer me.

"I'll have to take it," Jenny apologised, already reaching for the receiver.

She listened, intently, with one hand in her pocket as her face closed.

“Well, where is she? She can’t just have vanished.”

“Is there a problem?”

“My staff nurse has disappeared.”

Chapter Thirty-two

"When was she last seen?"

"Yesterday, here, at the end of her shift. She left as usual and presumably went back to the nurses' home."

"You saw her?"

"I did."

"How was she?"

Jenny Cullum had stood up to announce the disappearance of a member of her staff but now sat down again. She was thoughtful.

"Not herself, actually. She's had some problems recently and that may have affected her."

"What sort of problems?"

The alleged break-ins and Melissa's increasingly agitated state of mind were described. Catherine wanted more details, especially about the fob watch and missing underwear. Sister Cullum did not seem to have believed the girl, which might be interpreted as unfortunate, especially when Catherine spoke to the local police who had been summoned and made a search of first Melissa's room, then the whole nurses' home and grounds. There was no sign of her but she had clearly left in haste. Her bed had not been slept in, she had changed out of her uniform, which had been carefully hung up and put away, but had left without her handbag so had no money or identification. It was not clear what she would have been wearing – underwear certainly, but possibly only one stocking. She did not appear to be wearing shoes but her slippers could not be found. One of the nurses, a girl called Louise on the same corridor, had heard someone slam a door and rush out in what sounded like soft footwear as it was getting dark, but could say no more than that.

At first the police presumed that she was just running late for something, probably a date, and rushed off in a state of feminine fluster. Women, eh? Then they found the doll on the window-sill.

Catherine put a call through to DCI Martin to tell him what had happened. It was a disturbing development, despite the fact that it was so far out of their own area. Could it be connected to their investigation or was it just coincidence?

"I don't believe in coincidence, Scott, and nor should you. Stay there, talk to Potts and keep me updated. Technically, it's not our problem, but I want to know what's going on. Keep a low profile and don't get in the way; you may not be the kind of DS that they're used to."

A woman, you mean? Or because I have a skin condition? she wanted to say, but thought better of it. By now a full-scale search was underway. Melissa had been missing for over twelve hours; nobody seemed to have seen or heard anything after she had left her room, if indeed that had been her. She had simply vanished.

To her surprise, Potts sought Catherine out very soon after she had spoken to DCI Martin. He had thought, in the circumstances, that perhaps they should speak immediately. Wouldn't Scott be needed elsewhere? She would and was touched by his consideration. His secretary had rearranged his morning so he had about 45 minutes, he said. Not enough time to take Scampton for a walk unfortunately; perhaps another time? Now, where were these metal inserts?

There was only one, she said. She hoped that would be enough. They collected it from her car together, then she carefully placed it in the centre of the desk in his office. It felt strange to be studying a piece of metal that had inhabited the leg of a living man. It was shiny, stainless steel, about 30 cm (ironically a foot in old measurement) long with screw holes in both ends, by which it would have been attached to the bone. An alien, unseen internal splint, enabling a man to use his legs almost as normal, placed there by strangers. Potts began to enthusiastically explain the surgical procedure required but Catherine cut him off, politely, at the pass. Fascinating as that no doubt was, how could they track the source of the rod? Then they would be able to identify its dead owner.

Which did she want first? The good news or the bad? Well, the rod would be engraved with a unique identifying number and the manufacturer's name. Look. Together they bent their heads over the desk, almost touching. Catherine held her breath and tried to concentrate on the line of steel.

"We need a magnifying glass," Potts said, leaning back then to open a desk drawer. Catherine noticed that he sat in a rather shabby executive type chair, obviously expensive when purchased but now looking exhausted and overworked. Like the NHS she thought and wondered if it was the same in military hospitals.

They resumed their positions over the rod and located the marks. She wrote them down, very exactly, then read them back for confirmation.

The bad news was the difficulty of actually tracing them, Potts said. But if they did, they would be able to find out the hospital, surgeon, procedure, injury and above all, identity of the patient. Someone would have to do a great deal of searching but the answers were there for the finding. If anyone wanted his opinion, purely medical and speculative of course, about the injury the victim had received to need such an insert, he would hazard a guess at some major trauma to the lower leg. Crushed? Run over? An industrial injury or road traffic accident. Something of that sort. The victim would probably have walked with a limp after treatment, but at least he or she would be mobile. Probably a he? Ah yes, he remembered that Scott had said something of the sort on the phone and the dimensions of the rod indicated that the bone was likely to be male.

He was finding this type of medical detective work absolutely fascinating. Was there anything else he could do to help?

Catherine seized the opportunity. There was something, not strictly connected to the metal rod but nevertheless, of particular interest. She hoped it would not be a conflict of interest, but, well, it was about Sister Cullum.

"Sister Cullum?"

"Do you know what blood group she is?"

"Can't you ask her?"

"Not at the moment."

"Ah. Yes. The missing staff nurse. The one who works on Upper GI."

Catherine asked him what he thought of the absentee. Was her disappearance out of character? He really couldn't say, he replied. He hardly knew the girl except as a nurse on the ward. She had always seemed cheerful, perhaps a little flighty but was efficient and personable enough. Good with the patients; popular, especially with the men, but ward staff were really Sister Cullum's department. However, he could ask his secretary to try and find out the Sister's blood group, although he couldn't make any promises. Or better still, Scott could ask his secretary herself? Then she would be able to say hello to Scampton.

"Is there anything else?" He was looking at his watch as he spoke.

"Did you know or ever meet a woman called Linda Ruscombe, or she might have called herself Linda Gardiner? She worked here, in A&E as a receptionist, from mid-1975 until December 1976?"

"I've never heard of her," he answered. "But then I didn't start work here until September 1976. I did a stint in the RAF hospital at Halton after a tour in Northern Ireland and, as you see, I am not really involved with A&E. I don't wish to sound arrogant, but most of my acquaintances in the hospital are medics; I have very little knowledge about admin staff in anything but my own department."

He smiled, apologetically, sorry not to be of more help. And to be able to spend more time with her but, if that was all, he should really be getting back to work. If there was anything else, she would let him know, wouldn't she? He would be very interested to find out if they traced the anonymous vagrant. Hopefully they would meet again soon.

She asked if she could use his phone to check in with DCI Martin. Certainly; there it was, on the desk. Would she please pass on his regards to the Detective Chief Inspector? Then Potts was gone and as Catherine dialled North Yorkshire, she was left wondering what effect a place like Northern Ireland would have had on a caring and sensitive surgeon.

The news from North Yorkshire was not good. Catherine could only imagine the dejection of the hand knitted sweater and moustache. Forensics had come up with the blood results, at last, but they were not what anyone except perhaps Black and his mother wanted to hear. All the blood – yes, every last bloody drop of it – came from animals. Mostly deer, but a glorious variety of mixed fauna which read like the description of a bloody petting zoo the DCI said, gloomily, but nothing human. Not even Black himself, who never even appeared to have cut so much as a finger or thumb. He was clearly adept with a knife though, which was more encouraging and fitted the profile of the killer.

But not quite, Catherine had observed, which was met with an ominous silence.

"Our killer wasn't that skilled to start with and got better. Black's obviously been cutting up things proficiently for years."

DCI Martin grunted. At least there was a chance of tracing the dead vagrant he muttered, "'though it wasn't going to be easy, was it?" He'd put one of the lads onto it. Catherine read out the details from the metal rod and could almost hear him writing them down, carving them into the paper. Then the conversation moved on to the missing girl.

"Bottom line, Scott. Is there any connection with our case? What about Potts?"

"Not Potts, sir. But maybe Jennifer Cullum."

"But she's a woman!"

Now Catherine could hear the sweater and moustache droop even further with despondency as their owner breathed heavily and thoughtfully into the end of the phone.

"Bloody hell," he said at last. "Find out everything you can about this Jennifer Cullum woman then get back up here. Quickly. We're going to have to let Black go and I need something to take his place. We need a result, Scott. Do you hear me?"

Loud and clear, sir, but he had put the phone down so now it was her turn to sigh, then head straight for Pott's secretary.

Chapter Thirty-three

The search for Melissa had turned up nothing. Her family had been contacted and were in a state of panic but had no more information than anyone else. The grounds of the nurses' home had been scoured; the litter in the flower beds had been turned, lifted and returned; the grass flattened and the undergrowth among the trees prodded and probed until it hurt. Every room had been inspected and found empty of all traces of the missing nurse, although many other things were uncovered, including a great deal of alcohol that had mysteriously found its way there from the ward dispensaries. The doll had been removed for examination and Melissa's room dusted for fingerprints, of which there were hundreds. When accused of exaggerating, the police investigator who had logged them was very indignant and stood firmly by his assessment. The girl must have had half the hospital population in her room at some time or another and clearly never did housework. If they fingerprinted everyone in the hospital for matches, then they would see that he was telling the absolute truth.

The hospital. That was where they would now look. Everyone in the nurses' home was to be interviewed, then Upper GI, then, well, let's see what turns up. Yes, the police were very well aware of the disruption and inconvenience a search would cause in a large, working hospital but they had no alternative. Somebody must have seen or heard something; people didn't just vanish.

Pott's secretary was young, pretty and punk. Her lips were dark, her eyes weighted down with mascara and her hair short, upright and very yellow. Thank heavens it's summer Catherine thought, or she'd freeze. Her clothes were as skimpy as they were tight and black; perhaps that was why they needed the safety pins and metal bits. In her ears she had a ridge of coloured studs, travelling from lobe to top and around her neck, what looked suspiciously like a dog collar. Not unlike Scampton's, in fact, who patently adored her. He was slumped comfortably at her side, spread out on a large, chintz cushion from which he thumped his tail in greeting as he raised his head but did not get up.

"My Nan made it," the girl said apologetically as she noticed Catherine looking at the cushion. "From an old curtain. Horrible material I know, but Scamp loves it. I'm Charlotte." She held out a black-nailed hand in greeting. "Pleased to meet you. The GC said you would be calling in. What can I do for you?"

Catherine explained what she wanted, fascinated by Charlotte's appearance and, in particular, her face. Oh, to have the confidence to choose to look like that. Not to have to hide behind make-up but to use it like an offensive weapon: look at me! See what I am, what I have to say. If it unsettles you that's your problem, not mine. Charlotte, however, was oblivious to her visitor's curiosity. She was preoccupied with how to find out Sister Cullum's blood group and her sharply enunciated black eyebrows had gone fuzzy with concentration.

"It might be difficult," she said. "I'll have to apply to central stores and then there's no guarantee that they'll have the information. Not unless Sister Cullum has had a transfusion or a group and save. I can request her notes on behalf of the GC, as she's a member of staff but it's unorthodox and would have to be approved by the hospital administrator, who'll need to be convinced that there's a good enough reason. Is there?"

Straight to the point. I like you, Catherine thought, as she crumpled Scampton's ears.

"Helping with police enquiries?" she offered. Charlotte looked unconvinced but said she'd see what she could do; it might be acceptable in the light of current events but you never knew with the hospital administrator. He was, er, very protective. The two women looked at each other and shared a smile.

"How about Sister Cullum's address?" Catherine asked.

"Oh, that's easy." All it took was a visit to a filing cabinet. "Now what?"

"Does she drive?"

"I have no idea but I can find out. Anything else?"

"Not at the moment, thanks." Catherine exchanged her telephone number for the address and gave Scampton a final scrumple. "You'll keep in touch and let me know what you find?"

It would be Charlotte's pleasure, she said and then she had already returned to work, deciphering shorthand, typing at high velocity, dog-sitting, organising the lives of her two consultants, reshaping the world with make-up, clothes, bleached hair and safety pins.

Jenny Cullum lived in Selly Oak in the south west of the city, close to the hospital and the university: convenient, scruffy, drab and bleak. Hers was a small Victorian terraced house which opened straight out onto a subdued street behind the much busier high street. The area seemed remarkable for its large pubs, chip shops and open all hours, Asian shops serving the open all hours students and medics. There were a few cars parked along Jenny's street but it was difficult to work out whether she owned one of them. It seemed unlikely, what with the close proximity of the hospital, especially when there was a bus route so close by. The house was unremarkable and unassuming, as narrow and austere as its owner. It still had the original Victorian front door and sash windows, pristine, closed and sealed. Giving away nothing. Net-curtained, impenetrable, silent.

What had gone on behind them? Catherine wondered as she sat in her car and studied the blank façade. If there was noise the neighbours must have heard. Or maybe something had taken place elsewhere? What had happened to Lyn Ruscombe, as she called herself? How had she gone from this suburban backwater to the North Yorkshire Moors?

Time to ask the neighbours. No one answered the door bell of the house on the right but on the left, after several hefty knocks and a slight wait, the door was opened very hesitantly from behind a chain. Catherine found herself stooping down to speak to a boy, about nine years old, who wore the same sceptical expression as her own DCI. She explained who she was and what she wanted. Just to ask a few questions about the lady who lived next door. Were his parents in? Oh, only his mother but she didn't speak English. Never mind, perhaps he could translate? He obviously spoke excellent English and it would not take long. Look, she had identification, if he wanted to check. He did. Very carefully and seriously before closing the door to release the chain then opening it again, only just wide enough for Catherine to edge into a dark hallway and an assault on the senses. The aroma was tantalising: spicy, hot, exotic and seductive. It lit up the brown walls and thickly patterned floor, the dark woodwork and the mustard curtains in the front room where she was invited to sit. It made her warm and hungry and took her back to south London. North Yorkshire felt very far away.

Looking at the mother, who had all but covered her face with a corner of her sari, but speaking to the boy, Catherine learned that they had lived in the house for long enough to know Miss Cullum, but not well. She was a most quiet lady who did not mix. Her friend, Miss Ruscombe had been more friendly: a very nice lady. Always saying hello and smiling. The two ladies had seemed very good friends and always did everything together but, yes, there had been some noise. Not like the gun shots they heard from the range at the gun factory a few streets away but an argument, very loud with lots of shouting. Just before Christmas. It had been at night so they could not avoid hearing it, which was most unfortunate and they did not want to, but they could not help it. Then Miss Cullum had gone to work in the morning and slammed the front door, which she never did, so they could not but notice it. Usually, the two ladies went to work together but this day they didn't. And they hadn't seen Miss Ruscombe since then. No, not once. Not even at Christmas when all the English were at home.

"Did Miss Cullum drive a car?" The small boy looked amazed when Catherine asked the question. Of course, she didn't he replied, without even looking at his mother. Women didn't drive cars. Catherine thanked them for their time and hoped he would see her get into hers as she pulled away from the kerb at the start of her journey north.

Chapter Thirty-four

The hospital was in a state of upheaval. The hospital administrator had been delegated to oversee the police invasion which, he had been assured, would be as unobtrusive as possible. Well, if that was unobtrusive, he was a Chief Constable, which was where he was headed next if the chaos continued. They had been promised that the patients would hardly know the police were there, that order and calm would prevail and that it would be business as usual. Why then, were there uniformed officers on every ward, in every corridor, flooding the canteen, obstructing the porters and getting in everyone's way? Surely there was a limit to the number of places a staff nurse could hide? How was looking in a filing cabinet or through rubbish from the kitchen going to help find her?

When it was suggested to him that she might not be intact; that she might have been disposed of in more than one place and that, unfortunately, as time went on, the chances of finding her alive and whole became exponentially less, he went very quiet and let them get on with it. They had all heard about the goings on in Yorkshire. God help them if they were next.

The mood in Upper GI was subdued. They were short-staffed but Jenny Cullum did not want the assistance of an agency nurse or even someone else seconded from another ward. Not until Melissa was accounted for would they think about replacing her, difficult as it was, but they would persevere. It couldn't be long before she turned up. Time keeping and tardiness were her trademark. There was probably some perfectly innocent explanation, even now, for her disappearance and it was so typical of the police to spread dissent and rumour. Jenny was convinced that they did it deliberately, probably to justify their own lack of success. That was what she told everyone anyway. The police were not renowned for their intellectual abilities: big feet, anything above a certain height and the ability to walk in a straight line were their only pre-requisites. Perhaps if they had more women among their number, they might be more effective. Like that detective sergeant, what was her name? Scott; she seemed more intelligent than most but had now gone back to Yorkshire and they were left with Birmingham's finest and a still-missing staff nurse.

The assumption was that without money, shoes and maybe even a full set of underwear, Melissa could not have gone far. Certainly not of her own accord. If she had been abducted it would be a different matter but there was no evidence to support that theory - yet. It was a possibility; the fate of Linda Ruscombe was very much in the mind of the DCI leading the investigation in Birmingham. He had spoken with Derek Martin, at length, and depending on what DS Scott reported on her return to base, they would consider questioning Jennifer Cullum, as well as a search of her house. However, one thing was certain. Although she did not own a car, Jenny Cullum did have a clean, current driving licence which was proudly declared under the Additional Information heading of her CV. Personnel had checked, twice, once for the police and the second for Group Captain Pott's secretary.

Jenny herself was exceeding her own expectations of capability. Nothing like a crisis to bring out the best and most efficient in people she told everyone, especially Glenda O'Keeffe, who had a propensity to be sentimental.

"No need for that," she had reproved her remaining staff nurse who had begun to sniffle and get teary-eyed when she contemplated the fate of her colleague. "What good will it do?" However, when alone in her office, Jenny was less severe and more distracted. She fiddled incessantly with the contents of her pocket. When the ward round was over the day after Melissa's disappearance, Potts had himself taken his ward sister to one side to discuss the situation. He was concerned; how were they coping?

"A man down is serious. Do we have any more information?"

A shake of the head, a hand twisting in her pocket and Jenny Cullum had summed up the current hopelessness of the situation. Potts was supportive. He had every faith in Sister Cullum as a leader and an example. The ward was in good hands.

Catherine had arrived back in North Yorkshire and gone straight to the office. It was getting dark but the DCI was there, as she knew he would be. Although he sent the lads home, (to save on overtime he claimed) at the day's end, he himself stayed until late. He was still wearing the manky sweater she noticed, which must surely be too warm during these summer days and was now in great need of a wash. Perhaps she would be able to give him enough speculation, even if not information, to warrant a brief interlude in which Mrs Martin might be able to clean it up.

"You took your time," he said by way of greeting when she walked in. "I hope it's worth the wait."

Nice to see you too, sir, she thought as she began her debriefing. Sister Jennifer Cullum was a person of significant interest she said. There were anomalies, big ones, but also significant details that were more than coincidence and ought to be followed up. The connection with Linda Gardiner/Ruscombe, the medical knowledge, the opportunity to acquire drugs and equipment, as well as the mysterious disappearance of another woman close to Sister Cullum. Surely there had to be something in it?

DCI Martin studied his DS. Her make-up was as tired as her eyes and her complexion was getting blotchy. Her hair needed a wash, her blouse needed changing and she probably hadn't eaten a proper meal since she had gone south. Nevertheless, she was still talking.

"Jenny Cullum drives but doesn't have any visible means of transport. We can't prove where Linda went or what happened to her after she left the house and we don't have a motive. As for opportunity, yes, maybe for Linda Ruscombe, but what about the others? I bet she'll have alibis."

He was surveying the wreckage of his colleague. "Alright, we'll go with it. God knows we've precious little else and I need something to feed to the Chief Super. Did you find out her blood group?"

Catherine explained what had happened.

"That's not bloody good enough. Go home and tidy up then first thing tomorrow get onto the hospital and get it sorted. Tell them it's a priority, an urgent police matter. Or I will."

He had turned and was heading back into his own office. At the doorway he stopped and shouted over his shoulder.

"Nice work on getting a lead on the hobo's leg."

The following morning Catherine was, as usual, one of the first to arrive in the office. The DCI was already there, as always, or at least until this case was put to bed. Talking of which, Catherine thought as she greeted him, it looked as if he had not gone home last night and merely slept on his desk with his trusty sweater and facial hair for warmth. But then he always looked like that. She wanted to call Pott's secretary before anyone else, hoping that she had found out Sister Cullum's blood group. Otherwise, it would mean becoming officious and possibly insistent, playing the police investigation card with personnel or the records centre or wherever she would have to go. It was also important that Sister Cullum did not know what was happening; she had become a person of police interest and they did not want the horse to bolt.

Charlotte was in the office when Catherine called as soon as it turned eight. She was surprised, then felt ashamed. Why shouldn't a punk be punctual? And do an excellent job? She wasn't so different herself. The black lips and nails at the other end of the phone were delighted to hear from her, hoped she'd had a good journey and yes, did have news for her. Charlotte, who had not a trace of a Birmingham accent and would not have sounded out of place at an exclusive girl's boarding school, had had a bit of a job finding out the blood group. People were reluctant to divulge that kind of information as a rule and she had had quite a lot of ringing around. But the mention of the Group Captain worked wonders so yes, she could tell Catherine what Jennifer Cullum's blood group was. Actually, it had been a bit of a surprise. It was rather rare.

"Yes?" Catherine tried to be polite.

"She's AB."

"Are you sure?"

"Absolutely. She had a blood test some years ago, not sure for what, but that was the result and it's on her file at central stores. I'll fax it to you. Obviously, this is confidential information but I know that as a police woman you know that, so it's in safe hands. Oh, and she has a driving licence but no car so, yes, she drives but no, she doesn't, if you see what I mean."

Yes, Catherine did and was very grateful to Charlotte for her help. Really – she had no idea how much assistance she had given. The secretary said it was nothing, all part of the job, happy to help but had to go now – the Group Captain was in theatre with an emergency so his day needed rearranging, the other consultant had an important meeting and Scampton was panting for water.

The police in Birmingham were not best pleased to be asked to conduct a search of Jennifer Cullum's home. Didn't DCI Martin realise that they had a missing girl on their hands? Wasn't that search enough? Nevertheless, the order was given and it was agreed that in the course of turning the hospital inside out, very particular attention would be paid to Sister Cullum's office which would be re-examined. Thoroughly. Every inch, DCI Martin stressed. It might be that they would find something that would solve both cases – two birds with one stone – so the Birmingham force had plenty to gain. He and his DS and perhaps a couple of his team would head south to assist. Yes, hands on assist. Weren't they all in this together? No, the Press probably wouldn't be interested, not when they had the Yorkshire Ripper to focus on.

Chapter Thirty-five

The search for Melissa had so far produced nothing. It had now been extended into the more obscure recesses of hospital areas, grimly referred to as outer darkness. Most of the staff were familiar with the basement in that the canteen was located there, but only ever turned right at the foot of the stairs, (or the lift when it was working) in the pursuit of over-cooked cabbage and other subsidised delicacies. Just follow the smell, newcomers were advised and no one ever got lost. To the left of the stairs was another area, dark, gloomy and unvisited except by strange creatures such as suppliers, porters, those looking for replacement chairs or those with files, lists, trolleys and debris. It was a huge area, half the width and length of the main hospital building, endless rooms spidering off central corridors lit by flickering, overhead, fluorescent tubes, bright and harsh. The corridors were littered with the detritus of a busy hospital and the investigating police were required to climb, edge and shift their way through trolleys laden with linen and large metal bins on resistant wheels with opening lids, out of which protruded sacks of God knows what. Disused and broken furniture, dead mattresses and beds needing intensive repair spiked the way and obstructed the intruders like medieval fortifications. It was turning out to be the search from hell. Every bin, crevice, damp, mildewed mattress and sack had to be opened and examined, minutely. Likewise, the Central Sterile Supplies Department, placed between the wasteland near the canteen and the large, plastic, swing doors to the outside world: the stores' delivery area. With the incoming supplies came the weather, especially the wind and rain. Never the sun, thanks to the shade of buildings on three sides. The doors seemed unable to stand still, breathing in and out with the moving air.

The searchers had been permitted to leave untouched trolleys of obviously sealed and intact green-wrapped sterile instruments, secure behind locked doors, but were careful to make a detailed note of the wherewithal of all the dirty, used instruments awaiting sterilization. Just in case. They ignored the huge piles of clean linen, folded, lifeless and flat, piled high on trolleys but reluctantly opened the sacks of soiled laundry. Not quite what they had joined the police force to do, but all part of the job.

It was beyond the dirty laundry that they found her. Close to the linen room itself, lined with rows of white coats hanging like teeth and nurses' uniforms arranged according to rank, in descending order, from dark blue to auxiliary green. Above, shelves of hats to match marched in rows along the walls. Melissa was hidden in an unused side room, crouched, motionless beneath a row of outdated uniforms, a medical past consigned to history. It would have been very easy to miss her. She was lost in a doctor's white coat, far too large for her, on a bed of Sisters' uniforms. Their deep blue contrasted with her waxen face and body. She looked emaciated. Frozen. Her eyes had sunk into dark hollows, her cheek bones protruded like coat hangers upon which to hang pale lips and a tight jaw. But she was alive; sniffling and shivering, staring at the door with glittering eyes in a state of extreme agitation as it opened – with immense difficulty thanks to the chairs and trolley piled up against it from the inside. The girl was a picture of terror, picking at the white coat with scraggy nails, her feet in soiled slippers crumpled beneath her legs, one of which was bare, scratched and muddy. The stocking on the other was laddered, snagged and wizened. The officer who found her dared not go nearer. Even as he made to approach, she seemed to shrink further, her face to shrivel. A police woman was summoned, then a doctor.

The hospital hierarchy and Upper GI were informed that their missing staff nurse had been found. Alive, whole, but dehydrated, hungry, cold and catatonic. Only her eyes seemed capable of movement; restless, fearful and devious.

Less than ten minutes after word reached her, Jenny Cullum was on her way down to A&E to find her.

Chapter Thirty-six

"Where's Sister?"

It was Potts, on Upper GI, paying a visit to check on one of his patients and have a word with Jenny Cullum but she was nowhere to be found. Glenda O'Keeffe had picked up the mantle and was fussing her way around beds and student nurses, getting in the way and sweating heavily with the effort. She had dark semi-circles under her armpits which Potts ignored, but stood further back from her than usual. He did not like the way the moisture on her upper lip had darkened her moustache. The woman was too heavy; out of shape.

"She's gone to see Staff Nurse Sharp, sir. In A&E."

"When will she be back?"

Glenda really did not know; she was awfully sorry. Could she do anything to help?

No, thank you; she could not. Potts frowned.

"There's a document I want Sister Cullum to see so I'll leave it in her office. No, no, I'll do it. You're obviously very busy. Thank you, Staff Nurse." And he was gone, striding purposefully towards Jenny Cullum's office. Things to do, no time to waste said every exact step. Inside her office he placed the manilla file in the centre of the desk where it was sure to be noticed. How tidy and ordered it all was he noticed, approvingly, looking around. She ran a tight ship. This missing nurse was a nuisance but at least she had now been found and it was to Jenny Cullum's credit that she took such an interest in the welfare of her staff. Perhaps he should demonstrate some of the interest he felt in the situation. But when Charlotte had told him Jenny Cullum's blood group, he had been stunned. Blindsided. Who would have thought it? She, of all people. Was she really capable of murder?

That made him think of Scott. He had never met anyone quite like her. And he admired her. No doubt she assumed that he had not noticed the vitiligo she concealed with that heavy make-up, which he understood, but wished was not necessary. It was so artificial, like wearing another person's face. Perhaps one day she would be brave enough not to cover up but it couldn't be easy being a woman in an overtly manly man's world like the police. She would be back in North Yorkshire now. He could picture her sitting at her tidy desk surrounded by louts, engulfed in their cigarette smoke and lewd conversations, pretending not to notice.

The phone in the office rang. He let it ring and let himself out, shutting the door firmly behind him just as he had found it.

Glenda liked the feeling of being in charge, the way the other nurses now deferred to her and the patients viewed her with new eyes. Instead of their endless,

"Can I speak to/see/have a word with Sister?" it was now she, Senior Staff Nurse Glenda O'Keeffe who was the person they wanted. And she liked it. Very much. She would also suit a sister's uniform. Navy blue was so slimming. Her hair was thick and wavy, a perfect nest for the frilled white cap of sisterly seniority. Jenny Cullum had taken herself off to A&E to fuss over a silly flibbertygibbert of a girl who was no better than she should be. Well. She could stay there as long as she liked. And Melissa too. It would soon become apparent to everyone that Glenda was more than capable of running Upper GI as well as, if not better, than that skinny, sour faced Sister Cullum.

The ward was full and they were short staffed. Glenda had spoken to the nursing staff who were fully behind her; motivated, positive, determined. She was proud of them. The sudden absence of their leader had not gone down well, especially at such a busy time. Glenda had been unable to explain the desertion so did not try. The more abandoned they felt, the better.

She had not quite had the nerve to establish herself in the office, but marshalled her troops from the front as it were, striding purposefully up and down the ward: looking, listening, delegating and sweating. It was a warm day but that was no excuse for standards to slip; patients were still to be neat and tidy, beds to be straight, even the curtains at the slightly-open windows would not be permitted to break ranks. However, Glenda could at least smile as she governed. She had a nice smile; her father had always said so.

"Nurse. I don't feel well."

Glenda stopped, mid-stride, and looked over to the bed from where the complaint had come. It was a middle-aged woman, not one of the usual whingers and malingerers so probably worth taking seriously. A day or so ago she had arrived back from theatre after having her gall bladder removed and she had that listless, exhausted, postoperative look. Glenda glanced at the notes at the end of her bed.

“I feel sick.”

“It’s probably just the effect of the anaesthetic. It’s very common. Nothing to worry about. Do you have any pain?”

The woman shook her head as Glenda examined the dressing and then the wound on her abdomen. It was clean; there was no sign of infection or irritation.

“Nothing to worry about,” she diagnosed, offering her most reassuring smile. “But I’ll mention it to the doctor.”

The patient nodded, repressing her nausea. It would soon wear off.

Glenda headed straight to Jenny Cullum’s office, indicating to the student nurse who was fast approaching that she was otherwise engaged and that whatever it was, it would have to wait.

“I’ll be in the office,” she said. “I have an important call.”

The chair behind the desk was a perfect fit; it could have been made for me she thought as she picked up the phone and dialled. As she waited to be put through to the registrar, she opened the file on the desk. It was nothing of much interest, just a medical update from the Group Captain about one of their regulars but she did enjoy the feeling of intimacy and professional superiority it gave her to examine the handwritten note he had tucked into the front.

If the registrar was surprised to find not Sister Cullum but Glenda O’Keeffe on the end of the phone, it barely showed.

"Put in a nasogastric tube and then we'll get her X rayed. I'm tied up at the moment. Can you see to it?"

She certainly could. No sooner had she replaced the receiver when the phone began clamouring. It was Sister Cullum, who would surely be impressed at the speed at which her call was being answered. Glenda could sense her satisfaction.

"This is taking longer than I anticipated, Staff Nurse. Are you managing? Is there anything I need to know?"

Glenda barely had time to reply that all was well, everything was under control and she was managing very well: to the manner born, before Jenny interrupted. Really. So rude. No wonder people did not like her. When she was a Sister, Glenda resolved, she would be much more approachable.

"The equipment stores need checking and I want you to do it, Staff Nurse. I need to know that nothing else had gone missing ... Of course, you are busy. That's what responsibility is all about. If you want to progress in your career, you'll have to show that you can cope. As I do. Every day."

There was a knock at the door and the student nurse, who had finally dared to catch up with a Senior Staff Nurse, edged her head nervously into view.

"It's a catheter," she hissed with desperation. "The patient's in agony."

Glenda began to think that being a Sister could be quite demanding but at least she still managed to smile encouragingly at the student as they headed towards the recalcitrant catheter. The nasogastric tube would have to wait a few minutes.

“Nurse,” she called to the SEN. “Can you give our gall bladder in bed 7 some Omnopon? Just until we can get her sorted?”

Chapter Thirty-seven

The search of Jenny's house was in full spate. The small boy from next door and his mother, plus a grandmother, a grandfather and several other women in saris were an eager audience, positioned unashamedly outside their own front door for a better view. If asked, they would have said that the noise inside was so great from the machinations in the lady's house that they had been forced out of their own. Fortunately, the English lady had obviously refused her consent for the search. The ramming and battering down of the door were just as thrilling as it appeared on television. Miss Cullum had, indeed, absolutely refused to provide a key. She was defiant, furious and adamant; she was innocent. She had nothing to hide. Lyn Ruscombe had packed and left of her own accord and Jenny had never seen her again. Turning over her house was a complete waste of police time, which was why she would not be present but would continue with her important work at the hospital. They could search all they liked and they would find nothing, but woe betide the entire forces of justice if they did not replace her door, left the slightest mess or any other damage whatsoever. She would know. They had better believe it.

They did.

The Birmingham police were, somewhat disgruntledly, everywhere. The DCI from North Yorkshire, where they couldn't even catch that Ripper chap, had told them to look for any evidence of some bint who had not even died in the Midlands but up north. Especially – get this – earrings. Talk about needles in haystacks. Well, so far, they had found nothing. Not even a photograph. The woman who lived in the house was a nurse at the hospital and it didn't feel right, somehow, to be unwrapping her life like this. Not a nurse. They were the caring profession and plenty of police were married to nurses, who understood about shifts and anti-social hours and emergencies.

So, when the crew from Yorkshire finally put in an appearance, when most of the hard work had been done, there was little to report. And if they didn't effin' believe them, they could look for themselves. No earrings of any description, no photos, mementoes, letters, documents or personal touches of any kind. The house was an emotional void. Very clean, very functional and bitterly cold. There were finger prints but they were mostly Jenny Cullum's and no traces of blood of any type had been found, anywhere. If anything had happened there, the house was saying nothing. Some surgical equipment had been found – syringes, scalpel holders and some odd-looking scissor-type things but she was a nursing sister so, while unusual, it was not entirely unexpected. The only thing of any vague interest was an item of underwear which had been found in a drawer in the main bedroom, where Sister Cullum clearly slept alone in a double bed. The other bedroom was tidy and clean to the point of sterility, with a bed that appeared never to have been slept in. They had bagged up the underwear, a blue satin bra which stood out from all the other white cotton garments below which it lay. Not only did its colour stand out, but it was two cup sizes bigger than all the others.

Glenda was finding her stride. It was clumpier than Jenny Cullum's and not as fast, but sturdy and steady enough as she found her feet around the ward and the other staff. They were beginning to accommodate the new tread and to respond to its sound; they needed a leader and Glenda was actually astonished at how quickly she had slotted into the role. Mostly she had only to be there. The system worked. Jenny Cullum was beginning to look like a fraud: superfluous. Glenda glowed. She would even have time to do a quick inventory of the equipment store. After one final glance around the ward to make sure all was well, she slipped out to the store cupboard, just at the end of the corridor. She was pretty certain that nothing else had gone missing from it. When she had said she would keep an eye on things she had meant it and had already conducted several covert operations, as well as keeping a very close watch on her chief suspect. The link between Melissa Sharp's demise and the uninterrupted level of equipment supplies was telling. What an excellent detective she would have made. Never mind, she would settle for Sister and then, well, who knew? The thought made her smile and she stepped out surprisingly lightly for one of her BMI.

"Nurse. I think I'm going to be ..."

Sick

It was the woman in bed number 7. The stench of vomit made the student nurse nearby want to gag but she knew she mustn't, not if she wanted to qualify. The patient was lying on her back and had hardly managed to turn her head before she threw up. Violently. It was all over her face like a mask, slipping around her head like a halo.

She tried to speak but was caught by another guttering wretch which left her wet, frightened and breathless. So, she inhaled. Swallowed. Began to choke.

"Turn her over. Clear the airways."

Suddenly bed 7 was surrounded by hands and assorted uniforms. The student turned the woman onto her side as an SEN scraped at the sticky face, looping first one, then two fingers into the woman's mouth to try and find a way through the sludge.

"She's arrested!"

"Shit."

"Call 222!"

Running feet, shouting, vomit on hands, apron, hair and floor as the call was made and the arrest team were there, sprinting, sweating, ready for action.

Senior Staff Nurse O'Keefe appeared in the doorway just as the curtains were being drawn around the bed for the last time.

Elsewhere in the hospital it had been decided that Melissa, although physically unharmed, should be kept in for observation. It was her state of mind that was cause for concern. She lay motionless in her bed, as white as the sheets around her, the blue cotton bedspread as smooth as when the bed was made up but empty. Her blonde hair had been brushed and tied back to one side so that her head could rest more comfortably on the pillow. Her eyes, as blue as the bed cover, were fixed and vacant. Most of the time she stared at the ceiling, but even the slightest noise, interruption or movement would be greeted by darting glances and rapid blinking, accompanied by violent picking and plucking of the bedcover by crab claw fingers. Although she seemed to hear what was said to her, she spoke to no one. Not even Sister Cullum.

The police were desperately anxious to interview the little staff nurse but had been refused access. She was in no fit state to answer questions. Perhaps after a few days rest the situation would change but, at the moment, it was out of the question. For the second time the police found themselves up against Sister Jennifer Cullum, who stood between her staff nurse and the instruments of justice with as much vigour as she had defended her property. What was more, she had told them, Staff Nurse Sharp was to be transferred to a quiet side room on Upper GI so that she, Sister Cullum, could personally supervise her care. It had been unanimously agreed and approved by the doctors and psychiatrist, who all felt that Melissa would be best placed in a familiar setting surrounded by familiar faces.

The care and attention lavished on Melissa by Sister Cullum was a topic of much discussion on the ward and eventually, throughout the hospital. No one could have guessed that her severe angularity could be softened by anything less than a hammer and chisel but for Staff Nurse Sharp, she was all tenderness and consideration. Fresh flowers in her room, smiles, did Melissa want the curtains opened/closed? Was she warm/cool/comfortable enough? How about a nice cup of tea and a biscuit? It was generally agreed that Upper GI patients should never hear of this side of their ward sister or there would be no living with them. Potts too, was surprised but made no comment. He was glad that the girl had been found but what mattered was the continuity of high-quality medical care; Sister Cullum could do what she liked as long as this was not compromised. It seemed to him that Staff Nurse Sharp was suffering from some sort of PTSD, which was unfortunate, but she should try being under fire or being blown up by an IRA booby trap for a real understanding of Post-Traumatic Stress Disorder.

Chapter Thirty-eight

"When did you last see Linda Ruscombe, Sister Cullum?"

DCI Martin was sitting with his DS, opposite the interviewee, who had insisted on being called by her professional title. Between them the table was bare, bar the cassette recorder at one side. Sister Cullum was greatly encouraged by this. She had told them there was nothing to find and she had been right. She had also told them that, on that basis, she was speaking to them voluntarily because they had no cause, whatsoever, to suspect her. The male detective was doing the talking: she had nothing to worry about as she answered.

"As I have already told you, more than once," (really, they were more annoying than student nurses) "Miss Ruscombe, Lyn, left the house after I had gone to work and I never saw her again."

"After you argued so loudly that it kept your neighbours awake?"

"There was a disagreement, certainly, but that was all. I had no idea that Lyn was going to leave. It was a terrible shock."

"She gave no indication that she was going away?"

"None."

"And you have no idea where she went?"

"No."

"Isn't that rather odd? Two women, close friends, never a cross word, then one of them just disappears? Vanishes. And you say you have no idea where she went or even might have gone?"

"I never thought for one minute that Lyn could do anything so hurtful. But you have to understand that she was damaged. She wasn't herself. It was working in A&E that did it, and her past; that dreadful husband, the loss of her son. She was so vulnerable."

"When you weren't there to take care of her." It was the first time Catherine had spoken. Jenny looked at her very directly but showed no surprise. There was a pause, however, before she responded.

"I did look out for her, yes. Of course. Who wouldn't?"

"Did she threaten to leave you when you were arguing?"

"No. I told you, it came as a terrible shock."

Now the man joined in.

"Was it a very intense relationship, you and Linda - Lyn?"

"We were close friends, if that's what you mean."

No, not quite, but he let it go. For the moment.

"You must have been very angry."

"I wasn't angry. Just hurt."

"When?"

"When she left."

"Not when you were arguing?"

"Of course, when we were arguing. It was an argument. But that doesn't mean I killed her. You are making erroneous assumptions and jumping to ridiculous conclusions. It isn't even logical."

At this point any student nurse, staff nurse and most medics would have crumbled and thrown in the towel but neither Martin nor Scott seemed in the slightest bit put out. Jenny's mouth creased with distaste.

"Did she take all her things with her?" The female detective was speaking again, with a slight change of tone. Well, if that woman thought that she, Jenny Cullum, would be deceived by a change of tack, she was very much mistaken. Jenny knew exactly what was going on.

"No. she took just what she could carry in her suitcase. I got rid of everything else after she left. I needed a fresh start. That's why you couldn't find anything in my house, just as I told you. Just like you won't find anything in my office. You can search all you like."

"We are."

"There's nothing to find because I've done nothing wrong."

"Except this."

The man had reached down beside his chair and pulled up something in a plastic bag which he placed gently on the desk. It was a satiny blue bra.

Jenny stared at it, white faced. Silent.

No one spoke for what seemed like hours until the man split the air.

“I’m no expert, but this doesn’t look like your size.”

At that moment there was a knock at the door. The room burst like a lanced boil. A body appeared in the doorway and made some secret signal to the hairy detective who got up and went over to him. They disappeared, while Jenny studied the underwear on the desk and Catherine studied the nurse. Neither looked up when the DCI returned and sat down. He tugged energetically at his woollen sleeves and began to roll them up above his elbows. Catherine now took notice; something had happened.

“Well,” he said, conversationally. “That was interesting. We’ve just been searching your office, Sister. And found these.”

He put another, much smaller plastic bag on the table. It was so small that the two women had to lean over to see what it contained.

Catherine gasped.

Jenny seemed to struggle for breath.

It was a pair of tiny, gold stud earrings.

Chapter Thirty-nine

"It's not enough to charge her. You'll have to let her go."

Detective Chief Inspector Martin was on the receiving end of the telephone line from his Chief Superintendent in North Yorkshire. Catherine could hear him almost as clearly as her boss.

"I don't care if you find blood and prints on the earrings. It's not enough. And how long are you going to be in Birmingham?"

The moustache bristled as much as the sweater wilted as DCI Martin attempted to make his case, without success. It didn't matter if he could feel it in his water, the facts remained the same. The evidence was entirely circumstantial. Just what was the DCI proposing to charge the woman with? Murder? Based on a bra and a pair of earrings? The Chief Super rang off, muttering about overtime, limited resources and the fact that four bodies lay unaccounted for on his patch while half his force had apparently decamped to the Midlands.

"Bloody hell."

Catherine said nothing. The Chief Super was right. Jenny Cullum had motive and opportunity but precious little else. And even if she had killed Lyn Ruscombe, where had she done it? When? How did the deceased end up on the North Yorkshire Moors? And what about the other bodies? Their suspicions of Sister Cullum were generating more questions than answers.

"Ruscombe's wounds were different to the others, more frenzied. Could've been a mardy female. 'Ell 'ath no fury and all that."

Martin turned on the lad, one of his own team, who had spoken.

"Aye, and she was drugged and drained and laid out like Sleeping Beauty just for the fun of it. If you've nothing useful to say, bloody shut it. Right. We're heading home. Scott, you stay here and find out what you can about our suspect from that sawbones of yours. If Sister Cullum has alibis, check them out. See if that lost and found girl says anything useful then get yourself back up north. Fast. Or you'll have me and the Chief Super on your back."

"By train?"

"Unless you want to walk."

Ten minutes later, he, the two other members of the team and the car had gone.

Chapter Forty

"What do you mean, she's dead?"

Sister Cullum had returned to Upper GI as soon as she had finished speaking to the police. She had immediately noticed the closed curtains around bed 7 and wanted to know what was happening. It was most irregular to curtain off a patient like this in the middle of the day unless it was something serious.

"She was perfectly alright when I left? What happened?"

Glenda was standing in front of the desk behind which she had so recently sat and felt so comfortable. The manilla folder had been pushed aside, unopened, and Sister Cullum had both bony hands pressed on the top of the desk. Everything about her was braced, ready to pounce. She listened to the description of events without saying a word, breathing heavily, with her whole body, completely soundless. Just when she had thought that things could not get any worse.

Glenda finished speaking and there was silence. The air in the room felt sour, as if it too had been regurgitated.

Jenny spoke.

"You realise that there will have to be an investigation? I must accept some of the responsibility because of my error of judgement. My trust in you was misplaced. I cannot believe that you could be so . . . unreliable." She wanted to say 'negligent' but had already been advised by the legal department not to mention the word. "Not to follow a registrar's instructions because you were too busy! If that nasogastric tube had been put in, the patient would still be alive. I understand that you requested she be given Omnopon? An opiate? Which regularly causes nausea and vomiting as a side effect? Causing the patient to choke."

The sweat on Glenda's face was starting to form tears.

"You are, of course, Staff Nurse O'Keeffe, relieved of all Staff Nurse duties with immediate effect and if it were not that we were so short-staffed, you would have been placed under immediate suspension. You may, for the time being, continue basic nursing duties under strict supervision. What a pity Staff Nurse Sharp isn't here to take your place."

She stopped for a moment, as much to consider Melissa as to torture Glenda.

"Something like this reflects badly on all of us," she said, so softly that the offender had to strain to hear. "The whole department is brought into disrepute. Not to mention the distress caused to the patient's family. Do you have anything to say?"

"I checked the equipment cupboard. It's all there."

Jenny tried not to snort with disgust.

"I never doubted it." She said, more loudly. "Since we discussed the matter, nothing has gone missing. I wonder why that is, Staff Nurse O'Keeffe?"

Chapter Forty-one

The hospital administrator had offered Jenny annual leave but she had refused. Jenny was the sister in charge and that was the way it was going to stay. Besides, she wanted to keep an eye on Melissa Sharp. That poor girl had been through enough. Of her own troubles, she said nothing and showed even less.

Melissa was still in the secluded side room in Upper GI, unaware of the rumours and gossip flooding the hospital. Jenny Cullum had never been popular but now people could not get enough of her. Wherever she went, whatever she did, everything she said, wore, ate, drank or was reputed to wear was meat and drink to the hospital rumourmonger machine, which had never worked so hard. News of the missing woman, house search, earrings and the exotic brassiere had somehow got out. No one cared much about the earrings – boring – but the underwear! Who would have thought it? And Lyn Ruscombe had seemed so demure, sociable, in a quiet, unassuming way. Pleasant enough but not exciting. Those who had worked with her found themselves in hot demand, despite having virtually nothing to add to the discussion. Of course, what had happened was awful; terrible; but it couldn't possibly have been Jenny Cullum. Could it? And what exactly did it mean when she said that she and Lyn had just been 'close friends?' No one was more vocal on the subject than Glenda O'Keeffe.

Somewhat at a loss where to go and what to do first, Catherine headed towards Pott's office, dropping in at a ladies' toilet to check her face on the way. Charlotte would point her in the right direction to check Sister Cullum's whereabouts when the last three murders had been committed, as much as they knew, and she would see Scampton. Maybe even the Group Captain. She hoped she wouldn't have to go and find him in Upper GI. Sister Cullum would be there, which would be awkward but couldn't be helped, even though they'd only asked her questions. It had been nothing more than police enquiries; she was free to go and resume her duties at the hospital; they were grateful for her co-operation and if there was anything else, they would be in touch.

"Like bloody lightning," the DCI had said ominously into his jowls when she had left the room.

Charlotte showed no surprise at seeing Catherine. Word spread very fast in hospitals so when she heard that the policewoman had been left behind to continue asking questions, she had expected her to pitch up. In pursuit of Potts probably, not that she would have much luck there. The Group Captain was a cold fish. There was nothing, apart from Scampton and perhaps an especially tricky surgical procedure that seemed to blur his edges. He was so precise, a multi-dimensional diagram. Nevertheless, Charlotte liked him. No bullshit. Easy to deal with as long as you did the job right. He had never once referred to her punkness; not ever, not even when she had bleached and spiked her hair the first time and kohled her eyes right across her face to her ears. He was like Scampton in that respect; probably never noticed as long as water, walks, appointments, letters and messages turned up on time and she smelled right.

"He's in a meeting but it'll be over soon. You can wait here if you like. Hang on. Would you do me a favour? Scampton needs to go out, just for a quick stretch and a pee."

Catherine was taking the proffered lead before Charlotte had finished speaking. She'd love to.

"Come on Scampton."

"He'll show you where to go," Charlotte called after them as she returned to her typewriter with one hand and the ringing phone with the other. "I'll tell the GC."

Tell him, what? Catherine wondered casually as she followed the dog along a corridor. He did indeed know the way and everyone they encountered *en route* greeted him as some sort of four-legged medic. Outside she let him off the lead. There was a patch of lawn with which he seemed very familiar, so she let him wander as she stood at one side and enjoyed the fresh air. It was warm and sunny. She spent so much time indoors that Summer seemed like a stranger, or maybe a friend whom she had not seen for a very long time.

"Thank you."

Catherine tingled, all over. Potts came and stood beside her. "Scampton likes to get out of the office but Charlotte's often too busy. My fault probably, for giving her too much to do."

"She seems very efficient."

"She is. A consultant is sometimes only as good as his secretary; I couldn't manage without her."

"And very dedicated."

"Yes. You wouldn't think so to look at her, but I don't take any notice of that sort of thing. It's what people are like on the inside that matters."

"That's the surgeon in you."

He smiled and nodded his head in amused agreement, still focused on Scampton sniffing suspiciously at an empty cigarette packet. Catherine spoke again.

"Dedication is important to you."

Now he looked directly at her. Intently and seriously.

"Yes. Very. It's impossible to do a good job if you're not dedicated. You have to believe in it, heart and soul and know that what you're doing matters. That it makes a difference. Otherwise, what's the point?"

They looked at each other.

"Sorry," he said. "I'm preaching. But it's nice to talk to someone who understands."

"Have you always been so dedicated to your work?"

"Have you?"

Damn. She did not want to talk about herself. She wanted to know more about him, but maybe this was the way to do it.

She began to tell him how she had joined the police force not just to do good but to prove that you did not have to be a man to do it. That she hated the assumptions people made about, oh, all sorts of things. Not once did she mention her vitiligo; she did not need to. She was certain he knew but that it did not signify; that he did not care. Then it was his turn. She insisted. How did it start?

"I only ever wanted to do two things. Join the RAF and be a surgeon. When I was a medic at Cambridge, I worked with a surgeon called Roy Calne, a pioneer in the field of liver transplantation. He was an inspiration. Still is. Unfortunately, I had already committed to Queen and Country by that stage and it was made clear to me that I would not be able to specialise in the same way. I am what's generally referred to as a general surgeon." He smiled, wryly. "But I do my best."

There was a silence. Scampton was now selecting a suitable peeing point.

"Is that a regret?" Catherine asked, quietly.

"No. It's not about regret, just getting it right."

"What was it like being a surgeon in Northern Ireland?" Catherine pressed on, thinking that he was going to tell her to shut up and mind her own business. As well he might.

Another short silence.

"I was glad there was no one to worry about me." He gazed at the dog that took no notice of either him or Catherine. "What about you, Scott? What about your family?"

"Not really. Just me and my brother, who's in London but we're not close. I'd like a dog though. One day."

"Ah, yes. Scampton. I really am very fond of him. But don't be deceived. If anything happened to me, he'd survive; he's a dog. It's what they do."

He looked at his watch. “Talking of which, I must get back.”

“Sir, before you go, I’d like to ask you about Sister Cullum. What do you make of her?”

“Sister Cullum? Efficient, reliable, measured. Very professional. Caring but rather closed emotionally. Still waters run deep though. She’s careful and clever. Not to be underestimated I’d say. What you see is not what you get.”

“Is she capable of murder? Of killing someone?”

Potts turned his head to stare at the detective. He thought for a moment with an uncharacteristically creased expression, as if searching inside his head.

“Yes. I do,” he said eventually. “Now that you come to mention it.”

Chapter Forty-two

Melissa was still in her quiet side room, isolated and silent. Sister Cullum was a constant visitor, popping in and out, sometimes with doctors, sometimes alone, always solicitous and frequently bearing gifts. Small things but colourful: an apple, flowers in a painted jug, a fashion magazine. Initially Melissa took little notice but as the hours became days, the visits became something to look forward to. A moment of brightness in her black and white world, where fear hid in dark corners and safety was having the light on all the time. She rarely spoke but watched, catlike, with her eyes only as her head stayed inert on the starchy pillow and her hands clutched at the blue counterpane. She was no trouble and did as she was told. Not like she used to be at all the nurses on the ward agreed, and smiled gently when they changed her sheets and escorted her to the bathroom. Soon she was allowed to go there alone and would be seen shuffling nervously down the corridor, after darting henlike in and out of her doorway until the coast was clear.

At this point the police insisted on an interview. Yes, she could be accompanied and of course it would be conducted, gently and tactfully, at her bedside. Catherine's request to be one of the interviewers was refused. This was a Birmingham matter. No, nor could she sit in and observe. It would be too much for Staff Nurse Sharp. Sister Cullum was adamant about that and the doctors agreed. There would be a full briefing afterwards and that would have to do. Then DS Scott could get back to Yorkshire, the sooner the better; she must have so much to do there.

It had been decided that Sister Cullum would be present when Melissa was questioned. Catherine objected. Sister Cullum was not a reliable witness. She was still a person of police interest.

"Not the Birmingham police, chick," she was told. "And no charges have been brought against her. Anyway, it's what the little nurse wants. We asked."

Melissa had indeed been asked and Sister Cullum had answered. Melissa had then nodded her agreement, her eyes fixed on the safety net of Jenny's face.

At first, they could hardly hear what she said, she spoke so softly, as if trying out her voice for size. She shrank back into the bed linen as the male questioner leaned forward to hear her. Only when she had grasped Sister Cullum's hand did she seem to halt her retreat and stand firm against the enemy. Who could not have been nicer. Or more understanding. The sight of those troubled blue eyes gazing into his own as she described what had happened to make her bolt made the policeman melt. Poor kid; she must have been terrified.

"Just tell me, in your own words, in your own time, Melissa," he said, loving her name.

She told him about her fear; the Eyes, waiting and watching, all the time. How she had shut the curtains and locked the doors but they followed her. Everywhere.

"First, they were outside, in the garden, hiding in the trees but then they came closer. And closer."

Here she gripped Jenny Cullum's bony hand with her own white knuckles.

"Into my room," she whispered, glancing distrustfully around the room. "Even though the door was locked."

"She was burgled," Sister Cullum interjected as Melissa went silent, recalling the horror. "It was reported and additional safety measures were put in place. I saw to it myself."

"Was anything taken?"

Melissa leant forward, confidentially, to tell him in such a way that the eyes would not know.

"They took my watch but it came back. Then they took my clothes."

"What clothes?"

"My blue underwear with the flower." She looked tearful and sat back; the pillows would protect her.

"Now, Melissa, my dear. That's not quite right, is it?" Sister Cullum was still holding Melissa's hand and gave it a reassuring squeeze. "The underwear wasn't blue, was it? It just had a blue flower. That's what you told me, remember?"

Melissa wasn't sure. She tried again.

"It was brand new."

"Yes, it was. Still in the packaging, you're absolutely right. You hadn't even tried it on so it's easy to forget what it looked like." Sister Cullum spoke so soothingly. Melissa felt better.

"Yes. The flower was blue." She remembered now.

"A white bra and knicker set with a blue flower?" asked the policeman, writing it down.

"Still in the packaging," confirmed Sister Cullum.

He underlined some of the words and pressed on:

"These eyes that follow you, Melissa. Do you know who they belong to?"

No, she did not. But there was someone, maybe two, or three or more. She did not know but they were there, all the time, watching everything she did. She had thought it might be the doll but her eyes weren't real and she was still being watched."

"Can you tell me about the doll. Where did you find it?"

"Outside. On the window sill. There was a noise. It knocked on the glass but I didn't want to look and when I did, it was staring at me."

"And that's when you ran away?

"Yes. I was frightened." Her eyes expanded with the horror of it. "I had to get away. To go somewhere safe, where they couldn't find me."

"That's enough. She's exhausted." Sister Cullum was already ushering the man from the room. Outside the closed door he began to speak, but she put her finger to her lips and pointed him in the direction of her office. "Staff

Nurse Sharp doesn't need to hear us whispering, not in her state. Yes? What is it?" She pointedly looked at the watch on her chest.

"The doll. Dressed up to look like her with the over-painted eyes. Then deliberately placed where it would frighten her the most. Calculated and cruel. And it looks like it must have been done by someone from the hospital who knew where her room was and when she'd be there."

Chapter Forty-three

There would have to be more questions, but it was the nature of the questions that vexed Catherine when she discussed Melissa's interview with the Birmingham police. What the nurse had said was interesting, but it was the reaction of the other nurse, the senior one in navy blue, that she really wanted to know about. How had she looked when she spoke? She had clearly influenced the interview, but how much? The police couldn't tell her anything about that; it was the poor little staff nurse they had been talking to.

It was also discouraging news about the underwear. If the North Yorkshire Force had hoped to find a link between Linda Ruscombe, Jenny Cullum and the stalking of Melissa Sharp, they were disappointed. The blue satin bra did not fit the description of the garments stolen from Melissa. Both bras featured a blue flower it was true, but that was where it began and ended and if there were knickers to match the bra found in Sister Cullum's bedroom, where were they?

Nothing for it but to head north. Catherine went to the public phone in Upper GI and put a call through to the office. Yes, they'd tell the DCI she was on her way back and had nothing to report. No, he wasn't there. He'd gone straight to forensics when he got back. There wasn't any good news at their end. The Chiefs were doing their combined gold-braided nuts about rising costs and lack of results. The lads were still working on the dosser's leg and the Boss's jumper was beginning to smell. Taking the train might be an advantage Catherine thought, as she listened to the voice at the other end as it continued: they were doing surveillance on Dracula Black but all he did was carry stiffs, stuff stiffs and take his mother out to meet other weirdos to talk to the dead. Bloody odd but perfectly legal. They had interviewed every tramp, hobo, down-and-out and junkie from Redcar to Bridlington and still knew f-all about Nippy. He was well known, well liked but kept himself to himself except that he seemed to have some money. Not much, but regular, maybe a pension or summat, except no one knew where it came from and without an ID, they were stuffed. 'Course they'd tried to find out – what did she think they were? Banks, building societies, post-offices, the whole lot. But without a name it was bloody hopeless. You'd think they'd remember a smelly old tramp with a limp, but no one did.

"Problems?"

It was Potts. Catherine was just putting the receiver back on its cradle and turned around, surprised. She flushed and felt hot but resisted the temptation to wipe her forehead.

"Nothing new," she grimaced. "We're at a dead end."

"Nothing from the interview with the staff nurse?"

Catherine shook her head. He now grimaced in sympathy.

"So, what happens next?"

"I catch a train north and try to find out the owner of the leg."

"Can I offer you a lift? To the station?"

"That would be lovely. Thank you. If you're sure it's no trouble?"

"None at all." He would meet her outside the main entrance in, say, fifteen minutes?

She was surprised to see Scampton with him, tail wagging in polite greeting as he stood to close attention at the end of the slack lead. They were waiting for her, a short distance from the main entrance, unobserved, away from the surge at the large, endlessly opening doors. Man and dog stood on the grass in the sunshine, silent, watching the world move before them. If she hadn't been looking, Catherine might never have noticed them.

"Sorry about the mess."

Catherine looked around the car but could see nothing out of place, not even a dog hair. Scampton had been relegated to the back seat and his rug swiftly removed, shaken and folded back into its regimental creases before being consigned to a new position alongside its owner. Scampton seemed unsure whether or not to sit on it. This was an unexpected change of routine and he was not sure what the rules were. So, he sat, obediently, exactly where he had been put and awaited further instructions.

The Group Captain had held the door open for her, which was a surprise but then, when she thought about it afterwards, should not have been. He was a real gentleman, a senior officer in a proper military organisation. Educated. Polite. He probably did not even know he'd done it. Still, it had felt nice. She thought of the men she worked with, and sighed. The car was immaculate inside and out. Even the empty cubby holes in the doors were clean. That reminded her of her own shabby car, littered with the paraphernalia of her life: tissues, boiled sweets, tampons, (out of sight since the DCI had been a passenger), badly-folded maps and a budget-priced, tea-stained road atlas of the British Isles. Dirty wellingtons, jump leads, a shovel (for snow), warm clothes (for North Yorkshire) and God knows what other rubbish had made its home in the boot. She would have a proper clear out when she got back, maybe even give it a wash. Definitely get one of those air freshener things that you hung up on the rear-view mirror. Potts' car smelt so clean. Almost antiseptic. Just what she would expect from a surgeon.

The journey to the train station took longer than usual due to the evening traffic. Potts drove well. Smooth and sinewy. He chatted amiably but it was obvious that his attention was focussed on the road and Catherine was struck by the intensity of his concentration. Was this how he behaved in the operating theatre? Pleasant and unflustered, but utterly absorbed in the task in hand. Literally. When they arrived and he pulled in to drop her off, she immediately let herself out of the car – no, please don't - she had already inconvenienced him enough – thank you so much for the lift – sorry I took your seat, Scampton – thank you, yes, she would have a safe journey. She would let him know if there was anything else he could do to help. Thank you, again.

She did not watch the car pull out into the traffic but headed straight for the Ladies, then the ticket office. She did not see him when he left the train station and take the road out of the city.

Potts focused on the traffic. Scampton was still on the back seat, sitting beside his rug, awaiting orders. When none came, he lay down and put his head on his front paws. Lulled by the motion of the car and unable to see anything but what lay before him between the two front seats, he silently did what dogs do best and went to sleep. Once they were on the main road, they would stop at a service station for him to have a pee and change seats. As Catherine was aboard a train bound for York, Potts was pulling off the dual carriageway into the far side of the motorway services parking area, near a patch of grass. As he let Scampton out of the car, Catherine was just beginning to sip a cup of weak tea, most of which had slopped into a thick-edged china saucer as she carried it back from the buffet car to her seat.

Potts was standing at the end of the lead with Scampton in mid-flow when he noticed the young man. A squaddie. He had to be, with that hair-cut and stance. Even the police had longer hair than Service Personnel these days. Civilian clothes like his flared trousers and short-sleeved cheesecloth shirt always sat uneasily on military men. The wrong sort of uniform; tight in all the wrong places and lost, as if taking a break on their way to something more accommodating. The lad was sitting next to an army issue, canvas kit bag but as soon as he saw that he was being watched, he immediately stood up and all but stood to attention. Potts noticed that he was wearing heavy army boots, lurking behind the wide hems of his flamboyant trousers like thieves.

"It looks like rain."

"Aye, sir." The lad had a thick Yorkshire accent. He was fit and muscular, but not heavy. A plain face, clean, shaven, the shirt was open at the neck so that Potts could see the chain of his dog tags and a V of pale, healthy, hairless skin.

"You're waiting for transport?"

"Sort of, aye, sir."

"Hitching?"

"Yes, sir."

Potts did not ask why. They'd all done it; missed a connection or run out of funds on the way back to base. Fortunately, as an officer cadet he'd always been able to blag a lift or pull in a favour from someone so had made it on time, but this lad was clearly on his own and it was getting late.

"Where are you headed?"

"Catterick, sir. The camp."

"Need a lift?"

"Aye, please, sir." He had already started to pick up his bag to fling over his shoulder. The soles of his boots itched to march and began to clump impatiently at the tarmac.

"Hop in. Scampton, you're staying in the back. Put your kit on the seat beside the dog. Scampton. Move over."

Catherine had barely finished her tea and mopped up the spill from the saucer with a British Rail paper napkin by the time Potts, Scampton and their new companion were on the road again.

Chapter Forty-four

It was so humiliating. At least if she had been suspended, she wouldn't have had to face her former colleagues. That was how Glenda now viewed the people she worked with on Upper GI. Nobody, not one of the two-faced bastards had taken her side. There had been lots of sympathetic looks in the canteen but they came from other staff nurses, and had not been enough to offset the silence of her own ward. It was as if she had been sent to Coventry. Jenny Cullum had clearly got to them all and ordered them to make her life as unpleasant as possible – and yet they could not manage without her. She was still a senior staff nurse, innocent until proven guilty, and she had every intention of making it very clear in the investigation to come that none of this was her fault. The Sister in charge had gone AWOL; Glenda had stepped into her shoes, without warning or preparation, and they should be on their knees with gratitude. There had been no doctor on the ward, not even that scruffy HO who had had a thing with Melissa. The registrar had failed in his duty of care because he was too busy. Ha! He had dumped his job onto a Staff Nurse who was now expected to carry the can for his ineptitude. It was so unfair. A travesty of justice. She was being made into a scapegoat and, as if that wasn't enough, that bitch Jenny Cullum was suggesting that the missing equipment was Glenda's fault.

Glenda found herself sweating and stood up from the bed she was making to lift her arms. The air was cool against the wetness below her armpits. She sucked in her stomach to ease the pressure of her belt and made as if to stretch, in case people wondered what she was doing. It was already warm. Another hot day to come.

The patients on the ward were unsettled. Death always had that effect: an untimely reminder of their own mortality. Glenda's absolute refusal to be drawn on the subject had merely added to their disquiet. It must be very serious if even she was forbidden to speak; something to do with the missing nurse maybe? Or perhaps one of the student nurses? Why else would such a senior staff nurse be spending all her time with them? The ward routines continued, of course; they never failed. But there was an air of hesitancy; uncertainty; fuelled by hot weather and tight-lipped mouths. Even the Group Captain, that consultant chap, who was always calm and polite seemed to have disappeared. Away at a scientific seminar apparently, just for a few days. That's what Sister had said. Something to do with his work so it must be important and he would be back soon, so no need to worry.

They had run out of clean sheets but there were still beds to change. Could Staff Nurse O'Keeffe go to the laundry room and get some more? Take the trolley and come straight back. She knew where it was, didn't she? Glenda swallowed her fury, made an abrupt about turn with the trolley and only just missed the SEN who had spoken. Now was not the time, but when she was cleared, that bitch would pay. They all would. She propelled herself through the doors and swung violently out into the corridor, where she almost bumped into Melissa.

"Oh! Sorry! How are you?"

She looked dreadful. Vacant. Thin beyond slender. All her in-and-outness had gone; her curves had been replaced with bones and awkward angles. She was starting to look like Jenny Cullum, Glenda thought, and felt sorry for the girl.

“I was just going to the bathroom,” she whispered. Even her voice had changed. It had become lost and unsure, frightened; an echo.

“That’s alright. Shall I go with you?”

Melissa nodded and looked grateful. Relieved, like a small child waiting to be collected from school when their parent is late and everyone else has gone home. Glenda slowed her pace to a crawl to match Melissa’s shuffle and the trolley squeaked in protest.

“I hope they’re looking after you.” It sounded feeble, but Glenda could not think of anything else to say and at least it was a way in. There was so much she wanted to know; a very slow walk to the end of the corridor would give her more time. She noticeably slowed her pace so that Melissa was obliged to shuffle less quickly. “You mustn’t overdo it,” she fussed, offering her arm. To her astonishment, Melissa clawed at it and held on with white knuckles.

“You’re lucky that Sister Cullum is so caring. She’s doing a wonderful job.”

There was a slight pause.

“Yes. She’s very kind.”

Another pause.

“Glenda?”

"Yes?"

"What colour was my underwear?"

Glenda stopped walking; the trolley squeaked crossly to a halt on the lino floor at the same time as Melissa.

"Your underwear?"

What on earth was she talking about? She really was in a state.

"That disappeared."

"Oh! The bra and pants set! Blue, I think. Isn't that what you told Sister Cullum?"

"I thought so."

"Why do you ask?"

"I don't know. I don't know what's happening, Glenda."

"Scott. In here."

Catherine had only just sat down at her desk when she received the summons by sweater. She followed the voice into the DCI's office.

He was sitting behind the untidy desk. Perched on top of a pile of files and uneven papers were the earrings retrieved from Jenny Cullum's office. They were in a plastic evidence bag, far too large for them and looked forlorn. The DCI waved a sheet of foolscap at his DS.

"AB blood and that's about all. Too small for proper fingerprints but there're traces – Linda Ruscombe and one other - Jenny Cullum at a guess. Why're these earrings called sleepers?" Now he was waving the evidence bag at her.

"Because you wear them all the time after the ears are first pierced so the holes don't grow over. That's why they're gold, it's more hygienic."

"Bloody barbaric if you ask me. But it's a definite link between this Cullum woman and our victim."

"Although it doesn't prove anything."

Reluctantly, he had to agree, but there was other news.

"We've got something on our hobo. That serial number on his metal rod comes from a hospital in Northern Ireland; The Royal Victoria in Belfast, in 1972."

"Do we have a name?"

"Getting there. The manufacturer's told us where it went; now we just need to find who they put it in."

Glenda was tired. The day had dragged; gone on forever. Normally she did not mind that all nurses who lived off the hospital site were obliged to change out of their uniform before they left the premises. That was one of the only advantages of living in the nurses' home. It counted as on-site so you could arrive and leave work dressed and ready for action. Everyone else had to build in enough time to change in the horrible, smelly, small locker room before and after their shift. Changing time was not included in shift hours so everything took longer, not to mention the travelling time. At least she lived nearby, Glenda brooded, as she began to unpin her cap. It had been a long, boring, shift. All legwork and slops, clearing up patients and their bodily functions, fetching, carrying, obeying orders and worst of all, being watched. All the time.

She had been angry and hot all day. What she really wanted was a cooling shower but there were only a couple in the changing room and they were already occupied. Besides, they were disgusting. Badly-lit, black-rimmed with damp and mould and tiny. Far too small for ordinary people. And no one ever cleaned them. It was a disgrace. In a hospital! If it had happened on a ward there would have been an outcry but, because they were only nurses, no one took any notice. No one cared. Her feet ached; she was sure her ankles were swollen and probably her knees too. Her dress needed washing and, she peered into her metal locker, she would have to buy more deodorant. Even she had noticed the smell of stale sweat as she had lifted her arms. The young girls, silly things, all had those aerosol spray things that cost so much and smelt so artificial. They made such a show of caking their armpits with the stuff which left white marks on everything and made the air sticky. Some of them even used what they called intimate deodorant which they sprayed onto their private parts. It made her want to retch, but they were the ones who wore such unsuitable, unhygienic pants, if you could call them that. Tiny, skimpy and nylon with not even a cotton gusset, held up by a wing and a prayer. Disgusting. The sort of thing that Melissa Sharp would wear.

She stood for a moment in her own white cotton bra and proper pants that came up to the waist and remembered her conversation with Melissa. Why on earth would the girl want to know the colour of her own underwear? What a strange question. She had thought so at the time but now, well, it seemed even odder Should she mention it to Sister Cullum? Talking of which, there she was, just coming into the room to change. This would be an ideal opportunity for a quiet word with her and would also show those students that she was superior to them, whatever they might think at the moment. She had the ear of Sister Cullum and they had better not forget it.

As soon as she had entered the room, Jenny had seen Glenda and decided to ignore her. No more than she deserved. The hospital administrator had already initiated the internal investigation into the unexpected death on Upper GI. What Staff Nurse O'Keeffe did not yet know was that Jenny had been summoned to an interview with management to 'discuss the matter'. Staff Nurse O'Keeffe also did not know that Jenny Cullum had no intention of taking the blame and had every intention of throwing her staff nurse under the bus, ambulance, trolley or whatever moving object served her purpose. It was easy therefore, just to stride into the room towards her locker, which she would open with one decisive turn of the key that she kept in her pocket. Glenda O'Keeffe might not have existed for all the attention she paid her.

Jenny did not notice the flimsy, blue, lace-trimmed, satin panties that fell out of the navy-blue uniform pocket as she retrieved her locker key. Nor did Glenda, until her sister in charge had undressed and headed off for a shower in one of the now vacant stalls.

Chapter Forty-five

"Our dead vagrant was a soldier, a private, called Charlie Smith. He was in an RTA, a Land Rover, which crashed in 1972 when an IRA sniper took out its driver. He fractured his femur and was taken to the Royal Victoria in Belfast."

DCI Martin was reading from a fax. He had called a team briefing as soon as it had been handed to him by an over-excited policewoman seconded onto the case for admin support. Everyone had gathered around. Some had moved from their desks and one had even stubbed out his cigarette, all the better to concentrate. God! Surely it must be time for a breakthrough? It was not just frustration that haunted them, but fear. What if the killer struck again? They had an MO and plenty of bodies, but no motive, no idea who could be the next victim.

"He was discharged from the Royal Victoria and then the army on medical grounds about 6 months after he was injured."

"That explains why he had money, then," someone said. "He must've had an army pension or summat."

"Was he right in the 'ead?" asked another

"Must've 'ad a screw loose or 'e wouldn't 'ave been 'omeless."

"It doesn't say," the DCI replied. "But now we've got an ID I want to know everything there is to know about him. Family, school, where he lived, where he went, friends, enemies, girlfriends, wives, boyfriends. I don't care. We need to know everyone he knew and mostly, knew him. 'Specially when he came back from Northern Ireland. Poor sod. Well? What're you waiting for?"

The DCI headed back towards his office, fax in frilly-cuffed hand.

"Scott!" he called over his shoulder as he moved. "A word." Just as he spoke the phone on her desk began to ring.

"Leave it!" he shouted.

Catherine looked apologetically at her neighbour who was already reaching across his desk for the phone as she got up and followed her boss into his office.

"Shut the door. No, don't sit down. When was that RAF sawbones at the hospital in Northern Ireland?"

She had known the question was coming, even as she walked across the coffee-stained, nicotine-coloured floor. It was a reasonable question, so why did she feel so uneasy?

"I don't think he was there then, not until 1973, from what he said. But I'll check."

"You do that."

There was a knock at the door which immediately opened and the head of the Catherine's desk neighbour appeared.

"Scott. You might want to take that call. It's someone from Birmingham who'll only speak to you."

Less than five minutes later, Catherine was back in the DCI's office.

"Sir! That was Glenda O'Keeffe."

"Who?"

"The Staff Nurse on the Upper Gastrointestinal ward in Birmingham, who works with Jennifer Cullum."

"So?"

"She says Sister Cullum is trying to kill Melissa Sharp."

Chapter Forty-six

"Can you explain how an item of stolen underwear, belonging to Staff Nurse Melissa Sharp, came to be in your possession, Sister Cullum?"

Since Catherine had picked up the call from Glenda O'Keeffe, things had moved quickly. On behalf of DCI Martin and his team, the Birmingham police had immediately arrested Jennifer Anne Cullum on suspicion of attempted murder. Theft had been thrown in for good measure and she was now being held in a police station close to the hospital from which she had, unceremoniously, been extracted. It had been very dramatic; no one on Upper GI had ever seen anything like it. The Hospital Administrator was in a state of near collapse, not least because of the now critical staff shortage in Upper GI and hysterical Press coverage. Even the Yorkshire Ripper had been temporarily side-lined. A nursing sister! Trying to kill one of her own staff! The public were bound to be interested in such a story. They had a right to know. The Press had a duty of care. What if patients were next? No one was safe.

DCI Martin and Catherine had headed south to interview the suspect almost at once. They were being driven, at speed, in a police vehicle. Not quite blue lighted but almost. The sight of a fast-moving police car streaking down the A1 spoke for itself and, seamlessly, they found that their section of the dual carriageway was invariably clear. Martin was in the front beside the driver, Catherine in the back.

They had discussed their interview plan at length, which would be led by the DCI.

"Not that I don't trust you, Scott, but this is our chance to find out about Linda Ruscombe. And if we can pin that one on Cullum, then it might explain the others. I want you to watch her, carefully. Everything. Especially how she reacts when I ask questions. Look out for deflection instead of answers."

"Have you ever interviewed anyone like this before, sir?"

"A mass murderer? No."

There was silence after that, as they mentally rehearsed their roles and the driver took them ever closer to Birmingham.

Less than three hours later, there they were, sitting opposite Sister Cullum and the duty solicitor. She seemed completely unfazed. She had done nothing wrong; it was a simple misunderstanding. Yes, she had a pair of pants possibly similar to those lost by Melissa Sharp in her possession, but that meant nothing. Nothing. They could have come from anywhere. She could have bought them, or found them, in the locker room perhaps, like Glenda O'Keeffe. Who they did realise was a completely unreliable witness, didn't they? They were aware, of course, that Staff Nurse O'Keeffe was herself under investigation for death by negligence?

They seemed to be getting nowhere. There was no evidence to connect Jenny Cullum with any of the events relating to Melissa, stalking, theft, intimidation, and she knew it. On the contrary, Jenny said. Far from posing a threat, her care of Melissa since she had been found after her disappearance had been exemplary and widely witnessed. Melissa, herself, acknowledged it. It was Glenda's word against Jenny's. If Melissa had doubted the colour of the underwear, why had she agreed with Jenny that it was not blue, as Glenda asserted? As for the stud earrings. Well, so what? Jenny had had no knowledge whatsoever of their existence in her office. She had no idea how they had got there, but it made no difference. It proved nothing. Lyn had had pierced ears and studs but what of it? As for the small amount of surgical equipment, needles and such that had been found in her house, she had no idea how it had got there. It was nothing to do with her. How did they know that Lyn had not put them there? It was all circumstantial. Were her finger prints on them? No. Well, there you are then. They had searched her house and found nothing incriminating or suspicious so she should be released at once, with a full apology for wrongful arrest. Her solicitor would be pursuing the matter. (Clearly news to him his eyebrows said.)

To Catherine's concealed surprise, her boss hardly reacted at all. He sat, quietly, fiddling with his facial hair. She had been surprised that he had let Jenny Cullum speak, at such length, without interruption or contradiction. She appeared to have hijacked the interview and it felt as if they were the hostages.

"We will be talking further with Miss Sharp and Miss O'Keeffe," he said, finally. "In the meantime, you will be held in custody according to the law while we pursue our enquiries. However, before we finish, I do have just one more question."

Jenny clearly could not care less.

"How do you explain the presence of the blue satin bra, two sizes too big for you and also for Linda Ruscombe according to our forensic reports, that was found in your bedroom?"

Chapter Forty-seven

"I know Cullum did it. Someone must have seen something. It has to have been her. You can't just dump a doll with big tits and peroxide blonde hair, dressed as a nurse with over-painted blue eyes on an outside window sill in broad daylight and not be noticed, not in a bloody nurse's home. Check out her alibis. Yes, again. I'm going to talk to Melissa Sharp. Get forensics on those knickers and for God's sake, find me a witness."

The DCI had spoken. Now he stumped off and Catherine was left on her own, in the corridor, outside the interview room. Was she really back in Birmingham, already? She'd have to find a place to live there at this rate. What to do first? A quick visit to the Ladies, a cup of coffee and a confab with Charlotte would be a good place to start. Potts might be there and she would be able to discuss the soldier-victim they had finally identified. She would be able to use Charlotte's phone, away from the ears of the incident room, and get some info about Glenda O'Keeffe. Perhaps she could lead them to the witness the DCI wanted?

Charlotte was on the phone and, unusually for her, did not seem to notice Catherine as she appeared in the doorway, tapping lightly on the doorframe to announce her arrival. Whoever was on the end of the phone was unhappy, voluble and angry. Charlotte's black-rimmed eyes had retreated into their mascara and her brow was as dark as her mood. She was running black nails through her peroxide hair, tugging at the spiky ends as if trying to lift them off her head. Eventually the call ended and she put down the phone with a mutter and a sigh.

She had seen Catherine. Now she acknowledged her.

"That was the Hospital Administrator," she said, ruefully. "We're trying to find the Group Captain but no-one knows where he is."

"What d'you mean?"

"He's supposed to be in Cambridge, at a research forum at the university, but he's not. At least that's what they told me. Apparently, he never arrived."

"When did he go?"

"The day before yesterday, after he finished work."

"I saw him. He dropped me at the station. But he never said anything about going away."

"Did he have Scampton with him?"

"Yes. Of course."

The two women looked at each other.

"Oh God. Do you think something's happened to him?"

Charlotte spoke for them both.

That he was not in the hospital or anywhere on the premises was confirmed almost at once. His office was empty, his car had gone and most significantly, so had Scampton. Nor was he at the Officer's Mess.

"Gone away for a few days on a course," Charlotte was told, according to the steward prone to feed Scampton on the sly. "Asked that while he's away his room be properly cleaned for a change."

The details of his car and probable route to Cambridge were passed on to every police force between there and Birmingham but no accident, hold up or incident of any sort had been reported. Nor was he to be found in any hospital *en route*. Great concern was expressed as to the possible plight of the dog rather than the man, but the result was the same. Nothing. They had simply disappeared.

"Perhaps he didn't go that way at all. Perhaps he's gone somewhere else."

By now Catherine was speaking to the DCI, who really did not want to know. He had tried speaking to Melissa Sharp, who had practically refused to let him in her room, never mind talk to her. Not without Sister Cullum being there she had insisted, which had really annoyed the DCI whose sweater sleeves were rolled right up to his armpits as if ready to do battle. Eventually it had been agreed that Glenda O'Keeffe could play chaperone instead, but the hospital was unhappy about that arrangement. Staff Nurse O'Keeffe was under investigation. Surely someone else would do? No. Melissa was adamant. Either Sister Cullum or, reluctantly, Staff Nurse O'Keeffe could be present during interviews with the police or she wouldn't do them.

"Where the hell would Potts go?" Martin barked at his DS.

"I don't know."

"Sister Cullum hasn't got anything to do with his disappearance, has she?"

“I don’t know.”

“Stop saying ‘I don’t know,’ Scott, and find answers.”

Easier said than done. Catherine went straight to Charlotte. She must have a home address for Potts?

She did. Catherine looked at it and then asked for a chair to sit on.

“What’s the matter?” Charlotte said.

“Are you sure this is right?”

“Yes, of course. Why?”

“Have you got a road atlas?”

No, Charlotte hadn’t but she the ever resourceful, tracked down another consultant who drove a burgundy Jaguar XJ6, the love of his life, only just affordable even on his salary but with a twelve-month waiting list that no amount of money could shorten. He was very reluctant to help. No one but himself should touch the car. Was it really necessary? Oh, very well, but they would have to wait while he got it himself and no, he would not be persuaded otherwise. After an apparent eternity he finally arrived in the office with the unused road atlas and implored the girls not to tear or mark it any way. Most of all, they were not to fold the corners of the pages or crease the spine.

They took no notice and at once began to mark out the main routes from Birmingham in all directions north towards Yorkshire. The police would be alerted. Surely somebody must have seen something? - A distinctive car with a single male driver and a black Labrador in the front, more than likely sitting up and looking out of the window, knowing Scampton. They would have to stop at least once to let him out so all the service areas along the main north roads would have to be notified.

Catherine was ashamed and relieved that DCI Martin was not on hand to witness her ignorance. Her negligence. She had checked Potts out as the DCI had instructed – she even knew his blood group – but not to find out where he lived when he was away from work was at dubious best, a dereliction of duty and at worst, God alone knew. She felt herself burning under her foundation and hoped it would not shift. Not that Charlotte would have cared.

"Is there a phone number?" she asked, studying the address.

"No. He's incommunicado when he's there. Says it's the only way to get some peace. But he always rings me to make sure everything's ok."

"How often?"

"Every other day or so, give or take."

"Will he ring to tell you why he's not on the course?"

"I doubt it. Why would he?"

"Why isn't he in Cambridge?"

Charlotte shrugged. How the hell was she supposed to know?

"Personal reasons?" she suggested, lamely.

"Does he have any family?" Catherine was beginning to realise how little she knew about him. They had talked together, at length, but he had revealed so little. Years of doctoring she thought, must do that to you. And being in the Services. It's all about the others, listening, analysing, diagnosing, giving instructions and orders and taking them too. Being the one in charge and in control was costly. Perhaps keeping your private life concealed, completely separate, was a form of survival in such a public world. She could hardly blame him but she should have asked. Should have known.

"Just Scampton as far as I know. But I'm only a secretary." Who has work to do the phone reminded her, as it began ringing and a trolley appeared, with another pile of post for diagnosis and treatment. Catherine took the hint and headed back to the incident room to put out an alert for Potts and to tackle the mystery of the blue knickers. She would like to speak to Melissa Sharp, if she could. What she could not know was that Martin was at that moment looking for her to do just that.

"You're a woman. Maybe you can get through to her."

Chapter Forty-eight

"That looks revolting."

Both women were peering into the contents of the bowl in front of Melissa. She was out of bed, sitting in a plastic chair behind a narrow portable, Formica table which all but filled her small room.

"What is it?" Catherine genuinely had no idea.

"Rice pudding. I think."

They examined it.

"Are you hungry?" Catherine asked.

"Yes." Melissa was surprised to hear herself answer but realised that, for the first time in as long as she could recently remember, she did want to eat. But not that.

"Wait there."

Ten minutes later Catherine was back with a plastic carrier bag in her hand.

"Crisps, plain and cheese and onion, a Marathon and a Walnut Whip. And two cans of coke. I'll have anything you don't want. I'm starving."

Melissa had said little at first as she nibbled at the cheese and onion crisps. Nervously at first, as if they might bite back. Catherine had opened the packet for her, as if she were a small child, then sat down on another similar chair alongside her. It began to feel more comfortable. Catherine ate slowly, keeping pace with Melissa, who gradually seemed to find confidence enough to eat faster and more noisily and then, to find her voice.

"You don't look like a policewoman."

"That's a relief."

They smiled. Melissa indicated the food on the bed.

"Where did you get it from?"

"The canteen. Near where they found you."

So far, so good.

"Why did you go there, Melissa?"

The girl stopped chewing and looked at her inquisitor who smiled, and reached for one of the cans of coke, which she opened with a snap and began to drink. Look natural; like you don't care, Catherine was saying to herself as she tilted back her head to drink from the can and praying for a reply.

"I didn't want them to see me. There were no windows so I thought if I blocked the door, I'd be safe."

"What was it about them that frightened you so much?"

"The way they got in and moved things. I knew it wasn't me. And the way they got closer and closer."

"The doll?"

"Yes. And my watch and the clothes."

"The watch?"

Melissa explained. She'd thought it was her, that she was going mad but it was there, definitely, she knew it was, on the top of the chest of drawers and then it vanished. Just like the underwear but that never came back. Then she found the watch in one of the drawers, lying there as if someone had tucked it up in bed. But it wasn't her. She wouldn't do that. Sister Cullum said she that was untidy and careless and she was right, but Melissa was always very careful about her uniform and especially her fob watch. You got into so much trouble if you lost it or turned up for work looking a mess. Sister Cullum could be terribly fierce.

"You didn't tell us about the watch."

No, she'd thought it was just her, being careless or silly. Maybe she'd just imagined it. That's what Sister Cullum said. She told me to say nothing or everyone would think I was going mad."

Catherine waited.

"But I didn't make it up. It really happened."

"I don't doubt it. Is there anything else?"

Melissa was now leaning back in her chair, sipping coke. She selected the Walnut Whip which she opened herself and examined, before she carefully removed the nut on the top and put to one side. Then she bit into the chocolate peak and began to lick out the soft interior. Catlike. Her tongue curled and lingered over the sweetness, slowly, almost languidly, Occasionally, she took a tiny nibble of the walnut before washing it down with more of the silky mallow. Between each moment of pleasure, she talked; chatted. She began to tell Catherine about life on the ward, the scruffy HO and the chair that got broken, the porter who replaced it and fitted the bolts on her door. Then the parties, the contraband, some of which had also gone missing, the poppers and the blood all over the bathroom. Catherine let her talk. And talk. She did not make notes. It was more than enough to find out how much they did not know, particularly about the stolen drugs and equipment.

Back in the incident room she was in no doubt.

"We need to talk to Jennifer Cullum again. I may not have a witness, yet, but I know what questions to ask. At the very least Sister Cullum is guilty of perverting the course of justice. We also need to speak to Glenda O'Keeffe who I'm sure will corroborate Melissa Sharp."

DCI Martin did not ask how she had done it. Better not to know. Women were a strange breed. When forensics reported that the blue knickers were covered in Sister Cullum's fingerprints with fibres from a navy-blue nursing uniform, Catherine expressed no surprise and when she said that the bra would have fit Melissa perfectly before she had so recently lost weight, he knew better than to argue.

Chapter Forty-nine

"Potts has been seen!"

"Where?"

"Woodall Services on the A1. Northbound."

"When?"

The evening he left Birmingham, supposedly for Cambridge."

"What was he doing going north?"

Catherine said nothing. DCI Martin looked at her. What the hell is it that you're not telling me? his face said.

"Someone who works at Woodall, in the cafe, was taking a break outside. She's a dog lover and has a black Labrador of her own so it was Scampton that caught her attention. He was taking a pee on the grass with Potts."

"The dog?"

"Yes. They didn't stay long then got back into the car. She said they seemed to be in a hurry. There was no hanging around like people often do at the services, stretching their legs, having something to eat and drink, visiting the shop, that sort of thing."

"So, they got back on the road straight away?"

"Yes, but it wasn't just them."

"Whaddya mean?"

"They had a man with them, who got into the front passenger seat. The witness said he looked like a soldier. He'd been hanging around at the services for a while. She'd served him in the café and he didn't seem to have much money. He bought a cup of tea which he drank really slowly, then asked for a glass of water. She thought he was hungry because he put loads of sugar in his tea. She watched him and he pinched a load of ketchup sachets which he stuffed into his holdall. To eat later, she thought."

"Why did she think he was a soldier?"

"Short back and sides, the type of holdall he was carrying and his build - wiry and muscly. Quite a bit shorter than the Group Captain, she said, but they both walked the same way, sort of half striding, half marching. Plus, he was wearing army boots. She's seen loads of soldiers apparently, mostly going to Catterick where there's a big camp. The convoys often stop at Woodall because there's enough room for them to park. Creates havoc in the gents she said, but not as bad as the coaches."

"What was he doing getting into Pott's car? If it was his?"

"Yes, it was. She said it looked as if Potts was giving him a lift. He put his kit in the back with the dog and they drove straight off."

"Did they get petrol?"

"She didn't say."

"Find out. Find this soldier, hitch hiker, whatever he is. Get onto the army."

Catherine was already on it. She had contacted the duty officer at Catterick and was waiting for him to call back. She had also alerted the South Yorkshire Force for any further sightings.

"Why was Potts going north, Scott?"

Catherine inhaled, hard, and flung out the answer on the back of her outgoing breath. "He's got a house there."

"Where?"

"North Yorkshire."

A long silence followed, in which more was said than any words could have conveyed. Finally, the DCI spoke. Too quietly.

"Give me the address. I'm going to get the lads to pay a visit."

"Sir!"

"What is it?" DCI Martin shouted. He hated being interrupted. It had better be worth it. He glared at the young policeman, all acne and enthusiasm.

"Someone's come forward, sir. In Birmingham. A witness. A nurse, who said she saw someone who could have been Jennifer Cullum putting something on the window sill of Melissa Sharp's room. The witness thought it was odd because whoever was doing it had their head covered, even though it was warm and sunny."

"The doll?"

"It looks like it."

"How does she know it was Jennifer Cullum?"

"She recognised her when she turned round. Something about a pointy nose and skinny legs. She worked with her once and said she'd never forget it."

"Why didn't this woman come forward before?"

"She's been on holiday, camping in the Lake District with her boyfriend. She's only just got back and heard about what happened when she was in the canteen today."

"If it was Cullum, it's a bloody weird thing to do." DCI Martin was stroking his moustache down into his jowls as he concentrated. "And why put it on Melissa Sharp's window sill?" The jowls shivered as he tugged at his moustache. Come on, give me the answer they said.

Catherine now raised her head above the parapet below which she had been lurking since the mention of Pott's house.

"Control. By intimidation. She wanted Melissa for herself, like Linda Ruscombe. She was grooming her; making her totally dependent so that she'd do whatever she was told."

"Bloody hell." He would never understand women. "If that's the case, and that's what she's done to Melissa Sharp, what the hell did she do to Linda Ruscombe?"

Chapter Fifty

"He never arrived."

"Who didn't?"

"The hitch hiker that got a lift with Potts. The duty officer at Catterick has just called and told me that the guy that's missing is a soldier, a private, called John Slade, who was due back by midnight the night that Potts picked him up. He'd gone home on leave but never got back to base. He's been listed as AWOL and no one knows where he is. The last people to see him, apart from the waitress at Woodall services, were his family. Parents and sister who's just had a baby; that's why he was there. He got a coach to Woodall and was supposed to pick up a lift there with a mate, who says he never saw him. He waited, like they'd agreed, but the guy never showed so he went back to Catterick without him. It was only the following morning that he realised that Slade wasn't there."

Catherine stopped talking. DCI Martin had drawn himself and his sweater up to his full-just-meets-regulation-size and was staring at her. Everything about him bristled, including his moustache.

"And they haven't been seen?"

"Not since leaving the services."

"Where are we with Jennifer Cullum?"

"Her alibis stack up for the murders. All of them. Although she was the last person to see Linda Ruscombe, it seems she probably did just leave the house as Cullum says. She went to work; it's all documented, I've checked with Personnel. Linda never turned up and no one saw her again. There's no trace of foul play in Cullum's house and even if there was, how would she dispose of a body and get it to North Yorkshire without transport? She was definitely at work all the way up to Christmas, had Christmas Day off but was back in the hospital on Boxing day and even did the New Year shift."

The moustache drooped and the jowls sank.

"However, we can get her for what she's done to Melissa Sharp. Intimidation, breaking and entering, threatening behaviour, withholding vital information, theft ..."

"But not murder."

"No. We may never know what she did to Linda Ruscombe but it really doesn't look as if she killed her."

It was surprising how quickly DCI Martin could move when he put his mind to it, Catherine thought, as she trotted to keep up with him. He was fitter than he looked, without a trace of breathlessness as he gave instructions while he strode along the hospital corridor. They were to hand Cullum over to the Birmingham boys, wrap up their role in the incident room and get the hell back to Yorkshire. Fast. Blue lighted. Before it was too late.

Catherine's make up was beginning to sweat but it did not matter. She sat in the back of the screaming police car, hanging on to the door when they swerved around obstinate traffic. It did not happen much; most of it miraculously cleared as they appeared in rear view mirrors. Nobody would have had time to notice her variegated complexion as they went by so fast. The DCI was in the front passenger seat. He had rolled up his sleeves. The sweater was now more soiled than orange; it had started to smell and drooped down over his buttocks as if committing slow motion suicide by hanging. Death by despair and gravity.

Martin had jumped into the waiting car as soon as he had come off the phone to North Yorkshire. He had ordered the lads at the station, with back up, to get into Pott's house. With force if necessary. Yes, they were to go straight in, no, they did not have to wait for him. Now what the hell were they waiting for? He and Scott would meet them there.

And they were to get an ambulance.

Chapter Fifty-one

"Is he out of his mind?"

The Chief Superintendent had just heard about DCI Martin's instructions.

It was absurd. Power had gone to the man's head. That or something more sinister, as his disgusting taste in sweaters proved. What proof was there that an RAF Group Captain, a surgeon, who had a gong from the Queen herself, was a cold-blooded mass murderer? The man had disappeared yes, and reportedly picked up a hitch hiker. But he was only a person of interest, a respectable, professional man who had not turned up for an erudite medical conference at Cambridge. How could they be sure that it was him and not the hitch hiker who was a threat to life? And why assume that he had gone to his perfectly respectable home in a tasteful, residential part of North Yorkshire? He could be anywhere. No. A couple of sensible officers would be sent to make a routine enquiry and then, only then, further action would be taken. If required. The man was also a Freemason although the Chief Constable kept that to himself. No need for the likes of Martin to know such things and even if he did, he wouldn't understand.

The Volvo was parked on the hard standing outside the closed garage. The stone-built house stood alone, secluded, solid and decent. Upstanding, reliable. Unpretentious and well maintained. No roses around the door or superfluous colour of any sort. Blank-eyed, un-curtained windows ignored the men walking up to the heavy front door and never even blinked when they knocked on it.

Once.

Twice.

Again, louder. Inside a dog began to bark then, abruptly, stopped.

The door remained closed, so one of the policemen wandered around the side of the house and disappeared up the narrow concrete path between it and the garage. The back door was also shut. Tight. He stepped off the path onto the short back and sides grass and peered in through the first window he found, cupping his hands over his eyes to keep out the sun.

The kitchen was like an operating theatre. In the centre, on a long metal-topped table, lay the body of the soldier. Naked. Cold. Curiously flat and very pale; the dark hairs on his genitals and chest were like soft barbed wire, curled ineffectually over forbidden territory that had long since been invaded. The man's belly dipped into his spine. He was all knees, elbows and hip bones. With the blood that had been drained from his body had gone not just his life but softness, curves and cambers. He was all but empty. In a metal kidney bowl to his left lay his liver, juicy and plump. On his right was another bowl, awaiting the arrival of his right kidney and then his left. The incisions had been made and were pinned back, ready, like hair in salon clips waiting to be cut. A narrow tube hung from the body to the kitchen sink, immediately below the window. The policeman could clearly see where it had been fixed to the plug hole, down which the young man's life had neatly drained away, without mess or obstacle.

Potts was nowhere to be seen.

Nor did there seem anywhere in the kitchen for him to hide, unless he had put himself into one of the two large fridges standing opposite the sink, keeping watch over the dead soldier.

Within thirty minutes the armed response team, two ambulances, the Chief Super, a megaphone, a negotiator, the rest of DCI Martin's investigating team, forensics, two police photographers with the Assistant Chief Constable in hot pursuit, were on their way. Noisy, screeching, blue lighted. Armed Response arrived first and were already in place when the Chief Super picked up the megaphone to issue his first warning.

"Group Captain Potts. This is the Chief Superintendent of Police. Come out with your hands up. My men are armed."

Not even the dog barked.

"Potts. This is your final warning. Come out now, or my men will come in."

Nothing moved.

"Go, go, go."

The officers spread out and raced to the house which was completely surrounded. Escape was impossible. The heavy doors front and back surrendered almost at once under the barrage of bodies and battering and in poured the armed men, like water.

It was strangely quiet inside. Almost silent. Sepulchral. The soldier on the kitchen table might have been made of stone, sleeping on a tomb and the creeping policemen were worshippers, on their knees, come to pay their respects.

Where the hell was Potts?

"All clear!" shouted the men who had battered their way into the garage with the enormous coffin freezer.

He had to be in the house.

Not downstairs. The house was large enough, even for the torrent of padded armed men now edging its way forward room by room, but seemed suddenly small when they all converged in the quarry tiled hall at the foot of the stairs. Without words, they began to file up to the higher level, the clatter of heavy boots dulled by the carpet. Unfashionably pale and plain, the carpet unfolded before them, narrow on the stairs but wider, more dangerous on the landing at the top. Every door leading off it was shut. Locked? Shoulders braced, brute, boot force and weapons ready, they started to search, door by door.

He was not in the bathroom or the small bedroom opposite. Only another two doors lay ahead. Odds on he was in the alpha male master bedroom, but was the dog with him? No barking had been heard since their arrival on the scene but the danger of an animal attack could not be discounted. A frenzied moment of silent gesturing and the order for two armed men to enter the door in front of them was given, one to aim for the man, the other for the dog.

It was the door of the main bedroom, large, vacuous and cold. Like a dormitory but with just one single bed in its centre, guarded by a wardrobe, a chest of drawers, a trouser press and a hard backed upright chair. All standing to attention. No pictures, curtains or softness of any kind.

Not even a rug or a mirror. Potts stood tall and straight in the middle of the room, at the end of the bed. He might have been awaiting a kit inspection if it were not for the fact that there was nothing on the bed but a simple blue cover and he was wearing scrubs, with a plastic apron. One hand still wore the latex gloves he had been using but the other, the right, had been freed from its bonds and was tightly wound round a pistol. A Webley VI, held up against the right side of his head. He showed no fear. No concern.

There was no dog.

Just Potts, the lead surgeon. Always in control and calm, calculating his next move; a game of surgical chess.

No one moved.

"Drop your weapon".

The order came from behind the two men kneeling in the doorway, supplicants with guns, paying homage. Potts did nothing. Then from behind the one remaining closed door, the dog began barking.

"Scampton. Stop"

Potts spoke almost casually. He moved his left hand, very, very slightly. For the first time the intruders noticed that there was something in it.

"Don't move or we'll shoot".

He ignored them.

"Give this to Detective Sergeant Scott," he said, lifting his left arm. At the same time, his right hand moved the pistol muzzle to a point immediately below his chin. He tilted back his head and pulled the trigger.

The dog lead fell from his left hand. It hit the floor at the same time as his body.

Scampton began to howl.

Chapter Fifty-two

It is done.

They died so that others might live.

I regret that it had to be David Youde's child but she did not die in vain. One day he will understand. It was just a question of timing. They were given to me for my research.

It was meant to be. Their sacrifice was for the greater good and I thank them for it.

None of them suffered and now, thanks to me, liver transplants will become a way of new life. At first the world will censure and judge, but then it will rejoice.

Sing my praises.

I am the man who has shown the way.

Chapter Fifty-three

By the time DCI Martin and Catherine arrived, all haste, blue lights and anxiety, the armed response team had stood down and sent on their way. The Assistant Chief Constable had gone back to his carpeted office on the second floor, leaving the Chief Super to impatiently hold the fort until the arrival of DCI Martin. Had it not been for the untimely arrival of the Press (how the hell did they find out about these things?) he too would have gone back to the station, leaving the medics, forensics, photographers and uniform to begin the painstaking unravelling process that always took so much time, effort and report-writing.

But it was a result. At last.

Back at the station, the first thing the DCI did was to call a debrief meeting and take off his sweater. He flung it in a bin.

"You throwin' in the towel, Boss?" someone asked over the applause.

"Yes."

"He doesn't mean it," chipped in another voice.

"Yes, he bloody does," Martin muttered. "Right. Storytime."

Everyone who smoked now lit up and sat back.

Scampton had started howling the second Potts had shot himself and would not stop. The armed response team did not stand down until they had opened the last closed door in the house and entered the Group Captain's study. Scampton was leashed and led away, under armed guard, howling miserably. Not until Catherine had arrived and taken hold of his lead, did he quieten down. Only then would he consent to be led away from the house and the garden, now awash with strangers. Even the Volvo was being transferred onto a low loader to be taken away and taken apart for forensic examination. The RSPCA would be contacted to take Scampton but Catherine intercepted.

"No. I'll take him. I've always wanted a dog."

Yes, she was sure. She also thought it was what Potts would have wanted but she kept that to herself. Was there anything she had to sign or had to be done? She was after all, removing evidence from the crime site. Martin had wanted to laugh.

Potts' study was the Holy Grail. A small bedroom had been converted into an operations centre, meticulously clean and laid out, as orderly and neat as one of the corpses in their made-to-measure graves. It was the only room in the house with a window covering – wooden shutters, probably from the time when the house was built. They were half closed, so the room was cool in its semi-darkness, which threw the images pinned onto the cork board above the desk into sepia, like an old photograph album. There they were, in chronological order, from the body in The Gorge to the limping veteran. Even Sue Youde, whose photographs had that startled, over-lit look of having been taken at night. Only the soldier was missing, but he was downstairs in the kitchen. Images of their assorted incisions, wounds and organ extractions were attached, stuck with MOD wide-headed multi-coloured drawing pins, to their respective owners. The very body parts that had just been found in the freezer in the garage, neatly dated and labelled according to gender, age, physical condition and in the order of the death of their owners. None of whom had names. Had Potts even known their names? Probably not; what did it matter to him? All of them, except Sue Youde, had been photographed as they lay on the metal table in the kitchen below.

Pushed up against the wall, below the macabre picture gallery was the Group Captain's pedestal desk. Despite work in progress, it was exceptionally tidy and well ordered. The drawers were shut but unlocked and on the top was a journal, hand-written in a regular, modest script with the fountain pen that had been used placed horizontally above it. A dinner table, set for one, the journal the plate, its contents the food, a bottle of ink where there should have been a glass and blotting paper instead of a napkin.

It was all written down. Everything. Cut by cut. Medical murder.

They had been drugged with haloperidol and taken to the house where they had been exsanguinated and died. So at least they had not suffered, forensics had concluded. They wouldn't have known anything about it. Even the girl.

"All of them except the young girl were carved up on the kitchen table, then moved," the DCI said. "I've no doubt that the Volvo was the transport. It's big enough and although he'd cleaned it, you can't get rid of traces and fibres. No blood though."

That had all gone down the sink. All, except the bags of AB negative blood that had been found in one of the fridges and the coffin freezer. No wonder there had been a shortage at the hospital. With relief at having solved the mystery but infinitely more regret that it had been one of their own, the hospital administrator had to admit that Group Captain Potts must have been availing himself of copious supplies of blood, drugs and equipment for some time. Sister Cullum's disingenuous insinuations about Staff Nurse O'Keeffe as the thief were unfounded, which was something.

It also meant that everything Potts had said was,

"A bloody lie."

The DCI spoke with venom. "He deliberately misled us. He contaminated the bodies and the crime scenes with AB negative blood he had nicked, to throw us off the scent. It's the rarest blood type so of course we thought it was bloody significant – because he told us it was. He wanted us to think that the killer, who could not possibly be him because he had the wrong blood type, was either AB negative or was targeting people of the same blood group."

"Why drain them?"

DCI Martin shrugged his shoulders: you tell me. Convenience maybe? It was easier to see what you were doing inside a body without blood getting in the way; he didn't like mess; it helped mislead the police; he was bloody weird. Whatever the reason, it was part of his MO and that was how they had died.

"Boss, why wasn't Sue Youde carved up in the house?"

There was no clear answer, but if it was an experiment, it had not worked and Potts had gone back to his tried and tested method. Perhaps he had wanted to throw them off the scent.

Hadn't DS Scott gone with him to the Sue Youde crime scene? How had he reacted? Everyone looked at Catherine, pretending not to see Scampton at her feet, by her desk, staring mournfully at the filthy floor.

"There was no reaction at all," she said. "It was as if he'd never been there before although I must admit, now, that his analysis of the scene did seem rather well informed."

Every eyebrow rose.

"But he didn't say anything that a surgeon couldn't have worked out."

"Bastard". Scampton lifted his head to look in the direction of the voice that had spoken; Catherine tightened her grip on his lead. She did not mention the fact that she had left Potts alone in the farm outbuilding while she took Scampton out to stretch his legs. What would be the point?

"What I don't understand, sir, is why did he do it? I mean, he was a doctor. In the RAF. For Queen and country and all that." Scampton turned his head in the other direction from whence the question had come. It was one of the admin support staff who had spoken.

"That's a question," said the DCI, "to which I have no answer. He was a Freemason too, whatever that means. We found evidence of that in his desk – white gloves and a document about brotherhood and honour and integrity. Don't ask me how that explains anything but it seems he wanted to 'serve humanity' by finding a way of being able to retrieve organs – livers - from the dead and transplant them into the terminally ill. To bring them back to life."

The voice of the admin assistant was incredulous:

"He killed healthy people to work out how to keep dying people alive?"

"That's about the sum of it. He varied his choice of victims according to his research. What we thought was random was, in fact, a very carefully orchestrated selection process."

The silence threatened to crush them.

"Do the families know?"

DCI Martin sighed. There wasn't much in the way of families to inform. The Youdes, the Slades, Jenny Cullum and Peter Gardiner, not that he was likely to mourn. Nevertheless. No. Not yet. They would have to be told and that was something he had to do himself. A search of Pott's house had turned up a number of personal effects and belongings which would eventually be returned but it wasn't going to be easy. There was no clue as to the identity of the first body they had found. Nothing. He would probably always be known only as the body in The Gorge. A pair of stud earrings, almost certainly Sue Youde's, had been located in one of the desk drawers and it was considered that those of Linda Ruscombe that had been found in Sister Cullum's office, might have been planted there by Potts himself. He had the motive – to incriminate Cullum - and plenty of opportunity. There was no reason now to suspect the Sister of murder. They would never know how Linda had ended up in Yorkshire but perhaps she had been picked up off the street like the NI veteran, or at a service station like John Slade. Sue Youde had been abducted after she had left the café in Malton.

However, there was something else.

A letter addressed to Wing Commander David Youde had been found along with Pott's personal papers, in one of the desk drawers.

"According to the RAF, they knew each other. I've just found out," Martin said. "They served together in Northern Ireland in 1973, before Potts started killing. If there were other victims before then he would've documented it, so we can assume that he started after he came back from Belfast."

"Why then?"

Martin stroked his moustache and massaged his jowls, none of which could help with an answer. How did he know? He wasn't a shrink. The effects of being in a war zone? Perhaps he'd always been like that, but that's just when it came out? All that mattered was that he had stopped.

"Are you saying that Potts knew it was Youde's daughter that he'd murdered?"

Disbelief hung in the smoky air with the nicotine and cancer.

"I don't think so, at least, not when he did it. Not from the way he reacted when he found out who she was." Catherine spoke softly but everyone heard. Scampton kept his head down. "Perhaps that's why he wrote a letter. Maybe he felt sorry?"

"Bastards like that never feel sorry. They never feel anything."

It did not matter who had said it.

Martin looked at the clock on the wall opposite. Time to wrap this up. The letter for Wing Commander Youde would be delivered by him, personally. Yes, he had read it but that was as far as it went. There was nothing in it that added to the investigation except that it had clearly been written at the point when Potts had found out the girl's identity, so it was obvious that he had had no intention of stopping the killings. His affairs were all in order, as you would expect.

"His body – get this – is to be dedicated to medical research and all his property and effects are to be sold, with the money going to research into liver transplantation."

The disbelief settled on them like mustard gas. And became anger.

Hypocrite. Bastard. Bloody hell. Twisted git. Weirdo. I wish I could've got my hands on him.

Martin let them get on with it and moved across the room towards his office. He beckoned to Catherine to join him. She and Scampton got up together and trotted after him.

"Shut the door. Scott. You were told to check Potts out."

"I did, sir. No one could have known what he was like. No one did."

"You never went to his house, did you?"

No. She hadn't. She didn't tell him that she hadn't even known where it was. But she had seen no need to, she said.

He wasn't even a suspect. What was she supposed to do? Invite herself? Break in? God, she wished she had. Didn't the DCI know that she blamed herself, every second of every day, for letting it go on? She might have saved at least two lives, maybe more. She had to live with the guilt for the rest of her life and if she tried to forget, well, she had Scampton to remind her.

Blotches were starting to appear on her face as she spoke. Martin pretended not to see.

"It happens, Scott. You won't do it again."

No, never. He ignored the way her face tightened as she tried not to cry.

"I thought you might want to know what's going to happen to Sister Cullum. She'll lose her job and get a criminal record but she'll survive. The hospital's not pressing charges about the stolen equipment that was taken by Melissa Sharp, then nicked from her room by the twisted Sister. Seems that all the doctors and nurses do it, mostly for extra-curricular sexual gratification apparently. Don't ask. Cullum's also carrying the can for Staff Nurse O'Keeffe's negligence but at least that pretty little nurse will be out of her clutches. She'll recover, find a nice man and get married. The best thing for her."

If she heard, Catherine did not show it but she burned. There was one more thing that she had to know.

"The chap I spoke to from the BMA, who recommended Potts – was he involved? Did he know?"

In other words, was this all my fault? Was I the reason that the Group Captain got away with as much as he did?

"No. That was just coincidence, except I don't believe in coincidence. Let's call it Fate and..."

Catherine looked at him.

"Conspiracy."

"Conspiracy?"

Martin nodded and stroked the hair above his upper lip.

"Yes. In the name of brotherhood. I'll scratch my back if you'll scratch mine and all that crap."

Catherine had no idea what he was talking about.

"Freemasons. Potts. The Chief Constable."

"The Chief Constable? You're not serious?"

"I wish I was. Oh, he didn't kill anybody, not like that anyway, but he kept it quiet. If there'd been more of a fuss and publicity about Sue Youde, then Potts might not have been able to carry on killing."

"What are you going to do?"

"That, Scott, is the problem. No-one's going to listen to me. Or you. I'm not one of them and you never will be because you're a woman. I'll try, of course, but they're all in it at the top – white gloves, clean hands, blood bonds. That's how they get there. You and I are outsiders; the wrong type."

They looked at each other, in silence.

"Never mind!" Martin suddenly breezed. "At least I've got rid of my sweater."

Epilogue

Letter from Group Captain Potts to Wing Commander David Youde.

David,

I have broken my vow to the Masonic Brotherhood and must pay the price.
If I had known who she was, I would not have chosen her.

She did not suffer and she did not die in vain.

Leonard

Journal

Development of Liver Transplantation
Group Captain Len Potts RAF MB ChB FRCS OBE

Issues:

1. Harvest of the liver
    1. Access to porta hepatis
    2. Removal of inferior vena cava with liver
    3. Access to hepatic veins
2. Implantation of liver
    1. Reconstruction of IVC
    2. Reconstruction of portal vein
    3. Anastomosis of hepatic artery (Achilles' heel??)
    4. Biliary anastomosis

Subject 1
23 October1975
Male mid 30s
Approximate weight 12 stone
Approximate height 5'10''
Good physical condition
No external scars

Anaesthesia induced with direct injection of Haloperidol into internal jugular vein.

Circulatory arrest achieved by exsanguination.

Incision - long midline laparotomy
Findings – normal anatomy, healthy appearance of liver

Procedure – Careful dissection of porta hepatis to expose hepatic artery, common bile duct and portal vein. Liver mobilised from patients left by division of lesser omentum to expose left hepatic vein. Right liver lobe mobilised but access difficult because of steep costal margin.
(note to self; 1. consider sternotomy to improve exposure, this might be necessary in organ harvest in presence of normal circulation. 2. During implantation access would be improved by using Mercedes Benz incision)
Hepatic veins exposed from right, right kidney & adrenal gland visualised behind liver, IVC exposed along its length from right renal vein up to diaphragm.
(note to self; will need long vascular clamp to clamp upper & lower IVC)
CBD divided close to duodenum to give maximum length for implantation. CHA dissected down to aorta dividing gastroduodenal artery, left gastric artery and splenic artery, patch of aortic wall included on artery. PV divided at junction with splenic vein.
IVC divided above right renal vein and IVC dissected from retroperitoneal structures up to level of diaphragm.
(note to self; lumbar veins will need repair prior to implantation as numerous & significant in size)
IVC divided at level of right atrium.
Liver removed intact.

Closure – ½ pint of blood returned to body cavity. Mass closure with 0-silk suture.

Learning Points: As noted above. Further refinement on access will be important. Before moving to implantation phase further equipment will be required but overall a very successful start to the liver transplant programme.

Subject 2
4 January 1977
Female mid to late 40s
Approximate weight 10 stone
Approximate height 5'5''
Good physical condition
Lower midline scar consistent with previous Caesarean section

Anaesthesia induced with direct injection of Haloperidol into internal jugular vein.

Circulatory arrest achieved by exsanguination.

Incision - long midline laparotomy extended into sternotomy

Findings – normal anatomy, healthy appearance of liver, uterine scar

Procedure – Careful dissection of porta hepatis to expose hepatic artery, common bile duct and portal vein. Liver mobilised from patients left by division of lesser omentum to expose left hepatic vein. Right liver lobe mobilised again made easier because of flatter costal margin and midline sternotomy.
Hepatic veins exposed from right, right kidney & adrenal gland visualised behind liver, IVC exposed along its length from right renal vein up to diaphragm.
CBD divided close to duodenum. CHA dissected down to aorta dividing gastroduodenal artery, left gastric artery and splenic artery, patch of aortic wall included on artery. PV divided at junction with splenic vein.

IVC divided above right renal vein and IVC dissected from retroperitoneal structures up to level of diaphragm. Lumbar veins ligated during process.
IVC divided at level of right atrium.
Liver removed intact.
Careful dissection of right kidney to IVC and renal artery to aorta. Ureter dissected down to pelvis.
Decision to leave kidneys and heart in-situ for now. I have more time and will attempt to re-insert the liver.

Implantation Procedure – Liver returned to body cavity.
Upper IVC anastomosis using 3-0 silk. (note to self; explore other suture materials as the silk does not run very freely in IVC)
Lower IVC sutured using 4-0 silk. (note to self; will need to test integrity of IVC with saline before re-perfusion)
Portal vein sutured end to end with difficulty because of tension using 5-0 silk. (again, this is going to be difficult the PV is very delicate, and the silk suture tears the vein which will be a major problem of re-perfusion. In addition, at this point I will have to flush out the liver to reduce the impact of the re-perfusion hit, need to explore which fluids to use and get some heparin)
Hepatic arterial anastomosis using 5-0 silk. (note to self; this is very difficult because of access but should be easier in a real recipient because I can keep the recipient vessel long. I think that I will need some form of magnification and much better lighting to do this safely)
Bile duct anastomosis using 5-0 catgut. (note to self; this anastomosis is also difficult because of tension & access, will need to keep bile duct long in the recipient)

Closure – ½ pint of blood returned to body cavity. Mass closure of abdominal and thoracic incision with 0-silk suture.

Learning Points: As noted above. Overall, I am satisfied that with some adjustments and access to further equipment and materials implantation of the liver would be possible in a heart beating recipient.

Subject 3
23 February 1977
Female mid-teens
Approximate weight 7 stone
Approximate height 5'3"
Good physical condition
No external scars

Anaesthesia induced with direct injection of Haloperidol into internal jugular vein.

Circulatory arrest achieved by exsanguination.

Incision - long midline laparotomy extended into sternotomy

Findings – normal anatomy, healthy appearance of liver

Procedure – Dissection of porta hepatis to expose hepatic artery, common bile duct and portal vein. Liver mobilised from patients left by division of lesser omentum to expose left hepatic vein. Right liver lobe mobilised but access much easier on this occasion because of flatter costal margin and midline sternotomy.

Hepatic veins exposed from right, right kidney & adrenal gland visualised behind liver, IVC exposed along its length from right renal vein up to diaphragm.
CBD divided close to duodenum. CHA dissected down to aorta dividing gastroduodenal artery, left gastric artery and splenic artery, patch of aortic wall included on artery. PV divided at junction with splenic vein.
IVC divided above right renal vein and IVC dissected from retroperitoneal structures up to level of diaphragm.
IVC divided at level of right atrium.
Liver removed intact.

Closure – ½ pint of blood returned to body cavity. Mass closure of abdominal and thoracic incision with 0-silk suture.

Learning Points: As noted above. This procedure was much more refined than subject 1. The use of sternotomy was extremely helpful. I think that the major obstacles with organ harvest have been overcome, further equipment is being acquired in readiness to start the liver transplant programme. Conditions not ideal however. Lesson learned: Do not cut corners.

Subject 4
20 June 1977
Male early 50s
Approximate weight 12 stone
Approximate height 5'11"
Poor physical condition
Scar on right leg

Anaesthesia induced with direct injection of Haloperidol into internal jugular vein.

Circulatory arrest achieved by exsanguination.

Incision - long midline laparotomy extended into sternotomy

Findings – normal anatomy, fatty appearance of liver

Procedure – Careful dissection of porta hepatis to expose hepatic artery, common bile duct and portal vein. Liver mobilised from patients left by division of lesser omentum to expose left hepatic vein. Right liver lobe mobilised but access much easier on this occasion because of flatter costal margin and midline sternotomy.
(note to self; presence of sternotomy improves exposure, this would not be acceptable during implantation because of additional morbidity)
Hepatic veins exposed from right, right kidney & adrenal gland visualised behind liver, IVC exposed along its length from right renal vein up to diaphragm.
CBD divided close to duodenum. CHA dissected down to aorta dividing gastroduodenal artery, left gastric artery and splenic artery, patch of aortic wall included on artery. PV divided at junction with splenic vein.
IVC divided above right renal vein and IVC dissected from retroperitoneal structures up to level of diaphragm. Lumbar veins ligated during process.
(note to self; ligating lumbar veins in heart beating patient would significantly delay process therefore stick with plan to repair prior to implantation)
IVC divided at level of right atrium.
Liver removed intact.

Careful dissection of right kidney including patch of IVC on renal vein and patch of aorta on renal artery. Ureter dissected down to pelvis before dividing.
Heart removed en-bloc with vessel trunks (note to self; there might be a role in the future for heart valve usage).

Closure – ½ pint of blood returned to body cavity. Mass closure of abdominal and thoracic incision with 0-silk suture.

Subject 5
2 August 1977
Male early 20s
Approximate weight 13 stone
Approximate height 5'10"
Good physical condition
No external scars

Anaesthesia induced with direct injection of Haloperidol into internal jugular vein.

Circulatory arrest achieved by exsanguination.

Printed in Great Britain
by Amazon

38068770R00175